*He was the man
she'd married,
the man she'd loved
all her life, and
she was determined
to make him fall in love
with her all over again.*

Mary Morrell hand and wrist
Surgery. Brothers Medical Center.
Elk Grove Village. 847-437 9885

Just the Way You Are

"What time do you want me?" Sam asked.

"I don't want you!" Alli burst out. She put a shaky hand to her mouth. "I don't want you," she repeated.

"I thought we were going to forget."

"You shouldn't have kissed me."

"You shouldn't have kissed me back."

"Bad habit," Alli said.

Sam nodded. *Wasn't that the truth?* he thought. "Do you want an apology, Alli?"

Her eyes met his. "That's the last thing I want, Sam. Don't you know that yet?"

BARBARA FREETHY

Just The Way You Are

AVON BOOKS
An Imprint of HarperCollins*Publishers*

AVON BOOKS
An Imprint of HarperCollins*Publishers*
10 East 53rd Street
New York, New York 10022-5299

Copyright © 2000 by Barbara Freethy
Excerpt from *Here Comes the Bride* copyright © 2000 by Pamela Morsi; excerpt from *Heaven on Earth* copyright © 2000 by Constance O'Day-Flannery; excerpt from *His Wicked Promise* copyright © 2000 by Sandra Kleinschmidt; excerpt from *Rules of Engagement* copyright © 2000 by Christina Dodd; excerpt from *Just the Way You Are* copyright © 2000 by Barbara Freethy; excerpt from *The Viscount Who Loved Me* copyright © 2000 by Julie Cotler Pottinger
ISBN: 0-380-81552-4
www.avonromance.com

First Avon Books paperback printing: November 2000

Avon Trademark Reg. U.S. Pat. Off. and in Other Countries, Marca Registrada, Hecho en U.S.A.
HarperCollins® is a trademark of HarperCollins Publishers Inc.

Printed in the U.S.A.

OPM   10   9   8   7   6   5   4   3   2   1

*To Casey, Barbara, Sheila,
Carol and Lynn
for your endless support,
encouragement and friendship*

Prologue

"*Are* you ready to go for a sail?" John MacGuire asked his wife. A young, handsome man, he stood on the edge of a wide sandy beach, wearing summer shorts and his favorite T-shirt. He pointed toward the water behind him, to the sailboat that bobbed gently in the quiet bay. "It's the perfect day."

"I can't sail. I'm sick. I don't know what happened, but I can't seem to open my eyes." Phoebe MacGuire took a quick breath as panic filled her soul. "I'm seventy-six years old now, John. How did I get to be so old? I'm scared."

"No need to be scared, my darling, not when I'm here."

"But you're not really here."

"I miss you, Phoebe," he said softly, his voice as gentle as the morning breeze.

"I miss you, too. Nothing has been the same since you died. You were the one who kept the family together. It was you, your strength, your vision. Without you, we fell apart. Alli and Tessa are strangers now, and I don't know how to bring them back together."

"Do you still have the pearls, Phoebe?"

"Of course I do."

"Do you remember the one we found on our first anniversary? That's when we discovered you were pregnant. Then we had a son, and later granddaughters, and we taught them to love the sea, to cherish the family, and to treasure the pearls for the strength that they gave us each year to go on, to live life to its fullest, to complete the circle."

"But we didn't complete it," she said in despair. "Because you died. You left me."

"It was my time, Phoebe, but you must finish the necklace now. The pearls weren't meant to just be a symbol of our love, but of our family, our strength, our unity. The pearls are nothing on their own. But together in a strand, they are everything. It is the lesson we must teach Alli and Tessa." He paused, his expression as tender as a sweet blooming rose. "I wish for our girls a love as deep and as satisfying as the one we share."

"I want the same thing." But as his image faded away, Phoebe wondered if even the perfect pearl could save Alli and Tessa from themselves.

⛵ Chapter 1

"Daddy, did you ever love Mommy?"

Allison Tucker caught her breath at the simple, heartfelt question that had come from her eight-year-old daughter's lips. She took a step back from the doorway and leaned against the wall, her heart racing in anticipation of the answer. She'd thought she'd explained the separation to her daughter, but Megan still had questions, and this time it was up to Sam to answer.

Sam cleared his throat, obviously stalling for time. For the life of her, Alli couldn't move away. She hadn't intended to eavesdrop, but when she'd arrived to pick up Megan after her weekend with her father, she had been caught by the cozy scene in the family room.

Sam sat in the brown leather reclining chair looking endearingly handsome in his faded blue jeans and navy-blue rugby shirt. Megan was on his lap, her blond hair a mess in mismatched braids, her clothes almost exactly the same as Sam's, faded blue jeans and a navy-blue T-shirt. Megan adored dressing like her father.

3

"Did I show you the picture of Mommy when she dressed up like a giant pumpkin for the Halloween dance?" Sam asked, obviously trying to change the subject.

They were looking at a yearbook, Alli realized with dismay. There weren't just pictures of Sam and Alli in the yearbook, there were other people in there, too.

"Did you, Daddy? Did you ever love Mommy?" Megan persisted.

Answer the question, Sam. Tell her you never really loved me, that you only married me because I was pregnant, that your heart still belongs to—my sister.

Alli held her breath, waiting for Sam's answer, knowing the bitter truth but wondering, hopelessly, impossibly wondering . . .

"I love your mother very much—for giving me you," Sam replied.

Alli closed her eyes against a rush of emotion. It wasn't an answer, but an evasion. She didn't know why she felt even the tiniest bit of surprise. Sam would never admit to loving her. She couldn't remember ever hearing those three simple words cross his lips, not even after Megan's birth. Or after, in the days and weeks and years that followed, not even when they made love, when they shared a passion that was perhaps the only honest part of their relationship. Sam always held a part of himself back, a portion of his heart and his soul that he would never give to her.

Alli clenched her fists, wanting to feel anger, not pain. She'd spent more than half of her twenty-seven years in love with Sam Tucker, but he didn't love her, and he never would.

She'd lived in a dream, ignoring all the signs of disinterest, Sam's long hours running his family's charter boat business, and his desire to limit their family to the one child who bound them together.

Alli had told herself lie after lie—that Sam would change, that he would suddenly see her for who she was, that he would want another baby. Even now, a deep ache echoed through her soul at the thought of never having another child with the man she loved, but she could no longer live in a fantasy world.

The last straw came three months ago when it had become startlingly clear that Sam still held hopes of being with her sister. The realization that, despite years of trying to be the best wife, the best mother, the best woman she could be, Sam still loved Tessa had driven Alli to do the unthinkable— to ask for a separation.

Sam had been shocked, and no wonder. She'd chased after him forever. But no more. She couldn't keep loving someone who didn't love her back. Could she?

The niggling doubt ran through Alli's mind, her heart still battling her brain. She'd always acted on her emotions, forgetting about logic. Even her seduction of Sam all those years ago hadn't come from a master plan. It had been more like a crime of opportunity. And she'd paid for it a thousand times over.

Alli let out a sigh. She'd done so many things wrong, taking forever to grow up, as her grand-

mother was fond of telling her. Her biggest guilt
came from putting Megan in the middle of her battle with Sam, but there was no way to avoid it.
Megan had always been in the middle. And she
always would be.

"Damn," Alli muttered as tears filled her eyes.
She ruthlessly rubbed them away. She had to let go
of the past and focus on the future. Making sure her
daughter had a wonderful loving relationship with
her father was her main concern. In the long run,
Alli could only hope that it would be better for
Megan to grow up in two peaceful homes than in
one unhappy one.

Taking a deep breath, Alli smoothed down the
sides of her short-sleeve emerald-green dress, the
first new outfit she'd bought in years. It was tighter
than she would have liked, but married life and
childbirth had only encouraged her naturally curvy
tendencies. She took solace in the fact that she still
looked better than she had in ages, and there was a
small part of her, make that a big part of her, that
couldn't help hoping Sam would be floored by her
new look.

Clearing her throat with purpose and determination, she entered the family room and said, "Hello."

Sam looked at her, his light blue eyes filled with
annoyance. "You're early," he said. "You said seven-
thirty, and it's only six. Megan and I were planning
to have a pizza."

"I'm sorry." She knew his frustration covered
pain. Sam might not miss her at all, but he did miss
his daughter.

"This is *our* time together," Sam reminded her.

"I know." Alli tried not to feel anything for the man, but his physical presence had always overwhelmed her. A rugged, outdoor man, Sam had sun-streaked brown hair that was always windswept, never styled. His face was perpetually sunburned. His body was lean and fit, his fingers and palms callused from working his boats. She could still remember the way his fingers felt drifting down the side of her cheeks, her breasts . . .

She drew in a quick breath and looked out the window at the storm clouds about to descend on Tucker's Landing, one of the small seaside towns along the southern Oregon coast. Although it was late June, the weather was still unpredictable, and on days like today, summer seemed far away.

"It's starting to rain," she said. "The forecast said maybe an inch or more. I didn't want to get caught in the storm. You know I hate to drive in the rain."

Sam tightened his hold on Megan, as if Alli were attempting to steal his dearest possession. But she wasn't a thief; she was Megan's mother. Turning her attention to Megan, Alli could see that her daughter felt torn between them. Megan's blue eyes were worried, her mouth slightly pouty as she chewed nervously on the end of her braid. The last thing Alli wanted to do was make Megan feel like a wishbone, but sometimes it seemed impossible to avoid. They both loved Megan so very much.

"I'll bring her home at seven-thirty," Sam said.

"That's in an hour and a half."

"Exactly. And it's my hour and a half."

She sighed. "Come on, Sam. It's been a long day."

"Maybe Mommy could have pizza with us,"

Megan suggested. She put her small hands on Sam's face so he couldn't look away from her and gazed at him with bright, eager blue eyes. "Please."

Sam's mouth set into a hard line. "I suppose. If she wants to."

Megan looked at Alli, drilling her with the same relentless gaze.

Alli hesitated, knowing the last thing Sam wanted her to do was stick around. But she hated to disappoint Megan over something so small.

"I could stay, I guess." She glanced at Sam. "Are you sure it's all right with you?"

"Does it matter?" He didn't look her in the eye. Sometimes she thought he went out of his way to avoid looking at her. Maybe she did the same thing. It was easier to keep the distance between them.

Sam gently urged Megan out of his lap and rose to his feet. "I'll call Nina's. The usual?"

Why was it always the simple words, the familiar memories that hurt the most? "The usual," she agreed.

Sam walked over to the desk and picked up the phone. While he dialed the number for the pizza parlor, Megan handed Alli the high school yearbook.

"Daddy showed me your picture," Megan said. "You were really pretty, Mommy."

Alli stared down at her sophomore photograph. She'd been trying to grow her hair out, to be more like Tessa. But where her sister's thick, wavy blond hair grew like a weed, Alli's own copper-colored cap never quite made it past her shoulders, and was so thin and fine it almost seemed to disappear.

Once, a very long time ago, Sam had told her that her hair was like silk, and she'd thought, foolishly of course, that he'd found something about her that he liked better than Tessa.

Alli slammed the book shut. Megan looked at her in surprise.

"What's wrong, Mommy?"

"Nothing." She forced a smile on her face. "What did you do today?"

"We waxed the hot rod."

"Of course," Alli said. Because next to his business, waxing his 1955 red Thunderbird was Sam's favorite pastime. She wouldn't have minded so much if the damn car hadn't been just another reminder of Sam and Tessa. In her mind's eye she could still see the two of them tooling around town in it.

"Do you want to see it?" Megan asked.

"The car?" Alli asked in confusion.

"No, the thing I made you. Weren't you listening, Mommy?"

"I'd love to, honey."

"I'll get it." Megan ran out of the room, and Alli walked over to the bookcase and stuck the yearbook in a dark corner where she hoped it wouldn't be discovered for another decade.

As her gaze traveled around the familiar room, she realized that Sam had done some cleaning, made some changes since he'd moved back into his family home and his parents had retired to Arizona. His father's pipe no longer sat in the ashtray on the desk. The three-foot-high pile of fishing magazines had been tossed in a large open box along with some other knickknacks—obviously destined for storage.

The changes made her feel uncomfortable. The thought that Sam was finally accepting that this was his home bothered her more than she cared to admit. That he was changing the house to fit him as a man instead of a child was odd, too. This house had been a part of her own childhood, because she'd grown up next door.

When she was nine, and Tessa eleven, they'd lost their parents in a car crash and come to live with their grandmother, Phoebe MacGuire. They'd traveled between houses as kids do, and Alli had come to know this one almost as well as her own. Although she had usually been the one tagging behind, trying to catch up to Sam and Tessa, and somehow the door always seemed to slam in her face.

Sam hung up the phone. "The pizza will be here in fifteen minutes."

She nodded. "Great. So, how did the weekend go?"

"Fine."

"Megan starts summer school tomorrow. We'll have to redo our visitation schedule."

"I hate that word," he said with a fierceness that startled her. "Megan is my daughter. We should all be living together, not visiting each other."

Alli didn't know what to say. So much for thinking that Sam had accepted things. "I'm sorry; that was the wrong word to use. You know you can see Megan as often as you want, Sam. I would never keep you apart."

"Then why ask for a divorce? Why break up our

family? Why the hell do you have to be so selfish, Alli?"

His words hit her like bullets, each one hurting more than the last, and her only defense was to hit back.

"Don't blame it all on me, Sam. I wasn't the only one who wanted out, just the one who had the guts to ask."

"You don't know what you're talking about."

"The hell I don't," she said sharply. "When I found that box of clippings and photographs of Tessa, I felt like I'd just stumbled upon you in bed with another woman."

"I was never unfaithful to you."

"Maybe not in body, but in mind you certainly were. How do you think it feels to know the man who is touching you is thinking about someone else?" Her voice shook with the depth of her pain. She could still see herself sneaking into Sam's office to surprise him with an intimate anniversary dinner, only to find a box of Tessa's photos hidden away in the bottom drawer of his desk. She'd been looking for the corkscrew he kept there so she could open the wine she'd brought to celebrate nine years together. What a fool she'd been.

"It was never like that," Sam said.

"It was *always* like that."

"Alli—"

"And it wasn't just the box of photos. It's been so much more, and you know it. I wanted more children, Sam, and you refused over and over again. Because having another child with me, making a deliberate choice to add to the family, would mean you were planning to stay with me. But you couldn't make that commitment, could you? You couldn't cross that line, because you weren't planning to stay forever. Well, I just cut the time short."

Before Sam could reply, Megan returned to the room.

"Look, Mommy, I made you a candleholder out of a wine bottle, see?" Megan held up the papier-mâché-covered bottle with a proud smile. "Daddy helped me. Can we light a candle for dinner?"

"I guess."

"No," Sam said abruptly. "We don't need a candle."

Megan's smile vanished. "Why not, Daddy?"

"Candles are for special occasions, honey," he said more gently as he headed for the door. "I'll get some drinks."

Sam walked into the hallway and leaned against the wall, stopping to catch his breath, to steady his pulse. *Candles are for special occasions.* What a stupid thing to say. But the thought of a candlelight dinner with Alli . . . No, he couldn't do it.

Alli put his stomach in a knot every time she walked through the door, every time she opened her mouth. She'd destroyed his life not once but twice, for when he'd finally come to terms with being a father and a husband—after he'd struggled so hard to make it all work, she'd bailed out on him.

A twinge of guilt poked at his conscience. Okay, so maybe he'd kept up with Tessa's life, stored a few photographs. They were harmless pictures. Half the world owned magazines with Tessa's face on the

cover. And how could he tell Alli tha
mother had given him most of the
would only destroy their relationship, b
think her grandmother was favoring he

And what did it all matter anyway? He'd married Alli as soon as he'd found out she was pregnant. He'd been twenty years old, Alli only eighteen. But they'd had to grow up overnight. He'd thrown aside all of his plans of traveling and seeing the world and gone to work for his father, eventually taking over the business and working his ass off to provide for his family.

Damn it all. He felt as unsettled as the weather outside. He didn't know whether to be furious or relieved it was all over. He didn't know why he couldn't look at Alli anymore, why her voice made him so nervous, why he was so afraid that the merest touch of her hands would be the death of him. They'd lived together for a long time, but he'd never been as aware of her as he was right now.

Alli walked out of the family room and bumped into him, not expecting to find him still standing there. He automatically reached out to steady her, his hands coming to rest on her waist, his fingers burning as the warmth of her body seeped through the thin material of her dress.

She sucked in a short breath, and his pulse quickened. He didn't want to look into her eyes. It was bad enough that he could smell her favorite perfume—Passion—that he could feel her body under his hands, that he could hear her breathing.

He couldn't look into her eyes. He couldn't take that risk. He didn't know what he would see there.

e wasn't sure he wanted to know. She'd confused him since the day she'd moved in next door as a bossy little girl, changing personalities as often as a chameleon changed color. Just when he thought he knew who she was, she turned into someone else.

"Sam?" she questioned, her voice turning husky.

It almost undid him. He'd loved her voice in the dark of the night, whispering, promising . . . He drew in a breath and dropped his hands from her waist. "I'll get those drinks."

She stopped him with a hand on his arm. "Look at me."

He sent her a brief glance that barely grazed her face, then turned away. "I'm thirsty."

"Sam—" The ringing phone cut off her words, and Sam felt a great relief. He brushed past her, returning to the family room to find Megan on the phone.

"Oh, hi, Mr. Beckett," Megan said. "Yes, he's here."

Sam took the phone from her hand. "William? How are you?"

"Not too good, Sam." William's usually brisk seventy-six-year-old voice trembled. "It's Phoebe. I don't know how to tell you this, but she's—she's had a stroke."

"No!" Sam couldn't stop the word from bursting out of his mouth. He sat down on the edge of the desk, grateful for the support. Not Phoebe. Alli's grandmother was strong and vital and energetic, and he couldn't imagine the world without her. "How bad is she?"

"I don't know yet. We were walking along the

pier and all of a sudden she stopped making sense and she couldn't walk. I got help as soon as I could," he said helplessly. "We're at the hospital now. They said to call the family. I couldn't find Allison. She's not home."

"She's here."

"Then you'll tell her?"

"Yes. I'll tell her." Sam looked at Alli standing in the doorway and saw the fear draw sharp lines in her face.

"And Sam . . ." William hesitated. "I know there's bad blood and all, but I've called Tessa and asked her to come home. She agreed. She'll be here tomorrow."

Sam's entire body tightened, a knee-jerk reaction impossible to stop. He hadn't seen Tessa since the night he'd told her he was marrying her sister. And now she was coming home.

Because Phoebe was sick, he told himself. It had nothing to do with him.

"Sam?" Alli asked after he'd said good-bye to William. She'd wrapped her arms around her waist, as if she could protect herself from whatever was coming.

"Your grandmother has had a stroke. She's in the hospital."

Alli's eyes searched his. "Is she—"

"No one knows anything yet."

"I don't understand. Grams never gets sick. She's strong. I just spoke to her a few hours ago. I have to go. I have to see her." Alli looked wildly around the room, searching for something. Sam reached out and closed her fingers over the keys she still held in her hand.

"Easy," he said. "I'll take you."

She looked into his eyes with desperation. "She has to be all right. She has to be."

"She's a fighter, Alli."

"But she's seventy-six years old."

"Mommy, is Grams going to die?" Megan asked.

Alli opened her arms as Megan ran into a tight hug. "I hope not, honey. I really hope not."

They clung together for a long minute, and Sam itched to join them, but he couldn't. Alli had made it clear that she didn't want him in her life.

Finally, Alli set Megan aside. "Go get your things, honey. We need to leave."

Megan ran out of the room, and Alli slowly straightened. Sam dug his hands into his pockets to stop himself from doing anything foolish, like hugging her.

"I can't lose Grams," Alli whispered, her eyes filled with fear. "She's all I have left of my family."

Sam didn't say a word. It wasn't true, because Alli wasn't alone. She had a sister—a sister who was coming home. He couldn't stop the sudden quickening of his pulse.

Alli's eyes suddenly changed, and he wondered if she could read his mind.

"Oh, my God! William called Tessa, didn't he?"

Apparently she *could* read his mind, or she'd simply added up the equation. Despite the animosity between the two sisters, Phoebe MacGuire adored both of her granddaughters.

"Yes, he called Tessa." It felt strange to say her name out loud. And stranger still to think of seeing

Tessa again, her blond hair, her blue eyes, her generous smile. Not that she'd be smiling at him.

"Is she coming back?" Alli asked, her face so tense she could barely get out the words.

"Yes."

"Then those divorce papers can't come a minute too soon."

Sam touched her arm, but she shrugged him away.

"Don't touch me, Sam. You don't have to pretend you care about me anymore. We both know it isn't true."

"I married *you*, didn't I?"

"There it is again, your favorite refrain—you married *me*. That was your gift to me. And I'm divorcing you. That's my gift to you. Now I guess it's Tessa's turn."

⛵ *Chapter 2*

$\mathscr{I}$t was nine hours from Milan to New York, another six to Portland, and then a couple of hours more in a plush black stretch limousine to the southern Oregon coast. As a supermodel, Tessa MacGuire was used to waking up in one city when she'd gone to sleep in another, to living on black coffee, lemon water, and lettuce. She'd become accustomed to calling her post office box home, spending the holidays with strangers, and smiling no matter how tired or unhappy or lonely she felt.

Most people thought she acted only in front of the camera, but deep down inside Tessa knew she acted almost every day of her life. And no one suspected. No one saw through the smile or the laugh or the cheerful wave. And that's the way she liked it, easy, impersonal, safe.

As Tessa looked out the window at the passing scenery, she knew she'd long ago passed safe. The meadows and dairy farms had given way to the thick forested hills, the last barrier between the valley and the coastline, her new life and her old one. Even the rivers and streams had gone from lazy and peaceful to wild and reckless, the weather changing just as quickly, the clear blue sky suddenly taken over by gray, threatening clouds. She'd heard on the news that it had rained most of the night. Maybe it would storm again. Maybe she wouldn't be able to get home.

Home. The word slipped into her mind unbidden. Tessa didn't want to think of Tucker's Landing as home, but the familiar scenery had begun to awaken her dusty, musty memories from their almost decade-long cocoon.

On impulse, Tessa lowered the window and took in a deep breath of cold, crisp air that smelled of wet pine and fresh grass. A mile or two later, her breath caught in her throat as the forest gave way to sharp rocky bluffs, and as they turned south, the right side of the road fell away in a sheer drop to the blue-green ocean below.

The sea was magnificent—tall, booming waves hitting the rocky shore, spraying a fine mist over the rocks and a few sea lions basking in the sunlight. The coastline wove in and out, the tides pushing and pulling at the beaches below with a relentless beat. She'd forgotten how overwhelming the ocean could be, consuming everything within its reach.

It was all too familiar—and all too much. Tessa rolled up the window and leaned against the leather seat, closing her eyes against the view, steeling her heart against the memories, the hurt that went right down to her bones whenever she thought about Sam and Alli.

God, how she'd once loved Sam Tucker! He'd been her best friend, her boyfriend, and now the last man she ever wanted to see again. And Alli . . . how could she look at her sister and not think of her betrayal? How could she face either of them?

Sam and Alli were married now. They had a daughter together, a daughter who was eight years old. Tessa shook her head, unable to believe how much time had gone by. It seemed like only yesterday they had all been teenagers, young, restless, in love, with their lives stretched out before them. The future had been filled with possibilities; now there was only uncertainty and fear.

Tessa's thoughts turned to her grandmother. She hoped and prayed that the news wasn't as bad as Mr. Beckett had implied. Perhaps by the time she arrived in Tucker's Landing her grandmother would be awake and smiling and telling them it was all right. *"I can't die yet,"* she'd say, *"because I'm not through living."*

It had been Grams's favorite expression, Tessa remembered fondly, words meant to reassure her that unlike her parents, who had died in a car accident, her grandmother wasn't going anywhere. Every night before bed, they would look out at the stars and her grandmother would point out two that appeared to be winking at them and tell Tessa to blow a kiss to her parents. Then Grams would tuck her into bed and say, *"I can't die yet, honey. I haven't finished counting the stars, and don't you know, my darling girl, that you will never be alone, because there is always love, and love lives forever."*

But Grams was wrong. Love didn't always live forever. And there was a good chance Tessa would end up alone.

"Miss MacGuire?" the chauffeur said over the intercom.

Tessa opened her eyes, grateful to have her disturbing thoughts interrupted. "Yes?"

"I'm not clear on the turnoff after First Street."

"Left on Bayberry Drive, a mile down the road to the end. The house is the last one on the edge of the bluff. It has a widow's walk."

"A what?"

"A long balcony that winds around the front and side of the house overlooking the ocean." The place where her grandmother had once paced incessantly, watching and waiting for her husband's boat to sail into the harbor. How scared she must have been that last time when his boat hadn't come back after the storm—maybe as scared as she must be now.

"Do you want to go to your grandmother's house now or the hospital?" the chauffeur asked.

Tessa hesitated. She was hours earlier than planned, having flown all night. It was only seven o'clock in the morning, too early to go to the hospital. She needed a few moments to pull herself together, to get her emotions in check so she wouldn't fall apart when she saw Grams—or Alli or Sam.

"The house," she decided.

Tessa pulled out a brush from her purse and ran it through her hair, taking peace in the reassuring movements. She could do this. She could go to the hospital, make sure that Phoebe was being well cared for. She could be cool, polite, and impersonal when she saw Sam and Alli again. She'd mastered those traits over the years and no one ever suspected anything was wrong—why should it be any different now?

A tiny voice reminded her that there had been a time when she and Alli could read each other's thoughts, when she and Sam could finish each other's sentences. But it wouldn't be like that anymore. Sam and Alli were together, and she was on her own.

Tessa straightened up as the limo turned into the main streets leading into downtown. Tucker's Landing certainly appeared to be flourishing. Flowers were bursting out of window boxes, freshly painted signs proclaimed antiques, books, cafés, and other touristy nooks. A huge banner hung over the main intersection announcing the upcoming Fourth of July celebration, complete with kite festival, clam chowder bake-off, fireworks, and live music.

The Fourth of July had always been a special holiday, because it was also her grandparents' anniversary. Every year they would trek down to O'Meara's Oyster Farm to shuck wild oysters until they found a pearl. It didn't matter that the pearls didn't match in size or color or shape; they were making a necklace, a circle of love to last for all time.

It had been John MacGuire's idea to make the necklace for his beloved Phoebe. A man of the sea, Tessa's grandfather believed that the wild pearls symbolized hope, beauty, strength, and love, everything he wanted for the family.

Nostalgia ripped through Tessa as she thought about the times she and Alli had waded through low tide to find what they were sure would be the oyster that held the perfect pearl. They hadn't known then that perfection was impossible—or that the necklace would never be completed because John MacGuire would die just before his fiftieth wedding anniversary. The forty-nine-pearl strand remained one pearl short of completion.

Tessa sighed as each turn of the limousine brought new sights but old memories. The heart of the town was still the harbor, filled with fishing boats, small yachts, and sailboats. A long pier stretched out to the sea, a wooden strip filled with shops and restaurants, a place where fresh crabs and lobsters made friends with the tourists.

Down the road, next to the pier, was the sign for Tucker's Charter Boats, offering fishing, whale watching, and ocean tours. Her heart skipped a beat as she remembered running down to the harbor late on a Saturday afternoon to meet Sam after he finished helping his father for the day.

Finally, thankfully, the stores turned to houses and the sidewalks turned to grass, and the quiet, sleepy neighborhoods reminded her that she didn't have to face everything yet, not quite yet.

But she felt jittery, and the sudden ringing of her cell phone made her jump. She told herself that no one had this number besides professional associates. It was safe to answer.

"Hello?" she said.

"Where the hell are you, babe?"

Tessa couldn't help the smile that crossed her lips at the sound of her favorite photographer's voice. "You won't believe me if I tell you, Jimmy."

"I guess that means you're not on your way to L.A. for our meeting today."

"I left you a message."

"A very cryptic one," Jimmy Duggan said. "Something about a family emergency. I didn't even know you had a family. So what happened?"

"My grandmother had a stroke."

"I'm sorry."

Jimmy's simple words brought a lump into her throat. "I'm sorry, too. We were supposed to get together a few months ago, and I canceled out on her. Now I might never have a chance to talk to her again."

"Hey, you gotta have some faith there, babe. You gotta believe in what you want to happen. Then it happens."

Her lips curved into a reluctant smile. Jimmy was an incurable optimist. She'd watched him sit out a potential hurricane to get the perfect shot for a magazine cover. And damn if he hadn't gotten the shot. But then Jimmy was used to getting what he wanted. With his dark Irish good looks, he could have been a model instead of a photographer. Instead he'd opted to make a career and a fortune for himself with photographs that were always so much better than anyone expected.

Jimmy was almost too good, capturing her face, her eyes, in ways that seemed far too revealing. Sometimes, Tessa wasn't sure if it wouldn't be safer to work with someone else, someone who didn't see nearly as much as Jimmy did.

"You still there?" Jimmy asked. "Or have I once again bored you to sleep?"

"That's you, the ultimate in boring."

"Ouch. So, when do you think we can reschedule?"

"I don't know. I'll have to call you."

"My schedule is free right now. Just let me know."

"Thanks. You're a pal."

There was a momentary hesitation on the other end of the line. "Yeah, you're a pal, too, babe. See ya."

Tessa shut off the phone as the limousine pulled up in front of her grandmother's house. It was too soon. She wasn't ready. She wanted to tell the driver to keep going, to take her somewhere else, but he had already turned off the engine and come around to open the door.

She automatically smiled, but she couldn't move. Her gaze drifted past the chauffeur to the Tucker house next door. She remembered her grandmother telling her that Sam's parents had moved to Arizona, but the house looked the same. Whoever lived there now hadn't even put on a new coat of paint, hadn't taken down the basketball hoop over the garage or trimmed the rosebushes by the front windows.

Her heart caught again on the memories. How could she do this? How could she smell the flowers blooming with the scent of summers past? Even the breeze sang of long-forgotten songs and childish words from their neighborhood ball games. If she closed her eyes for just a moment, she could be right back there in the days of innocence, no problems, no betrayals, no fears.

"Miss MacGuire? Are you all right?" the chauffeur asked.

Tessa shook her head. She wasn't all right. Maybe it would be better to leave now, before anyone knew she was here. She could go back to the airport and call Mr. Beckett, make up a story, something. She'd been gone so long. Who really needed her now?

Sam walked into his childhood bedroom and smiled at the sight of his daughter lying in twisted covers on the same twin bed he'd slept on as a child. Megan's curls were as tangled as the sheets, her face as pink as a blooming rose, her dark lashes sweeping against her cheeks in the gentle motion of sleep.

At least one of them was at peace, he thought, remembering the night before. For long, tense hours he and Alli had been at the hospital, watching Phoebe MacGuire struggle to come back from a stroke, the damage from which they still had yet to determine.

It wasn't fair. Phoebe shouldn't be in the hospital and Megan shouldn't be asleep on his old bed. She should be at home, in the house he and Alli had bought together, and so should he. At least Alli had let him keep Megan for the night, instead of fighting to take her home.

It was funny, but whenever he thought of Alli, he saw a lioness, fighting for what she wanted, for those she loved. She'd fought for him, tooth and nail, down and dirty, willing to risk everything and everyone. So why wasn't she fighting now? Had she really stopped loving him after so many years? Had she really stopped caring?

He should be glad, he told himself. Hadn't he felt smothered by her never-ending crush on him?

Hadn't he paid the price of his freedom, his future, because of her reckless, relentless love?

He knew it wasn't fair to blame it all on Alli. He'd been there that night all those years ago. He'd drunk too much that Christmas, realizing for the first time in his life that he was nowhere near as important to Tessa as she was to him. If he had been, she would have come home with him instead of going to Aspen for a modeling job. The realization had scared the shit out of him. Without Tessa, he didn't know who he was, and stupidly he'd thought he'd somehow figure it all out by having sex with Alli.

He regretted a lot of things about that night, but the one thing he wouldn't regret was this child sleeping before him. Leaning over, Sam pulled a stray curl off her cheek and tucked it behind her ear. Megan's breathing didn't even catch. She was fast asleep. She didn't have to be at summer school for another hour, and he'd already asked Gary to take his early-morning fishing trip out, so they had some time.

Sam walked downstairs and into the kitchen, stopping short at the sight of the dirty dishes. The counter was as messy as his life. Megan was upstairs, sleeping in the wrong bed. Phoebe was in the hospital, Alli was paralyzed with worry, and Tessa was coming home. Nothing was normal, and he had a feeling it wouldn't be for some time. But his father had once told him that a man took care of his family first and himself second, and that's what Sam intended to do.

* * *

Tessa walked onto the back deck and stared at her grandmother's gardens and the wide green lawn that spread across the rest of the yard, sheltered by the branches of a massive oak tree. As she stared at the gnarly old trunk, Tessa felt a smile tug at the corner of her mouth. Could it be? Was it possible?

She bounded down the steps, suddenly filled with energy, with wonder. She stopped at the base of the tree and looked up. It was still there, battered, weathered wood tucked into the branches. A haven. A refuge. A treehouse.

The steps were pieces of board hammered into the trunk of the tree. She could remember handing Sam the nails while he flexed his thirteen-year-old muscles and tried to impress her with every swing of the hammer. At the time, she'd been far more interested in getting to the top of that tree.

On impulse she stepped closer. It would be silly to climb the tree. She knew that. She was a twenty-nine-year-old woman, for heaven's sake, but as she looked up at the shimmer of sunshine peeking through the branches, she knew she had to go up if for no other reason than to reassure herself there was nothing there she wanted to see.

It took her only a few seconds to climb the ladder. It had seemed so much higher before, so much bigger. As her head came through the opening in the floor, she saw that the huge treehouse was just a small cramped space. Tessa climbed all the way into the house and sat on the floor. She felt like a teenager again, hiding away in her mansion in the sky, as Sam had called it.

Tessa's gaze was caught by the carving on the

floor. It was a crooked heart with an arrow through it, and the words *Tessa* and *Sam* carved into the middle. She reached out to trace the heart with her finger, then frowned as she realized that someone had tried to cross out *Tessa*. On closer inspection, she saw that her name had been replaced with Alli's.

She wasn't surprised. Alli had been desperate to be part of the treehouse club. Never mind that she was two years younger and always an annoying little pest. She never stopped trying to be one of them. Maybe that was the problem. Alli had always tried a little too hard.

Tessa leaned back against the wall, but as she did so she knocked a loose board with her hand and winced as it clattered through the branches to the ground. Apparently, the treehouse wasn't quite as solid as it used to be.

It was then she heard the voice, *his* voice. Oh, Lord! Her toes curled into her shoes. How long had it been since she'd heard his voice? Was she simply imagining it now? Taken back to the past by a memory?

"I said, who's up there," Sam yelled with irritation. "If that's you, Tommy Hecklemeier, there's going to be hell to pay. You know your mother said you couldn't keep climbing up there. Last time you broke your arm."

Tessa held her breath, realizing he couldn't see her from the ground. Maybe if she stayed really quiet, if she didn't say a word, he'd go away. She didn't want to see Sam here. She couldn't meet him again after all these years—not now, stuck in a treehouse with her hair a mess and her eyes all puffy from crying and . . .

"Come on down, or I'm coming up. And if I come up, believe me, you will be sorry."

Sam's voice had deepened, matured. She wondered what the rest of him looked like, if his legs were still long and lean, if he'd filled in the hollow spaces of youth, if his blond hair had gone darker, or if his blue eyes could still see into her soul.

Tessa closed her eyes, willing him to go away as much as she willed him to come closer. She wanted to see him and yet she didn't. She wanted to talk to him and yet she had nothing to say. She wanted to feel his comforting arms around her, to rest her head on his shoulder, to have him tell her everything would be all right, but he was married, married to her sister, as unattainable as the man in the moon.

"Go away, Sam," she whispered. "For both our sakes, just go away."

⛵ *Chapter 3*

Sam felt a chill run through his body. Last night's storm had brought a cooling to the area and the sun had yet to burn off the lingering clouds and fog. But his wariness had less to do with the weather and more to do with the feeling that all was not right.

It was probably nothing. The treehouse had always been a magnet for the neighborhood kids. Phoebe hadn't minded the company, but six months ago Tommy had fallen out of the treehouse and broken his arm, and since then she'd decided it was time for the treehouse to come down.

Sam had told her he'd do it, but he'd been stalling. The treehouse was part of his youth, and it didn't belong to only him. He'd built it with Tessa, for Tessa. She'd called it her mansion in the sky, the place where she could go and dream of all the cities she'd visit, all the things she'd do. Tessa had said it was easier to dream when you were closer to the stars.

He shook his head at the foolishness of it all. Dreams were for kids. So were treehouses. And tomorrow he'd take the damn thing down. Just as soon as he got Tommy out of it.

"If you're not coming down, I'm coming up," he warned, but still he hesitated. He hadn't been up inside the treehouse since he'd married Alli, and for a brief moment he wasn't sure he should go now. But he heard another creak and knew that he couldn't leave without rousting the little trespasser.

"Mrs. MacGuire told you this place was off-limits," he said as he climbed up the rungs, praying they'd take the weight of a full-grown man. He put his head through the opening. "You have no right to be here. You—" He stopped abruptly as he took in the tousled blond hair, the blue, blue eyes, the trembling lips, the perfect oval angel face.

He stared at her in disbelief, then swung himself up into the treehouse, feeling the boards creak with the combination of their weight.

Tessa wasn't supposed to arrive for hours, and she definitely wasn't supposed to be here in the treehouse. He shook his head and blinked, wondering if he'd somehow conjured her up.

"I probably shouldn't have climbed up," she said warily. "But when I saw it was still here, I couldn't resist."

"I thought you were one of the local kids. Why didn't you say something?" He heard the words come out of his mouth and was relieved that they seemed to make sense when his mind was in total chaos.

She was more beautiful than he remembered, a woman now, he realized, taking in the slender curves accentuated by her designer jeans and short clinging sweater. Her face was thinner than he remembered, her eyes a bit more tired, her expression world-weary.

"I hoped you might go away. I wasn't planning on seeing anyone yet." She put a hand to her hair. "I must look awful. I can't remember when I slept more than a few minutes in a row."

"No, you don't. Look awful," he added, unable to stop looking at her.

Almost a decade had passed between them, a friendship gone, a love affair severed, a relationship destroyed forever. Yet here she was—in the one place he'd never expected to see her again and looking as beautiful, as desirable, as vulnerable as he'd ever seen her.

"Have you seen Grams?" Tessa asked. "How is she?"

"Last night," he said. "They don't know the extent of the damage yet, if there is any. They're hopeful that it will be minimal."

Tessa's eyes filled with fear. Her expression reminded him of Alli, of the way she'd looked at her grandmother, silently praying for a miracle.

Alli! She'd hate that Tessa was here. Hate it even more that they were together.

"Will Grams be all right?" Tessa asked.

Ten years ago he would have lied. It would have been expected. Tessa hated bad news, and he'd always tried to protect her. But now . . .

"I don't know," was all he could say.

"That's not the right answer."

"We're not kids anymore." He sounded like a

gruff old man, but he had to put some barrier between them. "I can't make this go away like a bad dream."

She stared at him uncertainly. "That's too bad, because I'd really like to wake up and not find myself here." She let out a sigh. "I'm surprised Grams didn't take this down years ago. There was no reason to keep it." Her words sounded offhand, as if she didn't care, but her eyes seemed to say something else.

"You loved this treehouse once." He felt sure she wanted him to remind her of that, although he couldn't have said why.

"A long time ago," she replied.

A silence fell between them. The treehouse swayed gently in the breeze, leaves drifting past the open windows like the cascade of memories that fluttered in his mind. He could see Tessa eating peanut butter on celery sticks, writing plays they would later act out, lying on her back staring through a square hole in the roof at the stars that peeked through, weaving stories and dreams that would take on a life of their own.

"The treehouse used to be bigger, didn't it?" Tessa asked.

"We used to be smaller."

She sent him a bittersweet smile. "Right. Well, we should go. I need to pull myself together, then get to the hospital." She paused, sending him a curious look. "What are you doing here anyway?"

"I was getting the newspaper, and I thought I heard someone in the yard."

"Getting the paper? Are you keeping an eye on Grams's house while she's in the hospital?"

She didn't know, Sam suddenly realized. Didn't know he was living next door. Didn't know Alli had asked him for a divorce. Although he *was* married, at least for the moment, and there was still a part of him that couldn't let go of Alli and Megan and the life they'd built together for the last nine years.

"Sam?" Tessa asked, a question in her eyes.

"I'm living next door now."

"I thought—I thought you and Alli lived across town in the new Seaside development."

"Alli still lives there. I moved out three months ago."

She stared at him, her eyes completely unreadable. "I—I don't know what to say. Grams didn't tell me."

He shrugged. "It doesn't matter. Do you want to go down first?" He stopped abruptly as her eyes widened, as they both remembered.

"You go first so you can catch me," thirteen-year-old *Tessa said with a laugh that sang on the wind. "You can be my hero."*

"I would never let you fall," Sam said gallantly.

"I know that. I trust you with my life."

The memory teased at his brain like an unwanted, irritating refrain. He certainly hadn't turned out to be her hero. He'd let her fall. In fact, he'd given her a push.

"I'll go first," he said abruptly, and lowered himself to the ground as fast as humanly possible.

Tessa reached the ground a second later, her willowy body so close to his he could almost touch her. Instead he put his hands in the pockets of his blue jeans while she brushed an errant leaf out of her thick blond hair. She was tall, almost five foot ten, at least a half dozen inches over Alli. But there was still a sense of frailty about Tessa that he'd never seen in her younger sister, a feeling that she needed to be protected, while Alli could fend for herself.

"Do you know where Grams keeps the keys to her car?" Tessa asked. "I got a ride from the airport, but I have no way of getting to the hospital."

"Her car is in the shop. It will be ready this afternoon."

"Oh. I'll call a cab, then."

"I can give you a ride."

She looked surprised by the offer. So was he.

"Are you sure?" she asked.

He hesitated. "You have to get there, don't you? I was planning to go anyway, right after I drop Megan at school."

Megan! It suddenly occurred to him that he had a daughter who was probably wondering where he was. "Come over when you're ready." He started walking toward the side yard as he spoke.

Tessa hesitated. "I think I should take a cab."

"Why?"

"Because it seems easier."

He turned back to face her. "Easier to find a cab in this small town than to get in a car with me? You really have been gone a long time, haven't you?"

"Being with you is complicated. Did I really need to say that out loud?" she challenged, her eyes suddenly coming alive.

"Life is complicated."

"I try to keep it as simple as I can."

"That's why you didn't come back."

"That's one reason."

"Don't you want to meet your niece?" He'd always found Tessa's lack of interest in Megan irritating. It wasn't as if Megan had ever done anything to hurt Tessa.

Tessa looked surprised. "Do you think Megan wants to meet me? I'm sure she can't have heard much good about me in your house."

"Alli hasn't talked much about you at all."

"Of course she hasn't. What was I thinking?"

"But you are family, Tessa, whether you want to be or not."

"Not anymore, Sam."

"You and Alli have the same blood running through your veins. I consider that family."

"I'm sure Alli wouldn't agree with you."

"Probably not. But then she doesn't agree with me about most things these days."

"I thought you'd stick by her forever." Tessa clapped a hand to her mouth. "Forget I said that."

"Alli doesn't want me to stick by her."

"I can't imagine that."

"No need to imagine. It's simple fact." He turned toward his house, not sure she'd follow, not sure it wouldn't be better if she didn't. He opened the kitchen door and found Megan sitting at the table eating Cheerios soaked in milk. She looked up, her mouth full of cereal, her hair tangled from sleep. "Hi, Daddy. Where were you?"

"Next door."

"Did Grams come home?"

"No." He hated the sad look that crossed her face. "But she will soon. You better eat so I can get you to school on time."

Megan looked past him, her eyes widening. Sam looked from his daughter to Tessa and wasn't sure who was more surprised. He'd shown Megan pictures of Tessa, but he'd never fully explained why Tessa wasn't part of their lives.

"You're Aunt Tessa," Megan said in delight. "The one who was the fairy princess in the school play."

Tessa looked taken aback. "I, uh, yes, that was me."

"I'm going to be a princess next Halloween," Megan continued. "Mommy thinks I should be a lion, or a Gypsy, but I think a fairy princess would be better. Because they're so pretty. You're beautiful," she added shyly.

To Sam's amazement, a flush of red swept across Tessa's face. How many people must have told her she was beautiful, with long blond hair sweeping past her shoulders, eyes the color of the deep blue sea, and a mouth that could pout or kiss or laugh with the best of them.

Looking at her now, in the light of the kitchen, he was struck again by the sheer beauty of her. And what he liked even better was that she could still blush.

"Thank you," Tessa said slowly. "You're beautiful, too."

"Do you want some Cheerios?" Megan asked.

"No, thanks." Tessa took a step back toward the

door. "Maybe I should wait at Grams's house until you're ready to go to the hospital, Sam."

"Don't leave," Megan protested. "You just got here. I have so many questions. No one ever seems to know where you are. Daddy says you're a model. And Grams showed me your picture on the cover of a magazine. I want to be a model when I grow up." Megan sent Sam a look that dared him to deny her that dream. "So you have to stay."

Tessa glanced at Sam. "Do you think it's all right for me to be here?"

"Why wouldn't it be?"

"You know why."

He did. But despite Alli's wish for the contrary, Tessa and Megan were family. Sometimes family ended up in the same room. And sometimes he liked to live a little dangerously.

Alli stared down at her grandmother's face. There was no tightness to her skin, no pucker to her lips, no humor, no joy, no pain, no anger. Phoebe MacGuire's face was as smooth as the face of a porcelain doll, the lines of age having vanished overnight. She looked . . .

Alli was afraid to let the words out, terrified that saying something out loud or even to herself would make it come true. She desperately wanted to see something on her grandmother's face, some emotion that would show she was still alive, still caring about them, still fighting to go on. But aside from the slight rise and fall of her grandmother's chest, there was no movement. And Phoebe was pale, her skin almost as white as her hair, translucent against the white sheet that covered her.

Alli wished for Phoebe to open her eyes, so the light would shine out of them like the lighthouse beacon on the rocky beach calling the sailors home, showing them the way to go, guiding them to safety. She wanted to feel safe again. She wanted all of them to be safe.

"Wake up, Grams," Alli said softly, stroking her grandmother's hand. Alli could feel the pulse beating in her grandmother's thin wrist, but she could also feel the fragility of her bones, and it frightened her.

Had her grandmother always been this thin or had she lost weight? And if Phoebe had lost weight, why hadn't Alli noticed? She felt an immediate surge of guilt at the thought that she hadn't been paying enough attention, so caught up in her own problems was she. Was this her fault? Could she have done something differently?

"You have to be all right," Alli said more strongly. "I don't want you to die."

"I can't die yet, honey. I haven't finished counting the stars. And don't you know, my darling girl, that you will never be alone, because there is always love, and love lives forever."

Alli could hear the familiar words as clearly as if her grandmother had said them out loud. But in truth the words had come from memories of those dark nights when the fears took hold and the only one who could soothe them away was her grandmother.

"You have to wake up. You have to say the words,

Grams. Otherwise, I can't believe them. Please," Alli begged.

The hospital room door opened and William Beckett walked into the room. He was an imposing man, tall, with a strong square face, sharp dark brown eyes, and thick brows that matched the pepper-gray color of his hair. He wore an expression that told everyone he usually got what he wanted. And he wanted Phoebe.

Losing her more than fifty years ago to John MacGuire, a man picked out for Phoebe by her parents, William had returned from Chicago after John's death, determined to win Phoebe back. He'd become a frequent visitor to Tucker's Landing, spending weeks at a time in a rented cottage, all the while wooing Phoebe. And while Phoebe seemed to care deeply for William, she had yet to commit to any sort of future with him.

Alli had no idea what their real relationship was, but anyone could see that William, despite his austere demeanor, was in agony. He had dark shadows under his eyes and wrinkles in his usually crisp tan slacks.

"You're back?" he said gruffly. "I thought you might sleep in this morning."

"I couldn't sleep at all. How about you?"

"There will be time to sleep later."

Alli looked over at her grandmother, then back at William. "Do you think . . ."

"I hope," he answered quickly. "And I pray."

It wasn't what she wanted to hear. "The doctors?"

"Haven't come in yet this morning."

"I guess I'll wait, then."

"What about work?"

"I can't leave."

"Your grandmother owns a stake in that shop of yours, doesn't she?"

William knew that the Alley Cat, a gift shop specializing in hometown treasures, was more than a business for Alli, it was a lifeline her grandmother had thrown her last year when she'd started to flounder in a sea of self-doubt. And it had been the lifeline that kept her going through her separation from Sam. It wasn't just a gift shop, it was her life, her future, her daughter's future. But Grams was more important.

"You can't do anything for your grandmother, Allison," William said. "Except to continue on with your life."

"I wish I could do something, though."

"We all do. But it will be as it was meant to be."

"I can't accept that. I was never very good at accepting things I didn't like."

For a moment there was a glint of a smile in his eyes. "So I've noticed. I actually understand the inability to accept something that seems completely wrong." He glanced over at Phoebe and smiled. "Your grandmother would tell you I've been bull-headed for longer than you've been alive. Unfortunately, it still hasn't gotten me what I want." His voice drifted away and he moved toward the bed, sitting down in the chair next to Phoebe. He picked up her hand and squeezed it. "But I'm not done trying," he said softly. "So you better wake up, Phoebe, if for no other reason than to tell me to go away."

"She wouldn't do that," Alli said, deeply touched by the despair in his voice.

"She hasn't yet, but I'm not sure she won't." He shook his head. "But there will be time for that later. Now we have to concentrate on getting your grandmother well. Giving her whatever she needs." He focused his piercing dark eyes on her face. "You will do that, won't you?"

"Yes."

"Even if that means accepting your sister's presence here at the hospital?"

Alli stiffened. "I would do anything to make Grams feel better, but Tessa turned her back on Grams years ago."

"That isn't true and you know it. They've seen each other many times over the years."

"On exotic vacations that only Tessa could afford," Alli acknowledged bitterly. It was just one more area in which she couldn't compete with her older sister. "But where was Tessa when Grams sprained her ankle last year? And where was Tessa when Grams turned seventy or during any of the last nine Christmas holidays? I'm actually surprised she's coming now. Tessa swore she'd never set foot in Tucker's Landing again."

"Never is a long time. I expect Tessa will do what she needs to do, same as you will."

Alli just wished whatever Tessa needed to do could be done in another country, miles away from here, from her, from Sam. How could she deal with her sister on top of everything else?

Alli paced restlessly around the cramped hospital

room, feeling angry and scared, more scared than she'd ever been in her life. "I can't lose Grams." She paused, looking into William's compassionate eyes. "I have to do something. I'm going to call her doctor and tell him to get over here. She needs . . . she needs something," Alli finished, feeling helpless despite her brave words.

"Dr. Price was here until late last night," William reminded her. "He's a good man and he cares about your grandmother. His credentials are excellent. I wouldn't entrust your grandmother to just anyone. But if Dr. Price doesn't give us the answers we require, I have no qualms about finding another specialist, even if it means flying someone in from across the country."

Alli felt better knowing that William was prepared to do anything to save her grandmother. She just hoped there was something that could be done. Tears pushed at Alli's eyes as she stared down at her grandmother's beautiful but cold face. "I feel like she's already gone. I can't reach her. I can't make her wake up. And I want her to wake up."

"She's a strong woman, your grandmother," William said, his eyes fixed on Phoebe's face. "She does what she has to do without complaining. And she doesn't give up. You must have gotten that from her." He paused. "At least that's what she always says."

"Grams said I was like her?" Alli asked in amazement. "She never told me that. Everyone says Grams looked just like Tessa when she was young."

William stood up and came around the bed. He puts a hand on Alli's shoulder. "Phoebe was blond and beautiful when she was young, same as Tessa. But she had fire in her heart, too, same as you."

Alli smiled back at him. "Thank you."

"Now, why don't you go home or go to work? I'll call you when Phoebe wakes up or if the doctor has any news."

Alli hesitated. "If you're sure. I can pick up Megan and take her to school, then come back."

"I'm sure. And Alli . . . whatever you may think, I know your grandmother loves both you and Tessa. That's why I called your sister. Because Phoebe needs all the support she can get."

"I know. And I can handle seeing Tessa again," Alli said, wishing she felt as confident as she sounded.

⛵ *Chapter 4*

*T*essa. Alli felt the word reverberate through her brain as she stopped and stared at the scene in her husband's living room.

It was Tessa, all right. Tessa of the long, glorious blond hair and the bombshell body and the seductive blue eyes. Her sister hadn't changed at all. If anything, she was more beautiful than ever. And Alli was nowhere near ready to see her.

Alli glanced at Sam. His jaw was set in granite, his eyes dark and unreadable. She wondered what had gone on between them before she'd arrived. Had they talked? Had they run into each other's arms like long-lost lovers? An old intense jealousy grabbed hold of her heart and squeezed.

"Mommy?" Megan asked in confusion.

The one word pulled her together like nothing else could. "Megan," Alli said quickly, trying to catch her breath. She'd known this moment was coming. She'd anticipated Tessa's arrival. But not like this. She'd thought to meet Tessa at the hospital, in cold, clinical surroundings, not here in the Tuckers' old house, and most definitely not with Megan in attendance, listening to every word.

Seeing the three of them together tore at Alli's heart. They looked like a family—the mother, the father, the child. It struck her that this was the way it would have been, maybe should have been.

Alli wondered if Sam was thinking the same thing, the way he was looking at Tessa, the way Tessa was standing with Megan's brush in her hand.

Megan's brush? Tessa was doing Megan's hair. Oh, God!

Alli struggled to hang on. She didn't know how she felt—angry, sad, ashamed, embarrassed, left out? The emotions flew through her so fast she couldn't keep track of them. She knew she had to say something, but she was almost afraid to open her mouth, completely uncertain of what words would come out.

"Aunt Tessa is making a French braid," Megan said uncertainly, picking up on the tension in the room.

"Maybe your mother should do it," Tessa said.

"Mommy doesn't know how to do it very well." Megan sent her mother an apologetic glance.

Alli's first inclination was to grab the brush out of Tessa's hand and take Megan as far away from her sister as she possibly could. Because Megan was *hers*! And Alli couldn't take a chance on Tessa's stealing Megan's affection the way she'd taken everyone else's.

Despite the childish emotions swamping her, there was a part of Alli that remembered she was an adult, a mother, and she couldn't lose control with Megan in the room.

"Alli, can I talk to you for a minute—in the kitchen?" Sam asked.

She looked at him in confusion and saw something in his eyes she hadn't expected—understanding. He knew she was about to blow, and he was offering her a way out. For Megan's sake, she had to take it. Mumbling something, she headed to the kitchen. She sat down at the table and desperately counted to ten. "When did *she* arrive?" Alli asked finally.

"A while ago," Sam said warily.

"I didn't expect her until later."

"She flew all night to get here as fast as she could."

"But she didn't go to the hospital. No, she came here instead. I wonder why."

Hearing the words fly out of her mouth, Alli knew they sounded like an accusation, but she couldn't help it. Why was Tessa here—brushing Megan's hair, chatting it up with Sam—when Grams was in the hospital fighting for her life?

"She thought it was too early to go to the hospital. She didn't realize they'd let family in at any time." Sam took the seat across from her. "Alli, you knew she was coming. Why are you so surprised she's here?"

"I thought I was ready. But it turns out I wasn't. She's still beautiful, isn't she?" Sam didn't look away, but he also didn't give anything away. "Isn't she?" Alli persisted.

"If I say yes, will that make you happy? If I say

no, will it be the right answer? Come on, Alli.
Tessa's looks aren't the question, and you know it."

"So she just fits right back in, like she never left."

"Maybe that's just the way it is with family."

"Tessa is not family—not anymore. She said it
herself when she left. She said she didn't want a sister. And since I feel the same way, I guess we agree
on one thing."

"Tessa was hurt. *We* hurt her," he said, reaching
out to cup her chin with his fingers. "You know we
did."

She hated that he was right, but he was. And she
could even admit it now, although it had taken her
years to come to grips with what she'd done. There
had always been ways to rationalize it. Tessa could
have come home that Christmas. Sam could have
said no.

"If anyone has a right to be angry, it's Tessa," Sam
added. "I was her boyfriend. You are her sister."

She shook his hand off her face. "Tessa made mistakes, too, Sam. She broke your heart when she
didn't come home with you. Yet you blame her for
nothing."

"That's not entirely true. And that doesn't excuse
what we did."

"I know that. But Tessa wasn't perfect, and I hate
that no one else can see that."

He uttered a short, bitter laugh. "No one else can
see it? Hell, Alli, you're the only one who ever
thought she was perfect. You couldn't see past
Tessa's pretty face. You were so consumed with jealousy, you never saw Tessa for who she really was."

"Because everyone treated her like she was a goddess visiting us from the top of the universe. And it doesn't look like anything has changed. Before she only had Tucker's Landing to rule, now she has practically the whole damn world at her beck and call. Even Megan . . ." Alli stood up, too restless to stay seated. "Even Megan has joined the ranks of the adoring."

"Megan is excited to meet her aunt. I don't think it would matter if Tessa had warts and a long nose. Megan would still want to meet her, because she's family."

"But she doesn't have warts and a long nose. And Megan wants Tessa to do her hair. How could you let Tessa do her hair?" she asked, her voice catching in her throat.

"I—" He shrugged. "I don't know. I can't make a French braid. And that's what Megan wanted."

His answer was so damn logical she wanted to scream.

"You're making too much of this," he added quietly. "You always make too much of things where Tessa is concerned. You've been doing it since you were nine years old. Can't you let anything slide?"

"It's not that easy. You don't know what she does to me."

"I have a pretty good idea," Sam said dryly. "I've refereed more battles between the two of you than I care to remember. But what you have to remember is that Tessa is here because of Phoebe. And that's all that's important."

"I know. I know." Alli pushed her hair out of her eyes. "I just wish Grams was all right and Tessa was on the other side of the world where she belongs."

Frustrated, she picked up the cereal bowl and carried it to the sink. She set it down more forcefully than she should have and it clashed with a glass, shattering it into several pieces. It was suddenly all too much, her grandmother, Sam, Tessa . . . Tears flooded Alli's eyes as she leaned against the counter.

A moment later, she felt Sam's hands on her shoulders, rubbing the tight muscles the way he'd done so many times before. It was familiar and loving and painful.

Still, Alli couldn't help leaning back against him. He felt so good, strong, safe. And she needed to feel him with her, behind her, supporting her, even if it was only for a minute.

"So, what now?" she asked with a sigh.

"I think I should take Tessa to the hospital, and you can take Megan to school."

Again, the green-eyed monster raised its ugly head. Of course he wanted to take Tessa, more time alone with his long-lost love.

She jerked away from him. "Fine. That's probably the way you want it."

"Yeah, I figure we can make out on the way to the hospital." Sam caught her by the arm, and this time his grip was not reassuring, it was angry. "What the hell kind of man do you think I am anyway?"

"I don't know."

"Don't you? Haven't we lived together for the past nine years? Haven't you folded my underwear and taken my temperature and seen me go to work every day and come home every night—to you, to my daughter?"

His eyes blazed with a fury she didn't begin to understand.

"I know what color your underwear is, Sam, but I don't know what you think, how you feel about me or Tessa or anyone for that matter. You don't talk to me."

"Maybe you don't listen. Maybe you don't want to hear me, because it would upset all your fantasies and illusions."

"I don't have any more fantasies. They died from lack of interest. So let me go, Sam, because we both know you've been trying to get away from me for most of your life."

Sam's hand fell from her arm. "Maybe you're right," he said. "Maybe it's time we both let go. Because I don't know what we're trying to hold on to."

Alli swallowed hard. She didn't really want him to let her go. But it was too late to take back her words. And it was better this way. Despite what Sam said, she knew his feelings for Tessa were unresolved. And now that Tessa was back, maybe it was time to resolve them.

"I'm out of here," Sam said, leaving her alone in the kitchen.

When she finally got up her nerve to return to the living room, she found Megan sitting all alone in the big armchair with her backpack on and her hair done up in a beautiful French braid.

"You look terrific," Alli said.

Megan's face blossomed into a smile as she moved her head from side to side. "Do you like it?"

"Like it? I love it. Are you ready for summer school?"

Megan nodded and got to her feet. "Are you going to take me, Mommy? I like it when you take me to school."

"You do?" Alli said.

"Yes, because Daddy always listens to the sports station and you listen to music."

It was the best compliment she'd gotten all morning. "You can listen to whatever you want, sweetie."

"Aunt Tessa is nice," Megan said.

Alli felt her body go tense. She couldn't come up with a response to save her life.

"How come you never talk about her? She's really pretty." Megan paused. "But you're way prettier, Mommy."

Alli swept Megan up into her arms and gave her a big hug. "I love you, baby."

"I love you, too, Mommy. But I'm not a baby anymore."

Alli gave her a teary smile. "I know, but you'll always be my baby."

Tessa tried to relax, but sitting next to Sam in the front seat of his Ford Explorer felt awkward and uncomfortable.

Sam had barely spoken to her, barely looked at her since they'd left the house.

She suspected he and Alli had had an argument in the kitchen, probably over her. No doubt Alli had not liked the fact that she was here, or that Megan wanted her aunt to do her hair. Well, big deal. Alli was acting like a child.

Tessa cleared her throat. Sam didn't even glance at her. "Sam," she said pointedly.

"What?" He didn't sound at all happy to be speaking to her.

"Do you still have the T-Bird?"

"Yeah."

"But you don't drive it?"

"Once in a while. It's not exactly a family car."

And he was a family man. How strange to think of him that way.

"Are you and Alli really getting a divorce?" she asked.

"It looks that way."

"Mind if I ask why?"

"Alli wasn't happy."

"Were you?"

He didn't say anything for a long moment. "Maybe not every second of every day, but who is?"

"That's an evasive answer."

He shrugged. "What about you? Are you happy?"

"Me? Of course I'm happy. My career is great. I travel all over the world. I make a lot of money." She cleared her throat, wondering why it didn't sound that good. She had a fantastic life, everyone said so. "I have two apartments, one in L.A. and one in New York," she added.

"Can't decide which city you like better?"

"It's convenient to have a place on each coast."

"Life in the fast lane," he murmured.

"There's a lot to see and do," she said, feeling defensive. She couldn't tell if he was impressed or critical of her lifestyle. "It's a big world out there."

"You don't get tired of the traveling?"

"No. Well, sometimes." She let out a breath, feeling especially weary today. She turned her head to look at him and was reassured by the familiarity of his profile. This was Sam. Why was she pretending? "It's hard to stay ahead of the pack," she said. "There are so many pretty young girls chasing me, I'm beginning to feel hunted."

"I doubt anyone can catch you."

Then Sam sent her a smile that took her right back to where they'd once been, when his every look could make her palms sweat and her heart race. There were better looking men in the world. She'd posed with many of them. But there was something about Sam that stirred her. Even now, dressed in blue jeans and a T-shirt, he was far too appealing.

"I appreciate the vote of confidence," she said lightly.

"It sounds like you've got everything you wanted."

Except you. Except a husband and children.

"Pretty much. So do you and Alli ever get out of this town?"

"We went to Los Angeles for a car show a few years back. That's about it."

"I remember when you wanted to hunt for shipwrecks in the Caribbean."

"I think I wanted to a professional race car driver, too, but I grew up."

"I also remember a time when you swore you'd never work for your father, but Grams tells me you've taken over his business completely."

"I like it better than I thought I would."

"Really? Or have you gotten good at making the best of things?"

He shot her an annoyed look. "You know, there was a time when you wanted to get married and have kids. What happened to *that*?"

Her body tightened at his question. She knew he was only getting a little back at her, but he had no idea how much his words hurt. Of course she'd wanted to get married. She'd wanted to marry him, have *his* children. She'd never found anyone else with whom she wanted to spend the rest of her life.

"I can still have all that. I have plenty of time. And I think it's smart to follow a plan, to make things happen when they're meant to happen."

"Bull's-eye," Sam said, putting a hand on his heart. "We're almost at the hospital. Any other darts you want to throw before we get there?"

She hated the fact that she'd said anything. It had been her intention to stay calm, in control, to never let him think she had spent one second of one day upset about what he had done to her.

"I don't want to talk about it," she said quickly.

"That makes two of us."

A few minutes later, Sam turned off the highway and entered the hospital parking lot. He pulled the key out of the ignition. "Ready?"

Tessa hesitated. "Sam . . ." She didn't know what she wanted him to say, but something.

"You can do this," he replied, in answer to her silent plea.

"Grams is the strong one, not me. I won't be any use to her."

"She needs you, Tessa."

"I'm not good with sick people. I never know what to say, what to do. I feel helpless."

"You'll be fine. Phoebe isn't expecting a tap dance. In fact, the doctor said it might take time for her to recover enough to speak or move."

"Oh, God! She's paralyzed. You didn't tell me she was paralyzed." A dozen horrible thoughts ran through her mind. Grams in a wheelchair. Grams unable to speak. It was too awful to contemplate, but she couldn't stop her imagination from running wild.

"Hang on a second," Sam said hastily. "They don't know the full extent of her condition, Tessa. She could recover completely. Don't jump off that cliff yet."

Tessa put a hand to her mouth, feeling suddenly nauseous.

"Come with me. Grams always liked you. I'll feel better if you're there."

"I can only stay for a few minutes. I have to get things settled at work."

"Thank you." Tessa opened the car door and stepped onto the pavement. Sam joined her a second later, locking the car doors with his remote control. She smiled at him and shook her head in amazement.

"What?" he asked curiously.

"You, me. I can't believe I'm here. After all these years."

"I can't quite believe it either."

"Grams says Tucker's Landing is turning into a tourist mecca," she said as they began to walk toward the hospital.

"That's right."

"So your business is doing well?"

"Yes, in fact . . . I haven't told anyone this, but I got an offer to sell out to a Japanese outfit."

"Really? Are you going to sell?"

"I don't know. It's an interesting offer, but completely impractical. What I *should* do is buy myself another boat and make it impossible for any outside operation to come in and take over my business."

"But if you sell, you could do something else with your life." She paused. "I know you had to go to work, Sam, that it was the most logical move to make, but surely you've wanted something more, something else over the years. I don't remember you ever dreaming about growing up to be your father."

"I'm not my father." He shrugged. "I'm a Tucker and I belong in Tucker's Landing. It's where my home is, my business is, and most importantly, where my daughter is."

"Alli works at a gift shop, doesn't she?" Tessa asked as they moved toward the hospital entrance.

"The Alley Cat. She doesn't just work it. She owns it with your grandmother."

"Alli as a businesswoman; that seems strange, too."

"She's actually very good at it."

Tessa raised an eyebrow. "Defending the woman you're about to divorce?"

"The divorce doesn't have anything to do with Alli's business capabilities. You know, you might find it hard to believe, but away from you, Alli actually acts like a grown-up most of the time."

"You're right, I find it hard to believe."

⛵ Chapter 5

"Five minutes around Tessa and I go from being a mature adult to acting like the nasty, jealous little sister I used to be." Alli tossed her purse down on the front counter of her store, thankful that the shop was still empty, because she needed to talk to someone before she exploded.

Mary Ann Whitman was not only Alli's assistant, but in the past year she had become a dear friend. At thirty-five, the slightly pregnant, brown-haired Mary Ann was eight years older than Alli. Where Alli was emotional, Mary Ann was cool as a cucumber. Where Alli was spontaneous, Mary Ann had a day planner that was detailed to the last minute. And when Alli took chances, Mary Ann usually had a backup plan just in case things didn't work out.

With such complementary strengths, they had developed a strong friendship and a good working relationship. And with daughters the same age, they also had the added advantage of sharing baby-sitting.

"You have to stop reacting," Mary Ann said as she finished straightening a display of shell jewelry.

"Tessa knows how to push your buttons, and I bet you're good at pushing hers."

"To be honest, Tessa barely said a word. It was just her presence. God! She's so disgustingly beautiful. Megan already adores her. And Sam, well, Sam is probably thrilled she's back."

"What do you think?" Mary Ann asked, motioning toward the display. "Kathleen really outdid herself with these necklaces," she added, noting the fine detail work of one of their local artisans.

"It looks great," Alli said without much enthusiasm.

"How is Phoebe?" Mary Ann pushed her constantly slipping glasses back up her nose and stared at Alli with concerned brown eyes. "Was she any better this morning?"

"No. In fact, William just called me to say that the doctor said it's a matter of time now to see how much damage has been done. They've run several tests, but they'll have to see what happens in the next few days before they can determine the full extent of the stroke." Alli sat down on the stool behind the counter. "I've never seen Grams so still."

"She's just getting her strength back."

"I hope so. William is staying with her."

"He's a good friend. Or it is more than that?"

Alli tipped her head. "Maybe. Grams is cagey when it comes to him. I do believe he has a thing for her, but I have a hunch that Grams is still in love with my grandfather."

"What are you doing here anyway? I thought you were spending the day at the hospital."

"Tessa and Sam are there now."

"And you don't want to keep an eye on them?" Mary Ann raised a questioning eyebrow.

"I don't want to upset Grams. And I'm not sure I can keep my mouth shut when Tessa is in the room."

"You know, I'm sure Tessa has all kinds of men dancing to her tune these days. She's a supermodel, for heaven's sake. Sam's just a small-town guy to her now. You have nothing to worry about."

"But she never married. Don't you think that's odd?"

"Tessa is living the jet set life. And she's not even thirty. There is plenty of time for her to settle down."

"I know. You're right. Tessa is free as a bird." Alli's mouth trembled. "And in a short while Sam will be free, too."

"Oh, honey," Mary Ann said with a compassionate shake of her head. "Why don't you call the whole thing off?"

"I can't."

"Sure you can."

"No. Tessa is back now. It's fate. Sam has to find out."

"Find out what?"

"Whether or not he still loves her."

Mary Ann looked at Alli with sharp, knowing eyes. "Are you sure you want him to find out? Because you could pull it in right now, take it all back, and I think Sam would go along with you. He loves Megan."

"But does he love me?"

Mary Ann sighed. "Maybe it's just enough that he

likes you a lot. Come on, Alli. You're not a kid any-more. You have a child, a job, a mortgage, bills to pay. That's the reality of your life—mine, too. Some days I'm not even sure I like my husband anymore, much less love him. And as for sex, well, jeez, the one good thing about pregnancy is that I can plead a headache as often as I want."

"You don't mean that. You're madly in love with Ron."

"I'm not 'mad' about anything or anyone. Passion is for teenagers. Something for them to do with all their energy. It doesn't last in any marriage."

"It's different for you. You know why Ron mar-ried you, and it wasn't because you were pregnant. Sam did the right thing by me. And I appreciate that. But we didn't marry for love."

"Maybe you didn't start off right, but you and Sam have made a life together. Why throw it all away?"

"Because this is the right thing for me to do—for Sam. When I saw that box of photographs and mag-azine covers, I felt like I'd stumbled on Sam and Tessa having sex together. It was awful." Alli shook her head, still feeling the pain of that moment.

"So he kept some mementos. Big deal. It's his past. You're his present, his future."

"They weren't from the past; the pictures were of Tessa today. Sam has been following her career, keeping his eye on her, probably counting the days until Megan turns eighteen," she said bitterly. "That's why he hasn't wanted to have any more children. He knows once Megan is an adult he can walk away, having done his duty. And you know what, he won't even be forty. He can start over, have another family—with Tessa."

"Whoa, slow down," Mary Ann said sharply. "You are way out there."

"I can't help it. I forced Sam to be a husband, a father, a provider. I thought I could make it work. I pretended for a long time that he would fall in love with me by the sheer force of my will, but I know now that Sam hasn't forgotten Tessa, and I don't think he's given up on her either. She still has his heart. And if she has his heart, she might as well have him. Because I can't go on living like this. I want my husband to be in love with me. I want to have more children."

"Then don't give up on your marriage." Mary Ann walked up to the counter and looked Alli straight in the eye. "You're not a quitter, Allison Tucker. Everyone in this town knows you fight for what you want. Why don't you make Sam see that you are still the best thing that ever happened to him?"

"Because I want Sam to fight for me this time."

Mary Ann sent her a sad smile. "Sometimes you have to be happy with what you have."

"I want more," Alli said simply. "I always have."

"And somehow you usually find a way to get it. For what it's worth, my money's on you."

"Even with Tessa in town?"

"Absolutely. It's much easier to fight a real person than a memory."

"I disagree. No one can diminish the memory of a first love. It's too strong. No matter what I do for

Sam, he'll always think that he lost out on the love of his life."

"But he didn't. He just doesn't know it yet."

Alli smiled at Mary Ann. "You're a good friend."

"And you're just going through a bad patch. Every marriage hits rocks. How many times can you pick up smelly socks and still want to suck on your husband's toes? We're talking about real life here."

Alli put a hand to her head. "You're giving me a headache. It's too early in the morning for toe sucking."

"Well, think about it."

"Thanks, but I'd rather not."

Mary Ann laughed as the bell over the door rang in a customer. "Saved by the bell."

"Can you keep an eye on things out here? I want to do some computer work in the office, check out the Internet and see what I can find out about strokes."

"No problem. Is Sam staying at the hospital with Tessa?"

Alli sent her a dark look. "I have no idea. Like I said, Sam is a mystery to me."

Mary Ann patted her on the shoulder. "You always did like a good mystery, honey. Just keep turning those pages, because I have a feeling this story isn't nearly done."

The late afternoon shadows danced off Sam's office wall, reminding him of the way Alli's wedding ring used to catch the light as she waved her hand around, each word she spoke accompanied by some rapid movement of her fingers.

Shit! Why was she back in his mind again? He rested his elbows on the desk, wondering if Alli still wore her wedding ring. He couldn't remember seeing it on her hand this morning. Had she taken it off? Why couldn't he remember? Why did he care?

Slamming his hand down on the desk in frustration, Sam got to his feet and walked over to the window that overlooked the harbor. By the Fourth of July there would be no empty slips, no quiet mornings. While a part of him missed the solitude of winter, the other part of him reveled in the chance to make some summer money. The next three months would determine the success of the rest of the year.

As Tucker's Landing and the towns to the north and the south began to spread closer to each other, there would be more long-term business as well, which was exactly why the opportunity to sell his charter boat service had arisen. But how could he leave behind what had become a part of him?

Saying it out loud to Tessa had only confirmed what he had instinctively known—that this was his life now, and he needed to start living it. Not just managing it, not just keeping his head above water, not just surviving, but taking charge, making changes. He'd invested his time in his business but not his heart.

Maybe that's what he'd done with his marriage, too. Maybe it had been easier to live the life that had happened to him instead of making it his own. But, hell, when had he had time to think about any of it;

he'd been too busy growing up, being a father, running a business.

Well, it was time now. In fact, it was past time.

The door opened behind him, and he didn't have to turn around to know that Alli had entered the room. He could smell her. He could feel her. Maybe it was because they hadn't had sex in months. Maybe that was why he was so attuned to her. He couldn't possibly miss her.

"Grams hasn't changed," she said.

He turned around and saw the shadows under her eyes, the tight lines around her mouth, the worry in her expression. Her hair drifted loose from its clip, and her black pants and matching sweater only emphasized her aura of gloom.

"The doctors said it was normal for Phoebe's body to shut down for a while," he reminded her. "She's suffered a trauma."

"It's been twenty-four hours since it happened. I think that's long enough to sleep, especially for Grams. She never sleeps. I talked to her, trying to get her interested enough to open her eyes and look at me, but she just wouldn't. It's so frustrating."

Sam looked at the clock on the wall, suddenly realizing it was after five. He'd meant to get back to the hospital but he'd let the work take over his mind, relieved to have something constructive to focus on. "When did you see your grandmother?"

"About an hour ago. William was still there. I don't think he's left her side all day." Alli cleared her throat and looked down at her shoes. "Apparently, he lent Tessa his car so she could go back to the house and rest."

Sam nodded, wary of Tessa's entrance into the conversation.

"I'd like to go back tonight, but I don't want to take Megan there again," Alli said. "She needs to be at home, watching television, playing, being normal. I don't want her worrying about Grams."

"I'll stay with her."

Alli hesitated. "At the house?"

"At *our* house," he said pointedly. "Of course."

"I didn't know if it would be uncomfortable for you to be there."

"It's uncomfortable for me to *not* be there," he said shortly.

"I told you I would leave and you could stay, Sam."

"And I told you it was better for Megan to be with her mother in her own house, her own bedroom. I still feel that way."

"Well, thank you,"

"Would you stop being so fucking polite?" he shouted, fed up with their conversation.

"Polite? You're angry with me for being polite?" she asked in amazement. "That's a switch. Didn't you call me selfish, childish? Now I'm in trouble for acting like a polite adult? I can't win, can I?"

For some reason he was relieved to see the sparkle come back into her eyes, the color sweep across her cheeks. She looked alive again. She looked like Alli.

"I'm the one who can't win," he said. "You get pregnant, so I marry you. But that's not enough. I work like a dog to make a life for us, but I don't spend enough time with you. I take care of you and watch over you, but because I don't send you love letters, I'm a bastard."

"I never asked for love letters. I asked for love," she cried, stepping forward as she shook her finger in his face. "Not once, Sam Tucker—not once have you ever said *I love you*."

Her wedding ring caught in the fading sunlight and sent sparks dancing off the wall, blinding him with memories. So she *hadn't* taken it off. He couldn't hear what she was saying. He couldn't remember what he was going to say, because her face was too close and her breath came in gasps that reminded him of the way she breathed when they made love.

He felt himself lean forward and saw her do the same. Suddenly her mouth was in reach, her lips were under his, and she tasted like his best dream, his best meal, his best kiss.

And she kissed him back. Her lips opened under his and he slipped his tongue between the seam before she had a chance to shut him out, before she remembered that she didn't like him and he didn't love her. But this wasn't about thinking, it was about feeling, wanting, taking, and he took, kissing her again and again, his body hardening with each taste, his hands seeking her soft curves.

She seemed to melt into him like a sail catching a breeze, going along for the ride, for the simple thrill of it all. It was so easy, so freeing, so—over.

Alli shoved him away hard, her hair flying around her face, tangled from his fingers, her eyes glittering with desire, with fear. "What the hell are we doing?"

It was a good question. A damned good question. He just wished he had an answer. The silence went on too long as he wrestled with an explanation.

"Let's just forget that happened," she said finally, crossing her arms in front of her chest, then uncrossing them, as she shifted from one foot to the other. "What time will you come to the house?"

"What time do you want me?"

"I don't want you," she burst out. She put a shaky hand to her mouth. "I don't want you."

"I thought we were going to forget."

"You shouldn't have kissed me."

"You shouldn't have kissed me back," he replied. "Bad habit."

He nodded. Wasn't that the truth?

"Come by in an hour," she said more decisively. "I'll feed Megan before you get there, and I'll be home by ten."

"Do you want an apology, Alli?"

Her eyes met his. "That's the last thing I want, Sam. Don't you know that yet?"

Chapter 6

"I wish I knew what to say to you." Tessa scooted forward in the chair next to the hospital bed. She wanted to take Phoebe's hand, but she was afraid to touch her, because this pale, lifeless woman did not look anything like her vibrant grandmother.

"I guess I should tell you how things are going, if you can hear me. The nurse thinks you might like some conversation." Tessa took a deep breath, then continued. "I saw Sam and Alli today. I knew I would when I got on the plane to come back here. I don't know what I was expecting. They look the same, and yet they don't. Sam felt like my friend. Alli looked like my sister." She paused. "But the truth is—Sam isn't my friend, and Alli isn't my sister. I don't want to feel anything for them. It hurt so bad the last time we were all together. How can I go through that again?"

Tessa settled back in the chair and crossed her legs, wishing her grandmother could tell her everything would work out. Then she realized how selfish that sounded. Grams was fighting for her life, and Tessa was worrying about an old love affair.

Maybe she really was as shallow as Alli had said.

Disturbed by her thoughts, she got to her feet and paced around the small room, which was sterile and frightening. Tessa hated the smells of medicine and disinfectant, the sounds of beeps and bells. She especially hated the nurses who were laughing in the hall like everything was fine, when there were people who couldn't laugh, who couldn't speak, who weren't fine.

"I don't want you to be here, Grams," she said, returning to the side of her grandmother's bed. "I want things to be the way they were."

Tessa's vision blurred with a sudden rush of tears. She couldn't cry. Models didn't cry, not ever. It was bad for the eyes, bad for the complexion. Crying made her human, and she wasn't supposed to be human, she was supposed to be super, extraordinary, out of this world. But right now she felt small and helpless.

Reaching for a box of tissues, Tessa deliberately blew her nose and wiped her eyes, just the way her grandmother had done after they'd buried Tessa's parents and gotten on with their lives.

"I'm going to get through this and so are you," Tessa said, resuming her seat. "I did meet Megan today. She's just as beautiful and smart and funny as you said. And she might have been the only one who was actually happy to see me arrive. Sam looked—shocked when he saw me, and wary. I don't remember him being so careful with his words, so quiet. And Alli was angry, guilty . . . I don't know. Sam says she has grown up. Maybe she has. It doesn't matter. We might be sisters in blood, but there isn't anything else there. Sometimes that's the way it is with sisters."

Tessa let out a sigh. "I really wish this hadn't happened to you, that we were sitting on a lounger on a beach somewhere sipping those piña coladas that you like so much. I wish I could hear you laughing and see you doing those crossword puzzles that drive you crazy or digging in your garden. I've never seen anyone who enjoyed being dirty as much as you do. I can't remember when I last had dirt under my fingernails.

"I hate this, Grams," she said with desperation. "I don't want you to be sick. I need you to tell me everything will be okay, just like when I was a kid. Please, Grams, can't you just tell me that? You remember how it goes: 'I can't die yet, honey, because I haven't finished counting the stars—'" Tessa's breath caught in her throat as her grandmother's eyelids began to flicker.

She sat up straight, her heart pounding against her chest with impossible hope. "Grams?"

Another flicker, then a blink, and Tessa was staring into her grandmother's light blue eyes. There was no recognition at first, but another blink seemed to bring Phoebe closer to awareness.

"Oh, my God. You're awake." She clapped a hand to her mouth. "It's me, Grams—it's Tessa."

Phoebe's mouth trembled but didn't open, and a silent battle went on in her eyes that grew more panicked by the second.

"Oh, no! You can't talk, can you?"

Phoebe didn't answer or couldn't answer, Tessa wasn't sure which.

"I don't know what to do. I should call the nurse or the doctor or William," Tessa said wildly, looking around the room for something, someone . . .

The door opened as her prayers were heard, and she looked toward it in relief. Even seeing Alli step into the room didn't diminish her feeling of relief. "Thank God you're here! She's awake. Grams is awake." Tessa jerked her head toward Phoebe. "But she can't talk." Tessa jumped to her feet. "We should get someone."

"She's awake?" Alli echoed, coming around the other side of the bed so that Grams lay between them.

"Isn't that what I just said?"

"I'll call the nurse." Alli pushed the call button lying on the mattress next to Phoebe, then she picked up Phoebe's hand and stroked it reassuringly. "Everything will be all right, Grams."

Tessa watched as Phoebe's eyes focused on Alli's face. It was plain to see that her grandmother could hear Alli, that she was listening with every last ounce of her energy.

Alli smiled down at her reassuringly. "Don't worry. You're just half asleep, Grams. It takes a few minutes for your muscles to catch up. You know, you've been sleeping all day. It's about time you woke up. Don't try to talk yet. You need to get your energy back first. Okay?"

Tessa stared at her younger sister in amazement. Who was this calm, supportive woman? She looked like Alli, but she certainly wasn't acting like the impulsive wild teenager she remembered. This woman in the black jeans and black sweater seemed graceful, assured, in complete control.

But when Alli looked across the bed at her, Tessa saw the fear in Alli's brown eyes and felt a shocking sisterly connection that she'd thought had died a long time ago.

"When did she wake up?" Alli asked.

"A few minutes ago. I was talking to her, and she suddenly opened her eyes."

"I tried to get her to wake up hours ago." Alli looked back at Phoebe with a more familiar and uncertain smile. "I guess you heard Tessa's voice and had to wake up, huh?"

Tessa heard the insecurity. It had always been that way. Alli putting her own ridiculous spin on a simple word or an innocent gesture. Before she could say a word, a nurse walked into the room.

"Can I help you?" the nurse asked.

"Our grandmother is awake," Alli replied.

The nurse smiled as she walked over to the bed. "That's good news, isn't it? Mrs. MacGuire?"

"She doesn't seem able to speak," Tessa interrupted.

"I'll call Dr. Price and let him know that your grandmother is awake." The nurse checked Phoebe's vital signs and noted them on the chart. When she was done, she patted Phoebe's hand. "You're doing great, Mrs. MacGuire. Just rest and don't worry about anything."

"Will Dr. Price check on her tonight?" Alli asked the nurse.

"I'll leave him a message, but Dr. Rogers is on call

tonight. I'll have him stop by to check on your grandmother. This is the first step, and sometimes there are just baby steps in the beginning. You'll have to be patient." The nurse sent them both another reassuring smile and walked out of the room.

"Baby steps. Be patient," Alli muttered. "These nurses drive me crazy. And they barely stay long enough to get one question answered, much less two."

"Do you think Grams knows what happened to her?" Tessa asked.

Alli's gaze returned to her grandmother. "You had a stroke, Grams. You're in the hospital, but you're getting better."

"Alli, do you think you should have told her just like that?" Tessa protested.

"She can hear you as well as me, you know." Alli turned back to Phoebe. "William will be back in a few minutes. He has barely left your side since you got here. He'll be so happy to see the roses in your cheeks."

Tessa's stomach clenched at one of her grandmother's favorite refrains: *Go outside and run around, put some roses in your cheeks. You don't need to wear blush to be pretty, you just need to live life.*

Tessa started shaking her head, feeling hot and cold, caught in the past, trapped in the present. "This isn't right. Grams shouldn't be here. She shouldn't be this sick."

Alli stared at her in amazement. "She will get better, Tessa."

"You don't know that."

"I do know that. I won't let it be any other way." Alli looked down at Phoebe. "You know how stubborn I am. Well, you and I are going to work very hard to get you back on your feet as soon as possible. We have too many things coming up for you to be sick. There's the kite festival and the Fourth of July, your favorite day of the year, and we have clam chowder to make, and you promised Megan you'd show her how to needlepoint this summer, remember?"

Tessa watched as Alli held Phoebe's gaze with her quiet confident words. Maybe Sam was right. Maybe Alli did act like an adult sometimes.

After a few moments, Phoebe's eyes grew tired, and she drifted off to sleep once again. It was then that Tessa realized she and Alli were truly alone, no one to act as a buffer. How long had it been since there had been just the two of them in a room? What on earth would they say?

Alli's eyes met hers and she saw the same conflicting emotions.

"She'll probably sleep for a while," Alli said. "You can go if you want. I'll stay with her."

"I can stay, too."

"You must be tired."

"No more tired than you."

Alli opened her mouth, then closed it, looking down at Phoebe as if seeking some guidance. A minute later her gaze returned to Tessa. "Sam and I are separated, did he tell you that?"

"Yes," Tessa said carefully, not sure she wanted to talk about Sam right now.

"I'm sure you weren't surprised."

"Actually, I was. I didn't think you'd ever let him go. You worked so hard to get him in the first place."

Alli looked at her in amazement. "Me not let him go? You're the one with the steel grip on him."

"I haven't seen Sam in years."

"And that only makes you more interesting, more desirable. You're the one who got away, the one he should have had if only he hadn't made that one stupid mistake."

Tessa felt her temper flare. It had been a hellish forty-eight hours, and the last thing she needed was this conversation. "For God's sake, Alli, you got Sam. You won. What more do you want from me?"

"I don't want anything from you," Alli said. "I gave up counting on your support years ago."

Tessa stared at her in disbelief. "Why are you mad at me? I'm the one who should be angry, not you. Why don't you just get over yourself?"

"That's right. I forgot. You're perfect, and I haven't done anything right my whole life."

"You do cause an amazing amount of trouble."

"I made some mistakes," Alli admitted. Her voice remained low, controlled, but Tessa heard the pain and anger there. "Sleeping with Sam was a big one," Alli added, shocking Tessa with the unexpected honesty. "I saw my chance, and I took it. I was young and stupid and reckless and I wanted him. At the time, it didn't really appear that you cared one way or the other."

Tessa joined her at the foot of the bed, her voice a sharp whisper. "I did care about Sam. I loved him."

"So did I," Alli said.

"Then why are you divorcing him?"

"Because he's still in love with you. Don't you know that?" Alli said in a rush of words that burst from her lips like a dam that had broken. "Oh, God, why did I say that?"

Alli walked away from Tessa to look out the small window. She barely took in the dark, dirty alley below, the trashbins, the laundry trucks. Her mind was repeating over and over again the words that she had never meant to say out loud.

"You're wrong," Tessa said from behind her.

Alli slowly turned around. "I'm not wrong."

"Sam doesn't love me. He couldn't. Why are you saying this? What game are you playing now?"

"I'm not playing a game."

"You always have something up your sleeve, Alli. I've been tricked too many times to believe anything you say."

"Then ask Sam. You trust him, don't you?"

"I did once," Tessa said pointedly.

Alli studied her sister's face, noting the lines of strain etched across Tessa's forehead, the shadows under her eyes, the remnants of berry lipstick on her lips. Tessa was still beautiful, of course, but she looked tired. She looked older.

Funny, but Tessa had never really aged in Alli's mind. Not even occasional unexpected glimpses of her sister on a magazine cover had prepared her for this woman, a woman who almost seemed as human and as confused as the rest of them.

"I don't understand you," Tessa said with a

quizzical shake of her head. "I didn't come here to get into any of this. I came here for Grams. And I'm sure the last thing she needs is to hear us arguing about Sam when she's the one who should have our attention."

"She's had my attention the last nine years. Where have you been?"

"You know where I've been. And I've treated Grams to some of the most spectacular vacations of her life. So don't act like I've neglected her, while you've been some sort of a saint. Just because you were too scared to leave home—"

"Scared? To leave home? Are you kidding?" Alli asked, waving her hand in the air. "Leaving home would have been a cakewalk. No. You want to talk about scared? How about having a baby when you're eighteen years old? How about trying to take care of a child when you barely know how to take care of yourself? How about marrying a man who's in love with your sister and trying to make a life with him? What have you done besides fluff your hair and say cheese?"

"You know nothing about my life. And if you were so scared to have a baby, maybe you should have used birth control," Tessa said pointedly. "But that was part of the plan, wasn't it? Seduce Sam and have his baby so he'd have to marry you. You couldn't have gotten him any other way except by being flat on your back."

"How dare you—"

"How dare *you*?"

"What on earth is going on in here?" William demanded, stepping between them like a referee.

He looked from Alli to Tessa, then back at Alli again. "Well?"

"I'm sorry," Alli mumbled, suddenly reminded of where they were and what they were doing. She'd been so caught up in their fight she hadn't even heard him enter the room. But dammit, why did William have to look at her like it was all her fault?

"I'm sorry, too," Tessa said quickly.

"I should hope so," William said reprovingly. "Your grandmother doesn't need you squabbling like children. You're her family, her support system. Don't make me wish I hadn't called you both down here."

"I really am sorry," Alli said again, feeling more guilty by the minute. "It won't happen again, I promise."

"Good." William walked over to the bed and glanced down at Phoebe. After a moment, he leaned over and kissed her on the forehead. "How's my sweet girl?" he whispered.

"Grams woke up for a few minutes," Tessa said. "She couldn't speak though."

"We called the nurse in," Alli added. "She said it was a good sign that Grams was awake, but that it might take some time before she is fully recovered."

"Could she speak? Could she move her hands? She wasn't paralyzed, was she?" he asked, standing up straight, his long strides taking him quickly to Alli's side.

"I don't know," Alli said, wishing she had the words to reassure him, but she had nothing.

William looked from Alli to Tessa, then back to Phoebe. "She can't be paralyzed," he muttered.

"She just can't be." His voice grew rough with emotion. "Her mother had a stroke, you know."

Alli vaguely remembered hearing something about it, but her great-grandmother had died years ago, and she'd never even known her.

"Phoebe didn't want to end up like this, trapped in her body," William said. "She used to say she'd rather be shot in the head than have her spirit suffocated inch by inch, second by second."

"Oh, God!" Tessa cried. "That's not going to happen to Grams, is it?"

Tessa looked like she was about to throw up. She also seemed to be seeking reassurance from Alli when just minutes before they'd been at each other's throats. But despite everything, Alli knew she had one thing in common with her sister, a deep and abiding love for their grandmother.

"Of course that's not going to happen," Alli said forcefully. "Grams will be back on her feet in a few days. You can't give up on her, Tessa. She never gave up on us. No matter what we did."

"She's really sick, Alli. This isn't just a cold. And you heard what William said. Grams must be so scared."

"Then we'll just have to reassure her. Grams is strong. She'll make it. She has to make it." Alli looked over at Phoebe and sent a silent prayer her way.

"Allison is right," William said, renewed strength in his voice. "Thank you for reminding me. Sometimes the fear takes hold, and it's difficult to make it disappear."

"You've known Grams a long time, haven't you?" Tessa asked him.

"Since we were seventeen. I met her at a party. I thought she was the prettiest girl in Philadelphia. She was wearing one of those floaty dresses that swirled around her legs when she danced. And she had this laugh, this incredible laugh that made everyone stop what they were doing so they could see what she was doing." He smiled at the memory. "We became friends that night, the best of friends. But a few months later her parents arranged a marriage for her with the son of their new business partner. His name was John MacGuire."

"Grandpa," Alli said softly. "But Grams never said the marriage was arranged."

"Oh, but it was, to solidify a business arrangement. John's parents had cash that Phoebe's parents desperately needed. John's parents wanted their son to have a wife, stability, a family. Phoebe's parents wanted the same thing for their child."

"But Grams loved Grandpa," Tessa said.

"She may have come to love him," William conceded. "But I can never forget how she looked the night she told me that she would have to marry to save her parents' business."

"I don't understand," Alli said in confusion. "Why didn't Grams tell us any of this?"

"It happened a long time ago."

A confused silence fell between them.

"Did Grams know that you loved her, too?" Alli asked.

"I was never in the running. I came from a poor

family. That party I mentioned earlier, when I saw your grandmother for the first time, I was a waiter, not even a guest."

"I can't believe that Grams would have married for money," Tessa interjected.

"She didn't marry John for his money. She married him because it was what her parents wanted her to do. It was a different world then."

"You didn't answer my question," Alli said. "Did Grams know that you loved her then?"

William tried to shrug off her question, obviously uncomfortable at the turn of events. "She never asked. I never said."

"But all these years . . ."

"I worked hard to make something of myself, to be someone Phoebe would be proud to know. I married twice, tried to find the happiness that she seemed to show me every time we spoke or exchanged a letter. But I couldn't forget her. And ever since John died, I've hoped that she might find her way back to me."

"Maybe she will," Tessa said. "Maybe that first love will win out."

Alli's stomach turned over at Tessa's words. She didn't want to think about first loves outlasting all others. Not that she didn't want Phoebe to be happy now, but Alli didn't want to believe that Grams had spent the better part of her life mooning over the absent William.

"I've always hoped that it would. But perhaps I've left it too late," William said heavily, moving next to Phoebe so he could stroke her forehead.

"I have to go," Tessa said abruptly. "I'll be back later."

"Don't rush," William said. "Your grandmother will probably sleep for hours. In fact, if you want to wait until tomorrow, that's fine. You must be tired from all the traveling."

Tessa picked up her purse from the floor. "I am tired." She opened her purse and pulled out a pen and jotted down a number on the pad beside the bed. "This is my cell phone. I'll keep it on. Call me if you need me, and I'll come back." She paused, her hands clenched tightly around her purse strap, as she stared at her grandmother. " 'Night, Grams. Sleep well."

Alli's eyes narrowed as Tessa practically ran from the room. She wondered where her sister was going in such a hurry. And the deep, sinking feeling in the pit of her stomach told her she probably didn't want to know.

⛵ Chapter 7

"What do you have for homework?" Sam asked as Megan finished her glass of milk, leaving an uneven white ring around her mouth. He leaned over and wiped her lips with his napkin.

"Well?"

"Daddy, it's summer school."

"I forgot. So you don't have homework?"

"Well, a little math, but we don't have to do it if we don't want to."

"You don't?" he asked in disbelief, for Megan was the queen of procrastination. "Why don't you get it and we'll do it together?"

"First we should have some ice cream."

"How about we have ice cream after we do your homework?"

"Before," Megan said stubbornly.

He recognized that fiery light. Sometimes Megan looked just like her mother. God help him! "Homework," he said calmly.

"Mommy doesn't make me do homework until after dessert. I want Mommy."

"She's at the hospital, you know that."

"Mommy loves me more than you do," Megan said.

He stared at her in amazement. Was this just a ploy for ice cream? Or did she really believe that he loved her less?

"That's not true. I love you very much."

"Then how come you don't live here anymore?" she asked, her eyes watering. "I don't like that you're gone," she said with a sob.

He pulled her out of her chair and onto his lap, giving her a tight squeeze, wishing he had something to say that would make her feel better. "I love you, Megan, more than anyone in the whole wide world. Wherever I live, wherever you live, that won't change. Not even when you grow up and you fall in love with some other guy. I'll still love you the most. You have to believe that."

She put her hands on his face, the way she loved to do, making sure she had his complete attention. "Can I have ice cream now?"

He laughed. "You're a bad little girl."

"Good girl," she said with a grin. "Good girls get ice cream."

He wanted to give in. He really did. And the little pout on her mouth was just too cute. "Compromise. I'll dish up the ice cream. You bring your math sheet to the table, and we'll do it at the same time."

"Okay," she said, skipping from the room.

He was a complete pushover, he decided, taking their dinner dishes to the kitchen sink. As he rinsed off the plates, he noticed that the garbage disposal was slow. He'd have to fix that.

His heart felt heavy as he realized he had no business fixing the disposal or even worrying about it. He and his wife were separated, on their way to a divorce. Three months ago he'd been living in this house, enjoying the kitchen he'd remodeled with his own hands, sleeping in the king-size bed they'd splurged on two years ago, kissing his daughter good night and waking up with Alli hogging all the covers.

He sucked in a breath and let it out slow. He didn't miss Alli. He just missed his life. He couldn't miss her. She was the one responsible for the god-awful mess that had become their lives.

As he turned off the faucet, the doorbell rang. He walked into the living room and opened the door, expecting to see one of the neighbors on the step. But it wasn't a neighbor, it was Tessa, and his heart turned over in his chest, making it difficult to breathe.

"Hi," she said softly.

"What are you doing here?"

"Can I talk to you for a minute?"

"Sure, come in."

She shook her head. "I don't think so."

"I can't leave. Megan is inside, and she'll probably be out here in a second."

"Maybe this was a mistake. I'm sorry." Her hair tumbled across her shoulders as she shook her head in indecision.

"What's wrong? Did you see Alli?"

"Yes."

She stared at him as if she'd never seen him before. What on earth had Alli said to her?

"I have to ask you something," she began, then stopped abruptly.

"What?"

"Do you still— Never mind. I shouldn't have come."

"Tessa, wait." He grabbed her arm.

She looked at him through big, blue, watery eyes, and he could no more let her go than he could stop himself from breathing. "What do you want to ask me?"

"Daddy?" Megan called out.

Tessa's arm jerked under his hand. "I can't do this."

He hung on to her, unwilling to let her go. "Wait. I'll be right there, honey," he called out to Megan, then stepped onto the porch and pulled the door closed behind him. "Tell me what's wrong."

She lifted her head, studying his face with an expression of pure confusion. He'd never seen her look so—lost.

"This is the house you and Alli bought after Megan was born, isn't it? Grams told me it was nice. Just what Alli always wanted, a white house with green shutters and window boxes filled with flowers, and even a front porch with a swing." She looked over at the white wicker two-seater swing. "It's perfect."

"You didn't come here to talk about the house."

"No, but right now it seems like a better idea. I'm tired." She tucked her hair behind her ear. "Really tired. And worried about Grams. She woke up, but she couldn't talk. It scared me. And then Alli started saying all these confusing things, and I never know what's real and what's in her head."

"What did she say?"

Tessa hesitated. "Did you miss me, Sam? I mean, did you ever think about me after we broke up?"

"Of course I did. How could I not?"

"I tried not to think about you. I threw myself into my life. I thought if I could run really fast, I'd get far enough away that I wouldn't be able to look back. And it was working pretty well, until now."

He knew exactly what she meant, for hadn't he done the same thing, pouring himself into his new family? But time had come to a crashing halt when Alli asked for a divorce. Now, with Phoebe's stroke and Tessa's return, he no longer knew how he was supposed to feel, what he was supposed to do.

The door creaked open behind him, and his daughter's head peeked out.

"Daddy? Who's here?"

He stepped aside, putting his arm around Megan's shoulders as he pulled her onto the porch. He was both relieved and disappointed by the interruption. There were things he and Tessa needed to say to each other. Then again, perhaps there were things better left unsaid.

"Aunt Tessa," Megan said with delight.

"Hi, Megan."

"Did you come to have ice cream with us?"

"Tessa just came by to tell me about Grams," Sam interrupted. "Phoebe woke up for a little while. That's good news."

"Then we should celebrate with ice cream," Megan replied.

Sam couldn't help but laugh. "My daughter has a one-track mind."

His comment drew a reluctant smile from Tessa. "Her mother's daughter?"

"Oh, yeah."

And they shared a connection that took him back to a time and a place where they'd always known what the other was going to say before it was said.

Megan jumped between them, grabbed Tessa's hand, and pulled her into the house as Sam slowly followed. "Can I get you some ice cream?" he asked Tessa as he walked into the kitchen.

"No, thanks, I don't eat ice cream."

"Since when?"

"Since a long time ago. The camera adds pounds. I can't afford any extra."

"I think you look too thin," he said as he put two scoops of ice cream in a bowl for Megan.

Her face tightened at his blunt comment. "A model can never be too thin."

"Right." He still thought she looked like a good stiff wind might blow her away. But he knew that discussing weight with a woman would only end in disaster. He gave Megan her ice cream, then sat down in the chair across from Tessa, keeping Megan between them. "How long are you staying in town?"

"As long as Grams needs me."

"You don't have any pressing business?"

"I do, but Grams is more important." She drew an idle circle on top of the tablecloth with the tip of her rosy pink fingernail.

Sam watched the graceful but nervous movement

for a long minute. "Phoebe must have been happy to see you when she opened her eyes."

Tessa shrugged. "I don't know. I'm not sure I even registered. I didn't know what to do when she couldn't talk. I sort of panicked. Then Alli walked in and took over."

"You saw Mommy?" Megan asked, as she quickly downed the ice cream.

"Yes."

"Mommy said I could stay up until she got home."

"She did not say that," Sam said sternly. "In fact, you need to do your math problems. Why don't you get started on them upstairs, and I'll be up in a minute to help you."

"Now?" Megan whined.

"Now." He smiled at Tessa as Megan left the kitchen. "She can think up more excuses to stall than anyone I know."

"You're a good dad."

"Thank you. But it's not hard to be good for fifteen minutes. You should have seen us a while ago. Megan told me she didn't like me anymore and she wanted her mommy."

"She didn't say that."

"She did. But we both knew she didn't mean it." He paused for a moment. "Are you all right, Tessa?"

"I don't know. I think I've been awake too long." It was a prevarication, but she wasn't sure what else to say.

"You should go home, get some sleep."

"I will. I don't really like being in Grams's house alone, though. There are so many memories there, and when I look in her room, I can see her, and I can hear her, and it scares me that she might not be there again."

He reached across the table and covered her hand with his, and her emotions almost bubbled over. She hadn't cried in years, but Lord, she felt like giving in, letting down. And Sam's gentle touch on her hand was almost too much.

She blinked rapidly and took a deep breath, wishing she'd had the courage to ask him the question that had driven her from the hospital to his house. But how could she ask him straight out—Do you still love me? How could she do that, sitting here in his house, the house he'd bought with Alli, and with her sister's daughter upstairs waiting for her father? However Sam felt about her now wasn't important.

Tessa got to her feet and stretched her arms over her head.

"I should go."

Sam stood up as well. "You never did tell me what Alli said to you."

"It's late. I don't want to get into that now."

He stepped forward. "Are you sure? If you have something to say . . ."

He was so close, tall, strong, real. It would be easy to move into his arms, rest her head on his shoulder the way she'd done a thousand times. This was Sam, her Sam. When she looked into his eyes, she saw the boy she'd once loved more than anyone on earth.

"What happened to us?" she murmured. "How did we let it go so easily?"

His expression filled with guilt. She wondered if he would ever look at her with any other emotion.

"Oh, Tessa," he muttered. "I'm sorry."

She didn't know if he was apologizing for the past or apologizing for now, but it didn't matter, because somehow her feet were moving and her arms were sliding around his neck and her head was resting on his shoulder, the cotton fabric of his T-shirt warm against her cheek.

He didn't say anything and for that she was intensely grateful. It was enough to be with him, breathing in his scent, feeling his body, so familiar, yet new, too. He wasn't a boy any longer, but a man. And it was that thought that reminded her what they were doing was wrong. They weren't friends anymore. And they weren't supposed to be holding each other.

"Sam, I want—"

"Don't," he said sharply, stepping away so abruptly her hands fell to her sides.

"Don't what?" she asked in surprise, wondering why his mood had changed so drastically. And then she saw it in his eyes, on his face, the wariness, the distancing. "What did you think I was going to say—going to do?"

"Nothing," he said quickly.

"It was definitely something. Did you—did you think I was going to kiss you?" she asked, taking a shot in the dark. To her surprise, a dark color flooded his cheeks. "You did. You actually did. That had to be the last thing on my mind," she lied, because the idea hadn't been that far away.

"You should go home, Tessa."

She stared at him, annoyed that he seemed to feel she was pursuing him, when he was the one who'd said he was sorry and had been sending out all sorts of mixed messages. He hadn't exactly run from her embrace.

"Maybe I don't want to go home yet," she said, just to be contrary.

"Go anyway."

Sam walked out of the kitchen, leaving her alone in the middle of the room. "Sam," she called after him, but he didn't return.

Resisting the sudden childish urge to stamp her foot, Tessa took a deep breath and counted to ten. As she did so, she took a good look around the room, and saw exactly what she didn't want to see—the signs of a family. There was evidence everywhere, from the dish towels that said HOME, SWEET HOME to the crayon drawings and photographs on the refrigerator, a stray belt on the counter, and a stack of bills on a small desk in the corner of the kitchen. Megan's shoes and socks had obviously been kicked off in a hurry under the round oak table in the breakfast nook.

Sam was right. She didn't belong here. She needed to get away and fast, before she started thinking about how this life could have been hers, how that little girl upstairs could have belonged to her and Sam, and the calendar on the wall could have had their dates written on it, their life, their plans.

She hadn't wanted this life, Tessa reminded herself. A small house in a small town had never been her dream. In fact, she'd spent many a day dreaming of a future far away from Tucker's Landing. But now that she'd come back, she realized how much she'd missed having a home, a real home, not a luxury apartment forty-two stories in the sky, but a house with creaks and groans and rusted pipes and peeling wallpaper.

She could see Alli in every crumb on the linoleum, every hastily scribbled recipe on a card falling out of a cookbook, every plate, every glass. This was Alli's home, Alli's life, and Sam was Alli's husband. At least he used to be.

"Tessa?" Sam stood in the doorway again, keeping his distance, his hands solidly in his pockets to prevent any accidental touch.

"I know, I'm going."

"I can't talk to you right now, not with Megan upstairs. She's notorious for eavesdropping."

"So was her mother. Alli and I used to eavesdrop on our parents after Alli discovered we could hear what they were saying in their bedroom if we stood by the heating vent in the laundry room. We once found out what they were going to buy us for Christmas."

Sam's eyes registered his surprise. "You never told me that before."

"This house reminds me of my parents' house. I wonder if Alli deliberately decorated it that way, or if she even realized what she was doing." Tessa sighed. "I never wanted to talk about them because they were gone, and once something is gone, it's easier if you just forget you ever had it in the first place."

"Is that what you did with me—forget?"

"I tried."

She walked past him, careful not to touch hi_
again, and she didn't pause until she reached the
front door. "Tell Megan I said good-bye."

He opened the front door for her, but still she
hesitated.

"Sam, if I had kissed you—would you have
kissed me back?"

He shrugged as if he didn't care, but she saw his
body tense, saw the light of desire flare in his eyes.

"Maybe it's better if we don't find out," he said.

⛵ Chapter 8

Alli returned home just before eleven. Every light in the house was on, but there were no sounds of life downstairs, so she went upstairs to Megan's room. Her daughter's bed had been turned down, but it was empty. Moving across the hall, she stopped outside her bedroom door, almost afraid to look inside.

She hadn't changed anything since Sam left. Some of his clothes still hung in the closet they'd shared. She'd told herself to get a new bedspread, new curtains, start over, but she hadn't found the time to do it. Now she wished she had.

For lying on his side of the king-sized bed was Sam. Fast asleep, one arm flung over his eyes; he looked like he'd looked every night for the past nine years when they'd shared this very bed. And curled up next to him in her pink pajamas was Megan.

Alli thought her heart might just break. For this scene, this moment, was all she had ever really wanted.

Taking a deep breath, she walked into the room and flipped off the television. Megan and Sam slept on, Sam making an occasional deep-throated snore that was so painfully familiar.

Her side of the bed was empty, waiting, the sheets still cool and crisp.

They'd slept this way, the three of them, many a night when Megan had a nightmare or a stomachache or just wanted to be close to her parents.

But Alli couldn't leave them like this, not tonight.

Megan needed to be in her own bed, and Sam in his bed at his house, far away from her own treacherous longings. Leaning over, Alli touched Megan on the shoulder. "Bedtime, honey."

Megan blinked sleepily, not really waking up, but alert enough so that Alli could get her up off the bed and walk her into her bedroom. " 'Night, Mommy," Megan murmured as Alli tucked the covers under her chin. "I love you."

"I love you, too," Alli replied, planting a kiss on Megan's forehead as the little girl drifted off to sleep once again.

Oh, to be so easily able to sink into oblivion. Alli would give just about anything for a few hours of peace away from all of her problems, but she doubted she'd be able to sleep even when she got to bed. There was too much going through her mind.

Returning to her bedroom, Alli stopped by Sam's side of the bed and stared down at him. He simply could not stay here.

"Sam, wake up. You have to leave," she said.

He grunted, then rolled over on his side, facing away from her.

"It's late, and I'm tired, and you can't sleep here." She slipped off her shoes and contemplated her options. She knew from past experience that Sam could sleep through anything. With renewed purpose, she put her hand on his arm. It was a mistake. She could feel the power of his muscles and for a moment briefly considered moving her fingers under the edge of his T-shirt so she could really touch him. Lord! What was she thinking?

"Okay, this is it, wake up, Sam!" She raised her voice loud enough to be heard but not so loud that she'd wake Megan. It wasn't enough. His breathing didn't even change.

"You just won the lottery," she tried. "A new boat," she continued. "You just won a new sportfishing boat. You'll love it. But you have to wake up, so you can go get it."

Sam slept on.

She leaned over, planting her mouth right next to his ear, determined to let loose a scream that would surely wake him. But as she opened her lips, she was caught by the sexy curl of hair that graced his earlobe. She could remember kissing that earlobe, sliding her tongue along the edge.

Her breath came in a ragged gasp, and she felt a sensuous warmth draw heat to her cheeks and her hands and her breasts and her thighs . . .

She fought against the instinct to kiss him. It wasn't right. It was wrong, absolutely wrong. She couldn't do it!

But even if she did put her lips against his ear, he wasn't going to wake up. Nothing could wake him up. She knew that. It was safe.

One little lick, she told herself, one tiny kiss for old time's sake . . .

Her tongue touched his ear in pure rebellion against her common sense. She kissed his earlobe, then moved over to his jaw, his strong, sexy jaw, bristling with the rough edge of a dawning beard. She trailed her lips along his jawbone, which ended so close to the curve of his lips.

She couldn't resist. She put her mouth against his in a soft, breathy kiss that couldn't possibly wake him up.

She let her tongue play along the line of his lips and when he opened his mouth ever so slightly, she had to fight to stop herself from slipping inside, from tasting him completely. He smelled so good. He tasted even better.

And then suddenly his mouth wasn't still beneath hers, it was hot and seeking, taking her own mouth with a hard surety that couldn't be compromised. Sam's arm came around her, and she was tumbled on her back on the bed next to him. Sam pressed his body against hers, every long, hard inch of him touching every short, soft inch of her body.

His mouth came down again and again and again, until she was trembling from the onslaught.

When his hand came up under her sweater, his fingertips brushing her breast, she gave a soft cry. She tried to tell herself to stop, but his fingers brushed her nipple, and his hard groin fit perfectly between her thighs, and her body started melting into liquid fire.

She wanted to make love with him, to bare her body, and then bare his. She slipped her hands up under his shirt and stroked the packed muscles in his back as he moved against her, as the sweet friction built between them like the start of a long, hot fire.

"Sam," she whispered. "Help me. I shouldn't. We shouldn't."

"Don't wake me up," he murmured, his mouth touching off more sensations in the sensitive curve of her neck. "Make love to me."

It was then she realized his eyes were still closed. "Sam?"

He didn't reply.

Was he awake? Or was he dreaming? And who— who was he dreaming about? A sudden terrible thought bolted into her mind.

"Beautiful," he said softly.

Her entire body stiffened. Beautiful was Tessa. He had to be thinking of Tessa. Oh, God! She pushed on his shoulders, trying to get him off her.

"Stop," she cried.

Sam finally opened his eyes, blinking quickly against the bright light in the bedroom. "What?"

"Get off of me."

"What the hell is wrong with you?"

She pushed him back so she could sit up, so she could catch her breath, so she wouldn't feel so dominated, not by him but by her own traitorous body.

"You were dreaming," she accused him.

He eyed her warily. "Was I? I thought you kissed me."

"You didn't know it was me. You were asleep."

"Who else would it be?"

"You know who else," she said, pulling her sweater back down, her breath still coming in breathless gasps.

Sam put a hand to his head and rubbed his temple. "I wasn't dreaming of Tessa. I wasn't dreaming of anything. You kissed me, and I kissed you back." He paused, sending her a thoughtful look. "Why did you kiss me?"

"I—" She swallowed hard. "I didn't mean to."

He pushed a piece of hair off her face in a tender gesture that almost undid her. "Why do you always have to fight—even if it's only yourself? Can't you give in once in a while?" He leaned over and kissed her on the cheek, leaving his mouth a whisper away from hers as he murmured, "We were always pretty good at this."

"It will only make things worse," she muttered.

"Can they get worse?"

"I can't do this." She rolled away from him until she found her feet on the opposite side of the bed. "You have to go home, Sam."

"I *am* home."

Alli felt the threat of tears behind her eyes. She wanted this to be his home. But he had to give her more than his body, he had to be able to give her his heart and his soul, and there were too many things unresolved between them.

Alli shifted from one foot to the next, filled with a restlessness she didn't know how to quench. Actually, she did know how to quench it, she just couldn't do it. Making love with Sam wouldn't solve anything. It would only make it that much more difficult to say good-bye.

"Come here," he said softly, holding out his hand to her.

"I can't."

"Sure you can."

"It's been a long, difficult day, Sam."

"That's why you need to come here. I'm not going to jump you."

After a moment in which she fought helplessly against her need for this man, she sat back down on the bed. He reached out his hand and pulled her across the mattress until she was cuddled up next to him, her head on his shoulder, his arm around her waist.

"This is better," he said.

It *was* better. It was heaven. And even though she knew she should get up, she just couldn't make her body move.

"Phoebe will make it," Sam said. "She's too strong to die." He stroked the top of Alli's head, a gentle, loving touch that made her eyes water.

"I hope you're right," she said. "I started to miss her today, and then I felt guilty for even thinking that way. I shouldn't have any negative thoughts, only positive ones. I can't let the unthinkable take over my mind, because then—"

"It might happen," he finished. "But this battle can only be fought by your grandmother."

"I know. But William told me that Grams worried about having a stroke, ending up like her mother, trapped in her body. I don't want that to happen to her. And she must be scared. When she looked at me, I could see the fear in her eyes, and I didn't know how to reassure her." Alli lifted her head to look at him. "She was always the one to reassure me, to take care of me. How can I take care of her?"

"You'll find a way. You always do. Your grandmother's strength runs through you, Alli." He smiled at her. "I remember when you were in labor with Megan. I've never seen anyone sweat so much."

"Gee, thanks."

He laughed. "And every time a contraction hit, you grabbed my hand and squeezed it so tight I thought you were going to break my fingers. But you never gave in to the pain, never cried, never stopped pushing even when you were exhausted. You were amazing."

She looked at him in surprise. "You never told me that before."

"Didn't I?"

"No."

"It was all those sleepless nights in the beginning. I didn't know if we were coming or going half the time."

"That's true." She thought back to those early days with both affection and sadness for the dream of family she'd had then, a dream that had ended three months ago.

"Don't," he said, tweaking her chin with his finger. "Don't go there now." He put her head back down on his chest. "Just relax and let everything else slide. In fact, I've got a joke for you."

She groaned. "Not another knock-knock joke, please."

"This is a good one. Knock-knock."

"Who's there?" she asked with a sigh.

"Boo!"

"Boo who?"

"Don't cry, it's only a joke."

"And a really bad one," she said with a smile that he couldn't see.

"Megan laughed for five minutes. Okay, I've got another one."

"Sam!"

"Knock-knock."

"I'm not playing."

"Who's there," he said, ignoring her.

"Who's there?" she asked.

"Atch."

"Atch who?"

"I didn't know you had a cold."

She raised her head again to see him smiling. "That was even worse." She grinned back at him. "But thanks for trying to make me feel better."

"Did it work?"

"You've always been able to make me laugh, especially when I'm trying to be mad at you."

"Maybe you should stop trying," he said more somberly.

"We can't make this go away with knock-knock jokes."

"You take everything so seriously, Alli."

"Someone has to."

She rolled over onto her back next to him and stared at the ceiling. "You have to go home."

He turned on his side to face her. "Are you sure you want to be alone tonight?"

"No, I'm not sure at all. But . . ."

"There's always a but."

"It will confuse Megan. She'll think we're getting back together."

"I'll leave before she wakes up."

She looked at him. "You will?"

"Yes." He put his arm across her waist and curled up to her, resting his head on the pillow next to hers. "Sleep, Alli."

She closed her eyes and felt the comfort of his body and his words seep into her soul. "Sam, I said something I shouldn't have," she whispered.

"Tell me tomorrow," he said.

She hesitated, but he tightened his hold on her, and she felt so warm and secure that she couldn't bear to let go of him, and she knew he would leave if she told him what she'd said to Tessa.

"Good night, Sam."

"Good night, Alli."

True to his promise, Sam was gone by the time Alli awoke the next morning. After taking Megan to summer school, she made her way to the shop, where she pretended to work. But in truth she spent most of her time worrying about Phoebe and thinking about Sam. Restless and too distracted to be of much use, she slipped out of the store just before noon and sat down on a bench outside.

The pier was alive with summer tourists, and the smells of fresh fish, baked bread, and chocolate chip cookies mixed in with the breezy salt air made Alli take a deep breath of appreciation. She loved the wharf, the sea, the town. Unlike Tessa, she had never wanted to leave. Tucker's Landing had been her safe place after her parents died, a warm blanket she wrapped herself in whenever the outside world got too close.

Only now, the outside world and Tessa were intruding on her safe place. Alli looked down the road toward Sam's boat dock. She could see his morning fishing boat transferring piles of fresh salmon to the truck for Petrie's restaurant, waiting to haul the salmon a few blocks down the road, where it would be seasoned and broiled for dinner that night.

It had been her idea to use the mid-size of their three boats for commercial fishing purposes. They used the large fifty-footer for deep-sea charters and whale watching and the smaller boat for friends and family looking for some sportfishing a few miles offshore.

Alli wondered if Sam had taken the morning charter out or left it to one of the other captains. Lately, he'd been more office bound than he liked, taking care of paperwork and bookings. She knew he felt more comfortable on the water. For Sam it was all about what he could touch, what he could feel. Which brought up a disturbing memory of his touch the night before.

It would have been so easy to make love to him. So wonderful. One kiss and she'd been blown away. It had always been like that, for her anyway.

"Alli?" Mary Ann poked her head out of shop. "I thought you were getting us a sandwich."

"I was."

"But?"

"I slept with Sam last night."

"You did what?" Mary Ann stepped out of the shop and pulled the door closed behind her. "Cassie can handle the customers. You need to talk to me about what you were thinking—if you were thinking."

"I wasn't," Alli admitted, pushing her short skirt down over her bare legs. There was a cool breeze coming off the water, sending goose bumps along her skin. She had the strangest feeling that a storm was brewing even though there were only a few puffy white clouds dotting the sky.

"So, what happened?" Mary Ann wanted to know.

"Sam stayed with Megan so I could spend the evening at the hospital. When I got home, Sam was asleep in my bed. I tried to wake him up, I really did."

"But instead, you . . . ?"

"Kissed him."

"Oh, Alli!"

"I know, I know. I was weak."

"For a woman who is trying to divorce her husband, you're certainly using some strange tactics. But the real question is—did he kiss you back?"

"Yes, but it was probably just instinct."

"So what happened next?"

"I told him to stop, and he did. I thought we were headed for another fight, but then he backed off, and instead he talked to me about Grams and was really comforting. He told me some of his stupid knock-knock jokes."

"Oh, please, those are terrible."

"I know, but they made me smile. Then we just went to sleep. It was nice."

Mary Ann shook her head in amazement. "Nice. You slept with Sam, and it was nice."

"It was. He can be a good guy at times."

"You don't have to tell me that."

"But I couldn't make love to him, because Tessa is still between us."

"Oh, my God, you've got Tessa on the brain. So where *is* your sister today, anyway?"

"I have no idea." Although even as she denied knowing Tessa's whereabouts, Alli was struck by the sight of a slender figure dressed in a figure-hugging sleeveless blue sundress and walking down the road toward Sam's boat dock.

"Hey, isn't that her?" Mary Ann asked, following Alli's gaze.

"And it looks like she's on her way to visit Sam."

"Or not," Mary Ann said as the figure paused along the rail to look out at the harbor and the boats.

"I told her Sam was still in love with her," Alli said.

"Why on earth would you do that?"

"It seemed like a good idea at the time."

"Do you ever hear a little voice in your head telling you to stop and think?"

Alli made a face at Mary Ann. "Obviously, I don't listen to it."

"Maybe you should talk to Tessa."

"And say what?"

"I don't know. She's *your* sister."

Alli's eyes narrowed as a man in black jeans

stopped a few feet away from Tessa and raised a camera to his eye. It wasn't just a drugstore automatic either; the camera looked to be expensive, with a zoom lens. Tessa stared out at the water, seemingly oblivious to his presence.

"I wonder what that guy is doing," Alli murmured.

"Probably trying to snap a photo of your sister. I imagine she ends up in the tabloids quite frequently. Maybe you should warn her."

Alli hesitated. It wasn't any of her business, and no doubt Tessa was used to photographers and other people trying to record her every action on film.

"Go on, do something nice," Mary Ann urged. "It will probably shock the hell out of her."

"True."

"That alone should be worth it."

"All right." Alli got up and walked down the road. She was a few feet away from the photographer when she heard Sam call Tessa's name and saw Tessa run down the street toward him. She didn't stop until she was in his arms, giving him a long, very friendly hug.

"Holy shit!" the man with the camera said loudly, lowering the lens from his face as he stared at Tessa and Sam.

Alli glanced over in surprise, wondering why the man seemed so annoyed. She started to tell him to mind his own business, but when he turned his head, she was caught off guard by his face. He was shockingly handsome, with light green eyes that lit up his black hair and dark olive skin. His face was beautifully strong, and very appealing. If he hadn't been holding a camera, Alli thought he probably could have made some money standing in front of it.

"Hi," he said simply, his frown fading when he saw her. "Who are you?"

"I was going to ask you the same question. Why are you taking Tessa's picture? Are you planning to sell it to some cheap supermarket paper?"

"I'd rather die than have one of my photographs in a rag sheet." He held out his right hand. "I'm Jimmy Duggan."

She ignored his hand. "You still haven't answered my question."

His eyes narrowed on her face. "You look familiar. In fact . . ." He rubbed his chin. "You look like Tessa."

"I'm her sister, and I look nothing like her."

"I didn't know she had a sister," he mused, his gaze swinging from her to Tessa, who had stepped out of Sam's arms but was still in deep conversation with him. "Who's the guy?"

"More importantly, who are you?"

"I told you."

"Your name, not why you're following my sister."

"I'm a photographer. I work with Tessa."

"I don't think Tessa is here to work."

"You're really her sister? Although I'm not surprised. There is something in your bone structure, your expression. It's astonishing, really. Have you modeled?"

"Oh, please, don't try to butter me up. I know what I look like. I have a mirror, and when I used to ask who is the fairest of them all, there was only one answer, and it was Tessa."

"Well, she is beautiful," Jimmy agreed matter-of-factly. "So who's the guy?"

"Sam Tucker."

"And he is . . ."

"He's my husband."

Chapter 9

*J*immy looked taken aback. "Your husband?"

"Yes."

"And he's close to Tessa?"

"He used to be."

"Looks like he still is," Jimmy said dryly. "Hey, Tessa, babe, sweetheart." He waved as Tessa turned and saw them standing there.

"Jimmy? Jimmy, is that you?" Tessa cried, coming up the road to meet them. "Oh, my God, what are you doing here?"

"Trying to keep an appointment with you."

"How did you find me?"

"Your assistant gave me the address. And when you didn't call me back, I figured I'd have a better chance of talking to you if I came here."

"I've been so busy."

"With your—grandmother?" Jimmy asked, casting Sam a suspicious look as he moved up behind Tessa.

Tessa cleared her throat. "Among other people. I see you met my sister. And this is Sam Tucker, an old friend."

"And your brother-in-law," Jimmy said.

"Right," Tessa said, clearing her throat. "How long have you been standing here?"

"Long enough, I'd say," Jimmy replied. "For a woman who claimed to have no family, you seem to be acquiring relatives by the minute."

"Yes, well, it's a long story."

"I bet it's a good one. I think I'll stick around to hear it."

"Really? You can stay for a few hours?"

"I can stay for a few days. We still have that assignment to complete—a day in the life of a supermodel."

"We can't do that here. This isn't my life."

"Oh, I don't know. You're breathing, you're alive, and this is a day in your life."

"Not one I'd like to have recorded. Why don't we get some lunch and talk about it?" Tessa suggested. "There's a great little clam chowder place at the end of the pier."

"Sounds good."

Tessa looked at Sam. "I'll see you later?"

"Sure," Sam replied, digging his hands into his pockets.

"Good."

Alli watched as Tessa slipped her hand through Jimmy's arm and they walked down the road together, two strikingly attractive people. It was like watching the Red Sea part, she thought. The crowd seemed to naturally move aside for them, some taking a second look after they'd passed. When she glanced back at Sam, she caught him studying her with curiosity.

"What?" she asked.

"Were you following Tessa?"

"No. I was standing in front of the store, and I saw that guy taking Tessa's photograph. I didn't know who he was, so I thought I'd warn her, but you got to her first," Alli explained, remembering their passionate embrace. "That was quite a hug."

"Well, believe it or not, the reason I was walking up this way was to see you."

"Really?" she asked skeptically.

"Yes. I wanted an update on Phoebe's condition."

"She's better. They're going to do a CT scan this afternoon. When I was there this morning Grams mouthed a few short words—my name, William's, stuff like that. You couldn't really call it talking. She seems able to move her right arm and leg just fine, but the left side is more sluggish. It's hard to see her like that."

Sam held out his hand to her and, after a momentary hesitation, she took it.

"She's going to make it," he said, wrapping his fingers around hers.

She looked into his eyes and saw a kindness that reminded her of the boy she'd first fallen in love with. "You're being very supportive about Grams. I appreciate it."

"I care about her, too. Listen, I have a whale watching trip in an hour with a newlywed couple. Why don't you come with me?"

"Come with you?" she asked in surprise.

"They'll want to be on their own. You can keep me company. Fishermen I can deal with. Young lovers are another story."

"I'm working," she said, even though she was tempted to say yes.

"You can't spare an hour or two? Mary Ann can mind the store."

"You never wanted me to come on your tours. Why now?"

"I told you, I'd like the company."

"*My* company?"

"Do you want me to take it back?"

"No, but there's Grams, and . . ." She waved her hand in the air, trying to give voice to the million reasons why she shouldn't go with him.

His smile faded. "Say no if you don't want to go. Say yes if you do. You don't have to make an excuse either way."

Oh, God. He was killing her with his eyes, with his question. She was supposed to be breaking away from Sam, but he so rarely invited her out on the boat, preferring to keep that world his and his alone, that she didn't want to say no.

"Look, we're leaving in an hour," he said. "If you want to come, I'll see you on board." He started to leave, then paused. "You never used to think this much, Alli. I don't believe I like it."

"I like the new you," Jimmy said as he sat down across the table from Tessa with a heaping portion of clam chowder in a bread bowl. He eyed Tessa's own smaller cup of chowder accompanied by a green salad with approval. "You're actually eating. I'm impressed."

"I shouldn't be," she said, then closed her eyes in delight as the first spoonful of clam chowder slid down her throat. "But this is so incredibly good. Tomorrow I will eat only lettuce, I swear."

He laughed, reaching across the table to wipe a drop of chowder off her chin with his napkin. "You could use a pound or two."

"No, I couldn't, and you know how hard I have to work to keep them off. Still . . . maybe just a few more bites," she said guiltily. "It must be the sea air."

"It's certainly all around us," Jimmy replied.

Tessa followed his gaze to the railing just a few feet away from them, to the harbor and the ocean beyond, the sails blowing in the breeze, the sound of sea lions mingling with the chatter of tourists. She shook her head, thinking how incongruous it all was, having lunch with Jimmy at a beat-up picnic table, dented with the carvings of a thousand teenagers who had sat at this point and looked out at the sea.

"What?" Jimmy asked.

"I was just thinking that four-star restaurants are more our style."

"But you've never enjoyed a meal more. Must be my company, huh?"

She laughed. "Must be. I still can't believe you're here."

"How's your grandmother?"

"A little better, I hope. I stopped in this morning. She said a few words to me, but the stroke has robbed her of her personality, her spirit. She seems to be struggling to just stay awake, to even say hello." Tessa pushed her bowl of chowder away, suddenly losing her appetite. "I shouldn't be this happy while she's in there, not for one second. It's not right."

Jimmy pushed the bowl back to her. "Not eating won't make your grandmother better. Tell me about her. What kind of woman is she? Is she like you?"

Tessa smiled again. "In looks maybe, but not in personality or in height. She barely comes up to my chin, but she's indomitable. She has a heart so big it crosses continents. When life knocks her down on her back, she gets right up again. She never feels sorry for herself, and she never asks, why me? She says, why not me? I've tried to be like her, but I just don't think I have it in me to be so brave, so courageous. It doesn't take much in the way of guts to strut down a runway."

"I don't know about that. I'd be terrified at the thought."

"You could do it. You're good-looking enough."

"Yeah, right. I'd trip and land in some matron's lap."

"More like a busty brunette."

"I've given them up for Lent."

"It isn't Lent."

"You know, you look tired," Jimmy said abruptly. "Let me take your picture now with those gray shadows under your eyes."

"Don't you dare. My career will be over. And I was serious before—you are not shooting a day in the life of a supermodel here. You'll have to wait until I can get down to L.A. Promise me."

"So who was that guy?" Jimmy asked.

Tessa didn't like the way he avoided making a promise. "I told you, he's my brother-in-law."

"You looked awfully cozy for in-laws."

Was there a chill in the air or had Jimmy's eyes suddenly gone cold? No. She was getting as imaginative as Alli. "Sam was my best friend growing up," she explained. "We've known each other for years."

"Where has he been?"

"Here. Sam and Alli live here with their daughter."

"They have a kid?"

"Megan. She's eight years old."

Jimmy studied her the way he did when he was searching for an angle to shoot. She laughed self-consciously.

"Stop that. Stop taking my picture in your mind."

"I took a few photos earlier, you know, even got the one where you ran into Sam's arms like a long-lost—"

"Stop."

"Tessa, the camera doesn't lie."

"Okay, he was my boyfriend when we were kids."

"But he married your sister. How did that happen?"

"It's a long story."

"Is that why you don't talk about her? Or about him? Is that why most of the free world thinks you're an orphan?"

"Maybe." Tessa took another spoonful of soup, but found it as unsatisfying as their conversation. "I don't want to talk about this now, okay? I've got more important things on my mind than the past."

Jimmy slowly nodded. "Whatever you say."

She sent him a suspicious look, his agreement coming to quickly. She'd known Jimmy for five years and he never gave up easily. But he was very good at biding his time.

"How did you get here anyway?" she asked.

"I rented a motorcycle at the airport."

"A motorcycle?"

"I needed some air."

"You've come to the right place for air. When is your flight back to L.A.?"

"I don't have one."

"You must have other jobs to do."

"They can wait."

"Jimmy, you're not going to talk me into a photo shoot while I'm in this place. This isn't my home. This isn't my life anymore, and I don't really want anyone to know about it."

"Why not? Why all the secrets, Tessa? Why not tell the world you have a grandmother and a sister and a niece? Why not tell them you grew up in a small town by the sea, that you still like a good cup of clam chowder no matter how many calories are in it?"

"No one wants to know that about me. They want to see my fancy apartment, and my new emerald-green Jaguar, and hear about my trip to Europe and my last date with the latest celebrity of the moment. And I thought we weren't going to talk about this."

"Maybe you sell your fans short. Maybe you sell yourself short. You're more than your photograph."

"Sometimes my photograph feels more real than me."

His green eyes seem to bore right into her soul, and she knew she'd revealed far too much. So she tried for the practiced smile, the artificial laugh, the uncaring toss of her hair that would draw attention to her beauty and away from her soul.

"You've been a good friend, Jimmy, the best photographer I've ever had, but this isn't your business. I'm not trying to hurt your feelings, but—"

"You want me to butt out."

"Yes, I do. I'm sorry, but this is personal."

"The least you can do is show me around your hometown."

She sat back in her chair, not sure she wanted to show him even that much encouragement. "There's not much to see."

"I don't know about that. It's been pretty interesting so far."

She saw his charming smile and knew she couldn't say no to his adorable face. Jimmy had a way of making her do things she never wanted to do, like wearing a bikini on an Aspen ski slope or riding a horse bareback down a Texas dirt road. She supposed this was an easy request compared to some of them. "You are nothing but trouble, you know that, don't you?"

He leaned forward, so close she could see the gleam in his green eyes, and she felt an unexpected tingle go down her spine.

"Sometimes a woman needs a little trouble in her life," he said.

She laughed. "Does that line really work on women?"

He grinned back at her. "You'd be surprised."

"I think I'd be more surprised if you ever stopped flirting."

"I keep hoping, that's all," he said lightly.

"Hoping? For what?"

He shrugged, a Mona Lisa smile on his lips that made her surprisingly uncomfortable. This was Jimmy, she told herself. A fun guy, a charmer, a man not to be taken seriously.

"You're not making any sense," she told him.

"Good, I'd hate to ruin my rep. Come on. Show me your old stomping grounds, where you went to school, what roads you took on your driver's test, where you parked to make out with all the boys."

She punched him in the arm. "Some things are private."

"Hey, if you can't tell your photographer, who can you tell? I know all your other secrets, babe, the freckles you hide behind powder, the way your hairline veers on the right side, that tiny little blemish under your left eyebrow." He leaned forward and cupped her face with his hands. "You can't hide from me, Tessa. Sooner or later, you're going to crack."

"Not even if you threaten to break my fingernails," she said, trying to lighten a mood that had suddenly gone serious. "Don't forget I know a few secrets about you, too, Jimmy boy. So, if you scratch my back, I'll scratch yours."

"How about your front?"

"Stop," she said, getting to her feet. "Enough. You're making me laugh. And I'm not supposed to be laughing right now. I'm supposed to be serious and concerned and worried."

"Not for the next hour. Give yourself a break, Tessa. The worry will be waiting when you get back."

"That's what I'm afraid of."

⛵ *Chapter 10*

"*R*elax, nothing will happen in the next few hours, except that you're going to think about something besides your grandmother and Tessa," Sam said to Alli as he steered the boat out of the harbor.

Alli wrapped her heavy sweater around her as the ocean breeze caught at her hair. She'd exchanged her skirt for a pair of jeans she kept in the back of the shop, and her sandals for white canvas tennis shoes.

"I feel so decadent," she confessed. "I should be working at the shop, or at the very least I should be at the hospital."

"You are working—for me," Sam said with a grin.

He'd looked downright pleased to see her arrive, and when he'd introduced her to the newlyweds, he'd called her his wife. Not his ex-wife, but his wife. For some reason, the distinction seemed important. "And you know Phoebe would want you to take a break," he added.

"I suppose." Alli rested her arms on the rail and glanced over at the young couple who were sitting on the bench seat in the stern of the boat, watching the white water kick up behind them as they gathered speed and left the harbor behind for the wide-open Pacific Ocean.

"They're cute," she said to Sam.

"Young love."

"Young? They're our age."

"Really? I feel older than they look."

"So do I," she admitted. She stared out at the horizon for a long moment. "Sometimes I wonder what it would be like to be twenty-seven and single, no child, no husband, no mortgage, no business to run, just myself to take care of."

"You'd probably be bored."

"Maybe."

"What's the point in looking back anyway? You can't change what happened," Sam said.

"I can't help it," she said wistfully. "Don't you ever wonder what it would have been like if we'd never gotten together that Christmas? I mean, what if you hadn't come to the party? Or if I'd left before you arrived? Things could have turned out so differently."

"But I did come to the party, and you were still there. I don't have time to wonder about what might have been, and frankly I don't see the point. We've got enough to do just dealing with the present." He stared out at the water, standing tall and straight, his hands firmly on the wheel in front of him.

She supposed that was one of the big differences between them: Sam didn't want to analyze any of it, and she wanted to pick it apart down to the last detail. "I guess the good thing about having a child young is that we'll still be young when Megan grows up."

"That's a long ways off."

"Not really, only ten years till she's eighteen. The last nine have gone pretty fast. And since we don't have any more children . . ."

"Don't start, Alli."

"I know you don't want any more children, but I do."

"You just said you wondered what it would be like to have no children. Make up your mind."

"I meant that hypothetically. I wouldn't trade Megan in for anything in the world."

"Neither would I." He sent her a brief look. "And I don't think you'd be happy with no one to take care of, to boss around, to get into fights with. You're not a loner, Alli, you never were. I was always tripping over you growing up. You were in the middle of things, stirring up trouble wherever you went."

"It was the only way I could get your attention," she admitted.

He laughed. "I think you had everyone's attention when you dyed your hair green."

"It wasn't supposed to be green, it was supposed to be blond," she replied.

He laughed. "What happened? Did you forget to read the directions? Oh, that's right, you don't believe in reading directions. Leap first, look later. That was always your style."

His tone was too gentle for her to take offense. "I was in a hurry."

"You were always in a hurry." He sent her a knowing look that reminded her of how many years they had known each other.

"You didn't exactly get through childhood unscathed," she said.

"Let's change the subject."

"Remember that party you had when your parents went out of town?"

"The one you talked me into having?" he asked pointedly.

"And somebody broke the picture frame that Tessa had given you to hold your prom photo?" she continued, ignoring the fact that she had been the one to encourage the party. "You thought Tessa was going to kill you for sure."

"So you went all the way to Portland with me to find an exact copy," he said quietly, turning to face her. "I'd forgotten about that. Why did you help me?"

"I didn't want you to get into trouble."

"Really?" he asked skeptically.

"Okay, I got to ride in the Thunderbird and spend time with you. But it was still a nice thing to do, even if my motives were a bit selfish."

"You were a pal."

She sighed. "And I wanted to be so much more."

"Well, it turned out that way."

For a few moments all was quiet between them. Alli leaned against the rail and watched him sail. Here on the water, he was completely at ease, master of his destiny, strong, powerful, a part of nature as much as the wind and the sea. It was how she always thought of him, the mist off the ocean dampening his hair, his cheeks burning from the midday sun, his eyes dancing with a joy that only being on the water could give him.

"You love this, don't you?" she asked, even though it wasn't really a question.

"More than I ever thought I would."

"So this part of your life turned out okay?"

He smiled at her. "Yeah."

"I'm glad." She looked out at the miles of water stretching before them. "Do you think we'll see any whales today?"

"I hope so or the Starks will be disappointed."

Alli turned her head to see the newlywed couple exchange a deep, passionate kiss. "I'm not sure they will come up for air long enough to see a whale."

"You might be right about that. By the way, we should talk about our kite. The festival is only a few days away. Have you thought about the design?"

"Megan wants to do a picture of our family for the design. She even drew three stick figures. Yours has great hair. Mine just looks fat."

"You always think you look fat."

"I have a mirror."

"You don't look in the mirror. Most of your impressions are stuck in your head from a hundred years ago. Maybe once you looked fat, so forever you're fat. That's the way it is with you. You never change your mind."

"That's not true," she automatically denied, although she had the vague impression that he might be somewhat right.

"Sure it is. Twelve people could say you were skinny and one person could say you were fat, and who would you believe—the one person who said you were fat."

She thought about that for a moment, wondering when Sam had gotten so good at analyzing her. "Maybe."

"Not maybe; it's true."

"It was different for me, Sam. Growing up, you and Tessa had each other for support. I didn't have anyone."

"You had friends."

"I didn't have a relationship like the one you and Tessa had. What was it about her that made you want to be with her every second of the day?"

He thought about her question for a moment. "Tessa was an incredible storyteller," he said finally. "We'd sit for hours in the treehouse and Tessa would talk about climbing the Pyramids and shooting the rapids and coming face-to-face with wild tigers in the jungles of Africa."

"Like any of that would actually come true," Alli said scornfully.

"It didn't matter. The story was enough."

"Did you really want to do all those things—shoot rapids, hunt tigers?"

"At thirteen, yeah. But there was one thing Tessa wasn't good at—"

"You mean there was one thing? I'm in shock. Catch me if I faint."

"Tessa never figured out how we were actually going to get to the African jungle, especially since at the time we didn't even have a driver's license." He laughed at some memory that was not hers, and it hurt. But Alli couldn't let him see that, because then he'd stop talking, and she needed him to talk, she needed to understand why he loved Tessa so much.

"You could still do it, Sam. You and Tessa could travel around the world, see all those things that you never got to see."

"And what about you? What about Megan?" His eyes grew more serious as he looked at her. "Wouldn't you miss me? We've been together for nine years. And they weren't all bad. Is it really so easy to send me away, Alli?"

His words created a lump in her throat that she had trouble swallowing. "Of course we would miss you, Sam, but . . ." She didn't know what he was asking really. Did he want her to ask him to stay, to walk away from Tessa?

She'd already forced that decision on him once before, and she couldn't do it again, especially now, since he'd reminded her of the past, of all the hours he and Tessa had spent in the treehouse with the flashlight and the telescope.

Alli had seen their first kiss. She'd heard their first fight. She'd watched them fall in love. And she'd broken them up. It was time to do the right thing, set Sam free.

"Alli?"

"What?"

"Look at the seagulls."

She watched a group of gulls dance off the water in search of food only to soar high into the sky as the boat drew closer to them.

"Beautiful," she murmured. "Absolutely free. I'd

forgotten how fun this is, to sail into the wind, feel the mist on your face, breathe in the fresh air. It's invigorating."

"It's spectacular," Sam said. "Out here, everything is so simple. Why do we have to complicate things?"

"Because we're human, and we need more than the seagulls to be happy." She paused. "You know what you said about Tessa teaching you how to dream? Well, since I spent most of my time standing on the ground beneath that damn treehouse, I always had to look up to see anything, and when I looked up, I saw you." Her eyes grew watery. "You were my dream, Sam. I wanted so badly to be yours."

"Come here." He held out his hand to her.

Alli hesitated, then walked over and let him slide his arm around her waist as he encouraged her to put her hands on the wheel.

"You can drive," he said.

"Since when?" she asked, feeling the power of the boat under her fingers.

"Since now. Besides, there's nothing around for you to crash into."

"Thanks for the vote of confidence."

He rested his chin on her head, his hands firm on her waist as she steered the boat. "Sometimes you need to forget everything, Alli—where you've been, where you're going, what you want, what you think you want. Sometimes you just have to be in the moment, or the moment passes you by."

"I think that's how we made Megan," she said dryly.

"And since then you've been trying to take it all

back. But you can't. I came to accept the fact that you were never going away, Alli."

"Hey," she protested, but his teasing laugh prevented any further protest.

"And you need to accept the fact that we can't change the past. Just stop and feel the sun on your face and the breeze in your hair and let everything else go. Be as free as those seagulls."

She turned her head, his face so close to hers. "Is that why you spend so much time out here, so you can feel free, so you can forget everything?"

He stared at her for a long time, so long she had to stop herself from fidgeting, force herself to not look away, because she really wanted to hear his answer.

"I used to come out here to forget. Lately, I've been trying to remember." Then he smiled his special smile . . . and Alli remembered how much she loved him.

"You'll remember how to do it as soon as you get on," Jimmy said, holding the two-seater bicycle steady as Tessa eyed it with distrust.

"Tell me again why I want to do this."

"Because it will be fun. Because it's here, and we're here, and what the hell."

"It's amazing how complex your thoughts are," Tessa said sarcastically.

Jimmy laughed, feeling better than he had in weeks. He'd missed Tessa, missed the way she didn't take crap from him, saw through all the bullshit and yet still remained one of the most beautiful, desirable women he'd ever met—and he'd met plenty in his career as a fashion photographer. In fact, after his first few years of sexual indulgence, he'd become vaccinated against the superthin, superbeautiful, superbitchy women who only wanted him because he made them look better than anyone else.

Behind the camera, he had all the power, and he'd used it unashamedly for a long, long time. But Tessa, Tessa was different. There had always been a vulnerability to her, a privacy, a secret side that even his camera had yet to unveil. Now, seeing her here in her hometown, he was beginning to believe she was nothing like the woman most people thought they knew.

Tessa straddled the bike, her short dress hitched up to mid-thigh. "I think I should be wearing jeans for this," she said. "I might stop traffic."

"Good. That will save me from running the lights."

"Maybe I should be in the front. Can I trust you to steer?"

"I don't know, can I trust you to pedal?"

She laughed. "Good question. Now, are we doing this or not? Because at some point today, I really need to get back to the hospital."

He flicked her chin with his finger. "You just called the hospital and your grandmother is sleeping, so don't start feeling guilty on me. I'm not used to seeing guilt on a model's face—unless, of course, she just scarfed down a pound of Godiva chocolates."

"My favorite."

"Mine, too. All right. Let's see if this thing works." Jimmy slid onto the front seat, balancing the bike by resting his feet lightly on the ground. "Where to?"

"Head down Main Street, hang a left at Carmen Avenue, and I'll show you the hot spots: Milton's Barber Shop, Lucy's Hot Curl, and Mrs. Davenport's Frank Sinatra museum."

He looked over his shoulder at her. "No way, I love Old Blue Eyes."

"You do not like Frank Sinatra."

"How would you know, babe? You don't know everything about me."

She made a face at him. "Fine, I stand corrected. But you won't be able to get into the museum, because Mrs. Davenport only opens it on Saturdays."

"Too bad. So are you on, or what?"

"Actually, I'm not." She laughed as the bike threatened to fall over. "This isn't going to work."

"Sure it is. You put your feet on the pedals. I'll keep us stable until you're ready. Then I'll push off and you'll start pedaling really fast."

"If you say so."

He waited until Tessa said she was set, then pushed off and started pedaling. After the first few wobbles, they were cruising down Main Street and turning quite a few heads, as well as stopping traffic as Tessa had predicted.

He wasn't surprised that people stared at them; he was surprised to discover that so many of the people seemed to know Tessa. He wondered why she hadn't come home in close to a decade and had a feeling the answer had to do with her sister and her sister's husband. He hadn't seen Tessa run into a man's arms with such confidence since . . . well, since never.

She usually kept everyone at arm's length. On occasion, he'd wondered if she had something going on, like an affair with a married man, or if she was nursing a broken heart. Hell, maybe it was both.

Her sister certainly hadn't looked happy to see her husband and Tessa together. There was a history among the three of them, he'd bet his camera on that.

"There's Lucy's Hot Curl," Tessa said. "In case you need a haircut."

"I'm not sure I'd trust this mane to someone named Lucy."

"Fine, be a big-city snob."

"Oh, sure, since when has anyone but Gerard touched your golden locks?"

"All right, you win."

"I always do." He began to whistle as they cruised around town. It was fairly flat and easy to get around, not too much traffic to worry about, and he couldn't remember when he'd had such a good, simple, cheap time. He felt . . . happy. "Daisy, Daisy, give me your answer true," he sang out.

"Oh, please, don't sing."

"I'm half crazy, all for the love of you."

"I'm totally crazy for doing this with you," Tessa interrupted. "Everyone is looking at us."

"Looking at you. Aren't you used to that by now?"

"Turn left. There's Carmen Avenue. I want to show you Central Park."

"Just like the one in Manhattan?"

"Except it's about fifty times smaller."

"Cool." Jimmy made a fairly wide turn as the long bicycle still seemed a bit unsteady beneath his hands. But then he hadn't been on a bicycle in about twenty years. He began to pump harder as the bicycle seemed to be dragging up a small incline. Having a sneaking suspicion why, he flung a look over his shoulder. "Hey, you're not pedaling."

"Of course I am," she said.

"Liar." But he felt a definite improvement in their speed as they hit the top of the hill and began down the other side. "No more loafing," he said with another quick look at her. He should have kept his eyes on the road, but the bloom in Tessa's cheeks, her hair streaming out behind her, was just too hard to resist.

"Jimmy!" she cried.

"Shit!" he swore as he looked back just in time. He had to make a hard turn to the right to avoid a woman, a stroller, and some kind of dog on a very long leash. The turn was too fast, and he had trouble recovering as the bike soared over the sidewalk and down a long grassy embankment, toward a pond— a pond? Tessa hadn't mentioned anything about a pond.

"Turn! Turn!" Tessa screamed.

But he couldn't make the steering work. He didn't know if Tessa was turning to the right or the left, but they didn't seem to be in sync. The bike began to fishtail, and they drew closer to the water. Then he felt the back of the bike flare up as if Tessa had jumped. The next thing he knew he was underwater, under ice-cold water. He thrashed his way to the top, only to realize he could actually stand up since the pond was only about five feet deep. He looked over to the bank and saw Tessa standing next to the pond. She had jumped and left him to his fate. Traitor.

"It's okay, I'm all right. Thanks for asking," he said, pulling himself and the bike out of the water.

Tessa didn't reply. She had one arm wrapped around her middle and he was suddenly afraid that she'd hurt herself.

"Tessa, Tessa," he said as her body seemed to shake. He dropped the bike on the ground as he came out of the water and rushed to her side. "Are you hurt?"

"I'm—I'm fine," she said, then burst into fullfledged laughter as she pointed at his head. "You have green moss in your hair."

"And here I was worried about you. Silly me."

"You should be worried. You practically killed me," she said with a grin that was so much wider and freer and more joyous than any he had ever seen on her face.

"You look pretty alive to me." He ran his hands through his hair, then winced as he pulled out some sort of weed.

"I'll be black-and-blue tomorrow," she said. "Probably won't be able to pose for any photographs for a while. I might have to sue you for lost wages."

"I might have to sue you for being so distracting."

"Excuse me?" she asked, planting a hand on her hip. "I didn't say a word. You weren't paying attention to the road. You almost hit that poor woman."

"I wasn't paying attention because I was looking at you. Besides that, haven't you ever heard of going down with the ship?"

"We were on a bicycle, not the *Titanic*."

"Same thing."

"It is not the same thing."

"Well, I'll give you this, you have great survival instincts." Her smile vanished abruptly, and the light went out of her eyes. "What did I say?"

"Nothing."

"Come on, you look like I just pulled the lights out of your Christmas tree."

"It's just something Grams said to me once about saving myself, surviving. Forget it."

"That's your secret?"

"I don't have any secrets," she said, flopping down on the ground.

Jimmy sat down beside her. "Sure you do. You never talk about your family. I didn't even know you had a sister or a grandmother, and I thought we were good friends."

"We should go back. You'll catch a cold. The afternoon wind can be brisk here on the coast."

He could feel the drops chilling his skin, but he was far more interested in hearing her story than in getting warm. "Why haven't you come back here before?"

She rolled her head on her neck. "You're not going to stop asking questions, are you?"

"Not until I get some answers. What happened? Did you suddenly get too famous for the old hometown?"

"No."

"Then, what?"

"I didn't want to see my family or this town because it's where everything fell apart." She let out a long breath. "When I was twenty years old, my sister slept with my boyfriend and got pregnant."

"Ouch."

"Sam did the noble thing and married her."

"After he'd done the noble thing of sleeping with her."

She sent him a sharp look. "I don't hold Sam blameless, but Alli chased after him for years. She finally caught him in a weak moment and made the most of it."

"Where were you at the time?"

"Aspen."

"I didn't mean geographically."

"Sam and I were supposed to come back here together that Christmas, but I got a chance to model in Aspen, and I took it."

"Bad decision?"

"Well, I lost Sam, but that modeling job got me a contract."

"And you never looked back."

"Not until now." She paused. "But I had to come home for Grams. She's the reason I'm here, not Sam or Alli. I don't care about either one of them."

"Then why were you in Sam's arms a few hours ago?"

"Sam was just being nice. He knows how worried I am about my grandmother."

"I can see that." Jimmy stretched out his legs in front of him. "So, any old feelings come back during that hug?"

"We should go." Tessa got to her feet.

"Just tell me to shut up, Tessa, I can take it."

"Shut up, Jimmy."

"You still have feelings for him, don't you?"

"You just told me you'd shut up if I asked," she said in exasperation. "Fine. I don't know what feelings I have. When I came back here, I thought Sam and Alli were happily married. But it turns out that they're not."

Jimmy felt his stomach turn inside out. When Tessa had told him that her old flame was married to her sister, he'd felt bad for her, but at least the guy was out of the running.

"Sam and Alli are getting a divorce," Tessa added.

He looked into her troubled blue eyes and had to ask. "Do you want him back?"

⛵ *Chapter 11*

*P*hoebe could hear them talking over her like she was already dead and buried, and she didn't like it one little bit. She suspected it was evening, but which evening she couldn't be sure. She definitely smelled food, spaghetti she thought, and she'd heard Alli ask William if he wanted to get a sandwich in the cafeteria.

Tessa was in the room, too, and Sam—she heard his deep baritone in between the two female voices. They seemed to be arguing about something.

Her mind drifted away with the weariness of it all. She'd wanted so badly to fix what was wrong between the girls. They were sisters, after all. They were family, and once she was gone they'd only have each other. It hurt her to think of them apart, separated by a wall of betrayal and distrust. But she didn't know how to make it better. Maybe if John had lived . . .

After his death, everything had gone to hell in a handbasket, as her own grandmother used to say. It was that Christmas after his death that Tessa hadn't come home. It was that Christmas that Alli and Sam had fallen into bed together, made a baby, and destroyed one family at the same time they were compelled to build another.

Phoebe prayed for John to speak to her again, to tell her what to do, for it was only in the strange dreamworld that she felt like a whole person, able to move freely, to speak clearly. But John was gone for now. He wanted her to finish the pearl necklace, to ask the girls to help, to remind them of what family and love were all about. But she could barely speak. Every time she woke up, she had to struggle to get small words out. How could she make them understand what they needed to understand?

But even as she worried, she felt the heaviness in her heart begin to lessen as the outside world grew louder and her dreamworld faded away.

"Look, her eyelids are fluttering." Alli reached out her hand to Sam.

He squeezed her fingers as he moved closer to her side. "She could be dreaming."

"I want her to wake up. It feels like forever since I've talked to her."

Alli leaned against him, and he felt more needed in that moment than he had in a very long time. She was such an independent woman, his wife, so strong, so bullheaded, that it was easy to think of her as totally self-sufficient. Only he knew better. He knew her insecurities, her fears lay just beneath the surface, and it didn't take much to turn her confidence into insecurity. Tessa could do that better than anyone. And he supposed he was a close second.

They'd had a love-hate relationship for eighteen

years now. They'd been so many things to each other—neighbors, friends, enemies, lovers—and now they were supposed to be separated, on their way to a divorce. What would they be to each other then? Strangers? It didn't seem possible that they could have ended up in this place.

He looked up as the hospital room door opened and Tessa walked in with William.

Alli stepped away from him immediately, as if she'd been caught doing something wrong, like holding his hand, like caring about him.

But why was that wrong? His definitions had changed, grown blurry. Marrying Alli had always seemed to be wrong. But divorcing her seemed wrong, too. And Tessa; he didn't know what the hell to do about her.

"Hi," Tessa said softly, her blue eyes seeking his for reassurance. "Everything okay?"

"Fine. But how are you?"

"I'm okay. Jimmy is in the hall. I didn't think it would be right to bring him in here since he's never met Grams. I wouldn't want to confuse her if she wakes up."

"That was thoughtful of you."

"Grams?" Alli questioned. "Are you awake?"

Sam looked to the bed as Phoebe's eyes slowly opened. Thank God, he breathed in silent prayer. Because if anyone could make the world right again, it would be Phoebe. She'd been as much a grandmother to him as she was to Alli and Tessa. And in the past three months she'd been a lifeline in a sea of confusion.

Phoebe's lips trembled and then moved into what looked like a smile. As her facial muscles seemed to respond to her command, her expression relaxed.

"It's all right, don't try to talk," Alli said.

"Maybe she wants to try," Tessa suggested, coming around the other side of the bed.

Phoebe's lips parted, and after several ragged breaths, she said, "Pearl."

Sam leaned closer to the bed, surprised by her word choice. Had he heard her correctly? Had she meant *Pearl* or were her brain signals all mixed up?

"Pearl?" Alli echoed. "What do you mean, Grams?"

"Don't push her," Tessa said. "Give her a chance to collect her thoughts."

"Tessa." Phoebe's gaze came to rest on Tessa's face. "You came home," she said slowly, looking more triumphant with each word.

"Yes, I came home," Tessa said with a laugh that was a half cry. "For you. You scared me. But you're better. I can see that you're better now."

"Alli," Phoebe muttered, moving on to her other granddaughter. "And Sam."

"And William," Alli added, moving back so William could stand next to the bed.

Phoebe smiled at her old friend. "William. I remember walking on the pier."

"That's when you fainted. I called the paramedics. They came pretty quick," William said.

"When? Today?"

"No, it was Sunday. Today is Tuesday."

A frown knitted her brows together. "So long?"

"You've been resting," William said. "For once in your life you've actually been sleeping in."

"Sleeping too much," she said, her words still a bit garbled.

Sam let out the breath he'd been subconsciously holding. Phoebe was going to get well. He could feel it.

"Favor." Phoebe struggled with the word. "Finish my necklace."

"I don't understand," Alli replied. "You didn't want to finish the necklace without Grandpa. Remember?"

"Wrong to stop. Need to finish . . . make everything all right."

"Why don't we talk about this when you're home?"

"When is the Fourth of July?"

"Monday," Alli replied.

"By then," Phoebe said. "Has to be done by then."

"But Grams—" Tessa protested. "We can find the pearl together when you're better."

"I'm sure the girls will do as you ask," William interrupted, sending both Alli and Tessa a stern look. "We want your grandmother to concentrate on getting well, nothing else, right?"

"Yes," Alli agreed. "If you want us to finish the necklace, we will."

"Together, you and Tessa," Phoebe said. "Can't go to the store. Have to find a wild pearl like we did before."

Alli leaned over and kissed Phoebe on the cheek. "We'll do it exactly like we used to."

"Exactly," Tessa added. "We want you to get better, Grams. Don't worry about anything."

"I'm tired," Phoebe said wearily.

"Then we'll say good night," Alli said. "Just rest."

Sam stepped up to the bed after Tessa said her good night. He kissed Phoebe on the forehead. "You take care of yourself, Phoebe."

"You take care of them," she said slowly. "Keep them together. I'm counting on you, Sam."

Keep them together—wasn't he the reason they were apart?

"I'll do my best," he replied, following Alli and Tessa into the hallway.

Tessa stood next to Jimmy. Alli leaned against the wall, her arms crossed in front of her like a shield. For a moment in Phoebe's room they'd been together, now they stood apart. Sam had a feeling it would take more than a pearl necklace to bring them back.

"Are you angry with me?" Phoebe asked the man sitting next to her bedside. William had been holding her hand since the others left, but he hadn't said much. He'd always been a mystery to her, keeping his distance during her marriage, then courting her like an old flame since she'd become a widow. He'd asked her to marry him, to move back East with him, to return to her roots, to take the place in his life he'd always thought she should have.

William cleared his throat and spoke. "Why would I be angry with you? I'm glad you're finally awake and talking. You scared me."

"I scared me." She drew in a breath and let it out. "Wasn't sure . . . I could make it back."

"Well, you did, and you're not going anywhere, except home."

Home. That sounded perfect. He must have seen her expression change, for his own grew more despairing. She didn't want to hurt him, yet she feared she did with every word she spoke, every breath she drew. He wanted her to be the girl he remembered, the one who'd almost married him. She could barely remember that girl.

"I've changed my plans, cleared my schedule," he said briskly. "I can stay here with you as long as you need me."

"You don't have to stay."

"I want to. I'm not leaving, Phoebe. Not without you. I've waited too long. Do you remember what you said to me Sunday morning?"

"No."

"You said you'd consider marrying me. It was as close to a yes as you've ever come."

She did remember. Because he'd been battering her resolve for so many years that it had become almost impossible to say no to him. And it wasn't that she didn't care for him, she did. But she still loved John, and William couldn't understand why. He was convinced she'd married John because of her parents, and not because she'd fallen head over heels, crazy in love with her husband.

"I can see that you do remember." William smiled tenderly. "I can make you happy, Phoebe. I have more money than I'll ever spend, houses in three cities, servants to take care of your every whim. It was the way you were supposed to live."

She was too tired to argue with him now. Too

weary to think beyond getting out of bed.

"It will be wonderful," he said. "Just as soon as you get better, we'll make plans."

She nodded, more concerned with the immediate future. "The girls must find the last pearl. It's important to me, to them."

He didn't want to talk about the pearls, about the symbol of her love for John. That was apparent from the sudden frown that turned his face to stone.

"Whatever you want," he said.

"I'm afraid."

The frown softened. "I know you are, Phoebe, but I'm here for you. I'm not going to let anything bad happen to you."

"Maybe you can't stop it."

"Don't talk like that."

"I'm not ready to die."

"Of course you're not."

She felt a tear slide down her cheek as she thought about all she wanted to do. Summer was coming, the Fourth of July. She wanted to fly a kite in the festival, eat clam chowder, sit on her deck and watch the fireworks.

She wanted to watch Megan grow up and see Alli's business take off, and read about Tessa in the magazines. She wanted to know how everything would all end, if Sam and Alli would get back together, or if Tessa would come between them. She didn't want to miss a second of what happened to her girls, her family. Yet there was a part of her that felt like she was slipping away, until William's tight grip on her hand yanked her back.

"You are not dying, do you hear me?" he said

forcefully. "We're going to be together. I know we are. I'm not giving you up."

"I want to go home."

"You will, soon."

"What if I have another stroke? Can't live like my mother."

"Stop worrying. The stress isn't good for you. You're not your mother. You won't have another stroke. This is our time, Phoebe. Our time."

His stubborn persistence made her feel better, anchored to the real world and not the hazy one in her mind.

"Those girls of yours are going to find the luckiest pearl in the entire Pacific Ocean and then you'll feel better," he promised.

"You're a good friend."

"I intend to be more than that."

⛵ Chapter 12

"Do you think Jimmy will come with Tessa today?" Alli asked Sam as they drove into the parking area next to O'Meara's Oyster Farm on Princeton Bay. It was almost lunchtime on the last Wednesday in June and unseasonably warm, Alli thought, as she rolled down the window and turned her face toward the breeze. "That feels better," she murmured.

"Is he still hanging around?"

"I think so. He didn't seem in a hurry to leave last night. I heard Tessa tell him she'd give him a ride back to the hotel. Do you think they're sleeping together?"

"How would I know that?" Sam asked, as he turned off the engine.

"Does the idea bother you?"

He sighed. "Does it bother you?"

"Why would I care?"

"I have no idea." Sam checked his watch. "What time is Megan's soccer game this afternoon?"

"Five o'clock."

"I don't want to miss it, so let's make sure we get out of here by four."

"Megan will be thrilled. I think she's playing forward today."

"Our girl likes to shoot," Sam said with a grin.

Alli smiled back at him, feeling warmed by the friendly look in his eyes, yet a bit unsettled by his nearness. They were so close, just a foot between them. If Sam slid over, if she moved a bit . . . no, she was absolutely not going to make that move. They were getting a divorce, for heaven's sake. They were supposed to be distant now, their relationship cooled by their obvious incompatibility and Sam's continuing interest in Tessa. But she didn't feel cool toward Sam. In fact, she felt as hot for him now as she had nine years ago, when she'd made the biggest mistake of her life.

Alli shifted in her seat, acutely aware of Sam's eyes on her. What on earth was he staring at? Her blue jeans weren't new, neither was the gray cap-sleeve T-shirt she wore. And she hadn't refreshed her makeup since she'd put it on at seven in the morning.

Finally, she drummed up enough courage to look over at him. "What?" she asked.

"I can't look at you?"

"You haven't in a long time."

"Well, maybe I feel like it now."

Alli took in a breath and let it out. In the past three months, she'd tried to separate herself from him. Slowly she was beginning to understand herself better, to believe that she could survive without

Sam. But surviving and being happy were two different things, and being near him made everything so much harder. She decided it was time to change the subject.

"Megan wants to know if you can work on the kite tonight after the soccer game."

Sam groaned. "I forgot about the kite."

"Is there a problem?"

"I planned to work on the Thunderbird tonight."

"You can't wax it another day?" She felt a bit peeved by his response. If Tessa had always had one half of his heart, the T-Bird had had the other.

"I'm not waxing it, I'm showing it to a potential buyer," he replied.

Her jaw dropped. "No way. You love that car. You've spent half your life caressing it with hot wax. I can't believe—"

"I'd hardly call a few weekends half my life."

"I'd hardly call it a few weekends." She searched his eyes for the truth. "You said you'd never sell the Thunderbird. When we had that horrible summer of rain and we had to repair the roof, you wouldn't even consider selling it."

He played with the keys still dangling from the ignition, his gaze fixed on the front window. "You said I was stuck in the past. Well, maybe you were right." He glanced over at her, his eyes serious. "I need some things for the business, equipment, maybe a new boat down the road. I could use the money. And the car is a good place to get it. I saw an ad for a Thunderbird on-line recently and the car went for thirty thousand dollars."

"Unbelievable."

"I know. It's a lot of money."

"Not the money, you. You're unbelievable."

He turned sideways in his seat. "Why?"

"Because you love that car. You worked forever to buy it from Mr. Carlton's widow—nights, weekends, summers. You were obsessed."

"I was sixteen. A car and sex were pretty much all I had on my mind."

"But I can still see you and Tessa driving around town in that car. You thought you were so cool."

"It was a long time ago, Alli. And you and I have driven in the car since then. Hell, we've done a few other things in that car as well, if you remember."

She cleared her throat at the piercing look in his eyes. She didn't want to be reminded of exactly what they'd done in that car. "I must admit you've surprised me."

"Maybe you don't know me as well as you think you do."

"Maybe I don't," she admitted. "When did you decide to sell it?"

He thought about her question for a few moments, then said, "Since I moved it out of our garage and into my father's garage. I started wondering why I was holding on to it so tightly when everything else in my life was slipping away."

She caught her breath at his words. "I never thought you wanted to hang on to me, Sam. I thought I was hanging on to you."

He opened his mouth to reply, but whatever he

was going to say was cut off as a loud motorcycle sped into the loosely graveled parking lot, kicking up dust and tiny pebbles. Alli was surprised to see Tessa hop off the back of the bike and pull the helmet from her head, shaking out her blond hair with a laugh. Tessa on a motorcycle? Tessa dressed in faded blue jeans with holes at the knees? Tessa?

Alli snuck a glance at Sam, who seemed as dumb-struck as she was.

"Hey," Tessa called out with a wave.

Sam opened his door and stepped out, leaving Alli to follow.

"I can't believe you're riding a motorcycle. What happened to thinking that was like riding down the road in a garbage can?" Sam asked her.

She laughed again. "Oh, I still think that, but Jimmy has a way of convincing me I should try new things."

"Nice to see you," Jimmy said to Sam, then he flung a charming grin in Alli's direction. "And I'm more than happy to see you again."

Alli couldn't help responding to Jimmy's sexy smile, especially since Sam was staring at Tessa like he'd never seen her before. So much for thinking he was having second thoughts about their marriage. "Likewise," she replied.

"So what do we do now?" Jimmy asked.

"We'll take a boat out to the far end of the bay and pull up some fresh oysters. Hunting for a wild pearl is a little like looking for a needle in a haystack," Alli continued. "We often had to try several oyster farms before we found anything."

"I do hope this involves some actual eating of oysters."

"By the time we're through, you'll never want to see an oyster again," Alli promised.

"Maybe, but I bet my libido will be in overdrive," he replied with a wink in Alli's direction.

"We better get started," Sam interrupted, his tone decidedly frosty.

Alli smiled to herself as they walked up to the entrance. Sam didn't like Jimmy. Good. Not that Sam was jealous on her account, more likely he was afraid that Tessa had something going on with the rugged photographer who had actually convinced her to get on a motorcycle. Oh, well, at least Jimmy would make things more interesting in what was probably going to be a long afternoon.

Jimmy dropped back next to Alli as Sam and Tessa spoke with Timothy O'Meara about going out in one of his boats.

"So, Alli," Jimmy said.

"What?"

"You and Tessa don't like each other?"

"Very good, Sherlock."

He tipped his head. "I'm intuitive. It's a gift."

"One of your many, no doubt."

"Why is it you MacGuire girls seem to be immune to my charm?"

"You mean Tessa isn't falling at your feet?"

"Does it look like she is?"

Alli glanced over at Sam and Tessa in deep conversation with Timothy, an old friend of her grandmother's. "They fell in love with each other when they were twelve, you know."

"Then how did you end up married to him?"

"I'm sure Tessa will tell you."

"Actually, she's not one for details. Why don't you tell me?"

"I could tell you it's none of your business."

Jimmy put a hand to his heart. "That would really hurt. I thought we were friends."

She shook her head in amusement. "Friends? I don't even remember your last name."

"Duggan. Jimmy Duggan."

"Fine, I know your name, but I don't know you well enough to share my private life with you."

Jimmy nodded. "All right. Maybe tomorrow." He stared at her so long she grew uncomfortable, since for the second time in less than an hour a man couldn't take his eyes off her. Was there something stuck in her teeth? She ran her tongue around the edge of her teeth in search of anything offensive. Finally, she gave up and asked, "What are you looking at?"

"Your face. You have incredible bones."

"Uh, thanks, I think."

"I'd love to photograph you."

"Oh, please, there's charm, and then there's stupidity. I'm not a model."

Jimmy rubbed his chin. "You don't like what you see in the mirror?"

"No, I don't. Especially since I grew up looking across the room at someone else."

Jimmy put an arm around her shoulders and gave her a quick squeeze. "I know how it feels."

"How could you possibly?"

"My brother is a state senator in Virginia. He graduated magna cum laude from Yale and made a fortune in business before he went into politics. He has the perfect wife, three incredible children, and a house with a foundation that goes back to the eighteen hundreds."

"Wow. What happened to you?"

He stuck out his tongue at her. "My parents ask themselves the same question. I think they sometimes wonder if they brought the wrong baby home from the hospital."

"I'm sure they love you anyway."

"What's not to love? But respect, that's a different animal."

"Yes, it is." They exchanged a look of complete and utter understanding. "You still try, don't you?" she asked.

"I shouldn't."

"Me either."

"They don't deserve us."

"No, they don't." She laughed and so did he. "You know, I'm glad you're here."

"I don't think I'll ask why."

"Jimmy," Tessa called impatiently. "Are you ready?"

"You bet." He looked over at Alli. "How about you?"

"I want to get this over with as fast as possible."

"Worried we won't be able to find a pearl?"

"No, I'm worried that with the four of us in one small boat, we may not all come back alive."

"Who do you think is the most likely candidate to go overboard?"

"You never know."

"Ooh, you are bad. I think I'm sitting next to Tessa."

"Big mistake," she said, laughing at his outrageous expression.

"Maybe I'll just stay close to you," Jimmy said hastily. "Somehow I think you may be more prone to violence than your older sister."

Traitor, Tessa thought, fuming to herself as Jimmy took a seat in the small aluminum boat next to Alli, sitting so close he was practically on her little sister's lap. And Alli was lapping it up like a cat with a bowl of cream.

"What's bugging you?" Sam asked, putting a hand on her shoulder.

"This whole pearl thing is crazy. It could take us days to find one—if we do at all." She looked away from Jimmy and Alli and concentrated on the water. Princeton Bay was beautiful, the water as still as glass with only a light breeze to ruffle its smooth surface. "I don't understand why Grams suddenly decided she needed the pearl now."

"Does it matter? You're still going to find it for her."

"I'll try, because Grams was always there for me, and I want to be there for her, even if it means spending the afternoon with *Alli*. She hasn't changed a bit."

"How would you know? Have you talked to her since you've been back?"

Tessa looked him straight in the eye, irritated by his defensiveness where Alli was concerned. He'd never been like this before. He'd always agreed with her on the subject of Alli. And now, with Alli kicking him out of his house, keeping him away from his daughter, his defense of her just didn't make sense.

"Why do you stick up for her, Sam?"

"Maybe because you seem intent on picking on her."

"Do you stand up for me when she rips me apart?"

Sam sighed. "I wish the two of you could figure out a way to get along."

"That's never going to happen." She took a breath. "Why are you doing this with us, Sam? Whose side are you on?"

"I'm here for your grandmother," he said sharply. "She asked me to help, and I owe that woman more than I could ever repay. As for sides, do we have to have sides?"

"We've always had sides. Since we were kids we had sides, and you used to be on mine."

"Looks like you already have someone on your side," he said pointedly. "Is Duggan your boyfriend?"

"He's a photographer. We have an assignment to do together. And you're avoiding my question. Why are you here, Sam? You could have made an excuse.

Grams would have understood. She knows it's awkward for the three of us."

"She wants us to do this together, Tessa."

"I just don't understand what is going on with you and Alli. You say you're getting a divorce and yet you're with her every other second." Sam stared at her, but she couldn't tell what he was thinking behind his dark sunglasses. "Well?"

"What do you want me to say?"

"I don't know—something. We used to be able to talk, to finish each other's sentences. Now it feels awkward all the time. I don't know who you are anymore."

"I don't know who you are either."

"Do you want to find out?" she challenged. Almost instantly she had second thoughts, but she couldn't take it back, wouldn't take it back. Ever since Alli had told her Sam was still in love with her, ever since she'd realized that if she was going to have a second chance with Sam in her life it would probably be now or never, Tessa had been unable to think of anything else.

"Why don't we spend some time together tomorrow?" she suggested.

Sam tipped his head in Jimmy's direction. "Your friend won't mind?"

"I'm asking you, not him. Jimmy came here on his own. I'm not planning my life around him. But if you don't want to . . ."

Sam hesitated for a long moment. "I want to," he said finally.

"Where?"

"Let's take that sail I promised you. If we go anywhere in town, we'll be the topic of conversation at every dinner table in Tucker's Landing. I'd rather be alone with you."

"A sail sounds perfect," she said, feeling an unexpected thrill run down her spine, another sign of a long-ago attraction that was starting to smolder again. She didn't know if she should throw a log on the flames or try to douse the sparks before they caught fire. Loving Sam could hurt. She knew that firsthand. And she certainly didn't want to go through that pain again.

Tessa looked over at Alli and wondered if the connection between Alli and Sam was truly broken. Before she could ask, the boat came to a halt at the far end of the bay, next to a long line of black buoys. In between the buoys oysters hung in bags off the lines that held them less then two feet under the surface of the water. Tessa moved to one side so Timothy O'Meara could pull up one of the yellow nylon lines.

"How come they're so shallow?" Jimmy asked her, drawing away from Alli for the first time since they'd boarded the boat.

"The oysters grow faster in warmer water," Tessa replied. "Plus, they can access the oysters at any time of the day. At some of the other oyster farms, you have to wait until low tide to wade in and scoop them off the bottom."

"Are we going to do that, too?"

"Depends on whether or not you're feeling lucky today."

He flashed her his patented smile. "I'm always feeling lucky, babe."

"Then it's a good thing we brought you along."

"Really? I thought you'd forgotten all about me," he murmured. "You seemed in rather deep conversation with Sam."

"We have some things to work out," she said evasively.

"I'll bet."

"What does that mean?"

"Nothing," he said innocently. "But . . ." His smile disappeared. "I hope you work it out."

She eyed him suspiciously. "Why do you care?"

"Because something has been holding you back all these years, and I think I just figured out what, or should I say who, it was."

Tessa was grateful when Timothy dumped a bag of oysters between them. She couldn't talk about Sam or Alli, not with the two of them standing just a few feet away.

"What now?" Jimmy asked.

"Now we go back to shore and start shucking," Tessa replied.

"Excuse me?"

"I'll show you how. It's easy."

"You know how to shuck oysters? You are full of surprises."

"I once shucked ten oysters in one minute. A family record," she said smugly.

"In case you haven't guessed, Tessa was the best at everything," Alli interjected.

"There's one in every family," he replied.

Tessa tensed as Jimmy and Alli shared a small smile that seemed filled with secrets. Then she felt Sam's hand on her arm and immediately relaxed. What did she care if Alli and Jimmy were getting along? It didn't mean anything. In fact, it would give her more time with Sam. And wasn't that what she wanted?

Chapter 13

"Okay, I want a kiss," Jimmy said to Tessa a few hours later as the four of them sat at a picnic table overlooking the bay with piles of empty oyster shells in front of them.

"I have eaten more oysters today than I have in my entire life and I am definitely in need of one juicy, wet kiss." He puckered up his lips and waited for Tessa, who was sitting next to him, to kiss him.

She put a finger against his lips instead. "No way. I am not giving you a kiss just because you got turned on by a mussel."

"You are an unfeeling woman, hard, cold, absolutely no compassion," Jimmy said.

"My God, someone who actually knows the real you," Alli mocked from her vantage point on the other side of the table.

Tessa sighed, realizing their unspoken truce had come to an end. For most of the afternoon, their conversation had centered on the oysters and the scenery, with Alli and Sam on one side of the table, Jimmy and her on the other. Now the gloves were apparently off.

"I'll kiss you, Jimmy," Alli offered, leaning forward.

"Okay," Jimmy said easily.

Tessa had to bite down on her tongue to stop herself from shouting "No." She looked over at Sam. "Aren't you going to stop her? She is still your wife—at least for a few weeks."

"Alli pretty much does what she wants," Sam said tersely.

"Come here," Alli said.

Jimmy met her halfway across the table, planting a brief kiss on her lips.

"You're never satisfied, are you?" Tessa couldn't help asking Alli. "If there's a man around, and he's with me, you have to have him."

"But they always ask you first, don't they, Tessa? I just get your leftovers." She stood up abruptly. "I think we've done enough for today. I'm going to wash my hands." She glanced over at Sam. "I'll meet you at the truck. We should go if we want to get to Megan's soccer game on time."

"Fine," Sam said, getting to his feet. He paused and looked back at Tessa. "I'll see you tomorrow."

She nodded. "Ten o'clock."

"Tomorrow?" Jimmy asked as Sam walked away. "What's tomorrow?"

"I'm going sailing with Sam. I'm sorry, but you can always go back to L.A. if you're bored."

"You sound like you're mad at me," Jimmy said with a quirk in one eyebrow. "Now, why would you be angry? Alli was right. I did ask you to kiss me first. You turned me down."

"I thought you were kidding. You're always kidding. But I don't care who you kiss."

"As long as it's not your sister."

Tessa played with one of the empty shells in front of her.

"Alli stole Sam from me. I'm a little touchy where she's concerned."

"She's a little touchy where you're concerned." He paused. "Do you really think a divorce is in the works?"

"That's what they both say. Are you that interested?"

"Oh, I'm interested, all right."

She sent him a wary look. "Because you want Alli or because you want me?"

He turned sideways, putting his leg over the bench so he was straddling it, so he was facing her. "That's the first time you've ever admitted that you even noticed I want you."

She swallowed uncomfortably. "You flirt with everyone, Jimmy. It's part of your DNA."

"I'm not flirting with you right now. I'm serious."

"How would I know that?"

"Because you know me." He put one hand on the side of her face, his thumb caressing her cheekbone. "You know I want to kiss you right now."

"That's the oysters talking."

"That's me talking."

"Jimmy, don't."

"Don't what?"

"I like our friendship."

"I want more from you than friendship."

"I can't."

"Because of me or because of Sam?"

She wanted to look away, but his hand slipped into her hair and held her in place. "Maybe a little of both," she admitted.

"Tessa." Jimmy shook his head, his eyes disappointed. "Where has he been all this time? If he wanted you . . ."

"He's been with my sister. They have a little girl. She's the reason they got married, the reason they stayed married."

"Until now?"

"Until now," she agreed. "I don't know what happened. No one has said. But Alli seems to think that . . ." Tessa couldn't bring herself to say the words.

"Seems to think what?"

"That Sam still has feelings for me."

"I see." His hand fell away from her hair, and he stood up. She felt suddenly chilled.

"I have to talk to him, Jimmy. I have to understand what happened. That's why we're going sailing tomorrow. We need to have a conversation that we probably should have had nine years ago." She paused, feeling like she had to explain herself. "Sam was my first love, the guy I dreamed about marrying when I was twelve years old. I owe him—I owe myself at least this much."

"First loves are tough to get over," Jimmy said, his voice cool and remote. "But I think you should be careful."

"Why?"

"Because you could get hurt again. Sam might have married your sister for the wrong reasons, but that doesn't negate the fact that they've spent the past nine years together."

"If their marriage was good, they wouldn't be splitting up," she argued.

"Maybe they didn't know how good it was."

"I'm not breaking them up. And by the way, you're not helping."

"I'm not trying to. I'm trying to make you think with your brain instead of your heart."

"I loved Sam," she told him, looking him straight in the eye. In fact, it felt strange to say the words out loud, strange but good. She'd been biting them back for a very long time. "And he loved me."

"Then why did he sleep with your sister?"

"Because I let him down," she cried, getting to her feet. "Because Alli was there, ready and waiting to take advantage of him. Because he was stupid. I don't know the answer. But it only happened the one time, and it changed everything."

"Sex will do that."

"I know it sounds silly to be carrying a torch for some guy who cheated on me, but Sam and I were inseparable from the time I was twelve years old until I was twenty. Eight years. He was the first one to get me to smile after my parents died. Sam saved me that winter. He listened to me for hours on end and helped me make friends here in town. Sam was my anchor, Jimmy. Through everything, he was the one who was there. I'll never forget what he did for me."

"Tessa, that was a long time ago. People change. They grow up. Sam did a lot for you when you were a kid. But let me ask you this." His eyes bored into hers. "What does Sam do for you now?"

She opened her mouth to answer, but nothing came out.

"Does Sam even know anything about you?" Jimmy persisted. "Does he know that you sneak cream into your coffee when no one is looking? Does he know that you hate that moment when the plane takes off, that you pretend to be calm while you're gripping the armrest as if it were a lifesaver? Does he know you love those little apple tartlets at that bakery in Denmark? Does he know how you can work a camera, work a room with just your smile and the flick of your finger?" Jimmy grabbed her by the shoulders and gave her a little shake. "Does Sam know what you think, what you care about, what you want out of your life?"

She looked at him in amazement, caught by his uncanny assessment of her quirks. "How do you know all that about me?"

"I've been there, paying attention, babe."

His eyes were too intense, too personal, so she looked at the water, at the horizon that had once beckoned to her in a way she couldn't resist. "I don't know what to say."

"You don't have to say anything. I can see right into your head when I take your picture."

"You cannot," she said, but his words were disturbing. He knew her better than she'd realized. Somehow Jimmy had snuck in when she wasn't looking.

"The eyes are the windows to the soul. Don't you ever look at your own photographs?"

"I don't see anything but the makeup hiding the blemishes and the powder lightening my eyes and the hair spray holding my hair in perfect position."

"What do you see when you look at your sister?"

She stared at him for a long minute. "Alli? I don't know."

"Come on, give it a shot, describe her to me."

"You just spent the afternoon with her, and I saw you taking photographs of all of us, so I'm sure you can see her for yourself later on."

"You don't look at her, do you? Funny, she doesn't look at you either."

"We prefer it that way."

"Weren't you ever close?"

"Maybe a hundred years ago."

"What happened?"

"I told you."

"Besides Sam—what else broke you apart?"

"It wasn't any one thing."

"Come on, Tessa, talk to me."

She hesitated. "All right. The beauty pageants started the competition between us. My parents entered me first, because I was the oldest, and Alli, well, she wasn't the prettiest baby. I'm not saying that to be mean, she just wasn't. And she was cranky all the time. I knew to smile at the right moment. Alli usually picked that moment to pull down her socks or burst into tears. Pretty soon, my parents took me on my own and left Alli behind. But I never tried to make her feel bad."

"But she felt bad anyway."

"I suppose. We didn't talk about it back then. And when our parents died, we were really close for a while. We shared a bedroom at Grams's house, and we'd talk for hours into the night. We felt like we only had each other."

"Until Sam came along," Jimmy said somewhat dramatically.

She made a face at him. "Yes. Sam lived next door. He was my age, and we were instant friends. Alli couldn't stand it. She did everything she could to make trouble for us."

Tessa paused, lost in the memories.

"Do you blame her for feeling left out?"

"I guess not. But you can't make someone like you. Alli couldn't ever figure that out."

Jimmy smiled to himself. "That's a tough concept to accept when you want someone badly enough. For what it's worth, I don't think Alli is so horrible."

"You've only spent one day with her."

"Yeah, but I looked at her, you didn't. I bet if you ever did, you'd be surprised by what you saw. In fact, while you're at it, you might want to take a good look at Sam, too."

"You just can't stop yourself, can you?" Sam said to Alli as the Ford Explorer sped down the highway, his foot heavy on the gas pedal. "You had to goad Tessa. Or was it me you were trying to get a reaction from?"

Alli ran a brush through her hair, checking out her reflection in the mirror on the sun visor in front of her.

"I was having a little fun. It was no big deal."

"Just a little fun, yeah, right. You knew kissing Jimmy would hurt Tessa and you did it anyway." He glanced over at her and immediately wished he hadn't.

Her eyes were sparkling with mischief, her cheeks a rosy pink, her hair a glorious tangle of reds and golds that reminded him of incredible sunsets over the ocean. He'd always thought Alli was pretty, but today she looked spectacular.

He tried to regroup, to remember that he was mad at her. But he was so distracted he wanted to stop the car and run his hands through her hair, kiss her sunburned lips, unbutton the three pearls on the T-shirt that even now strained against her breasts and . . . Talk about straining, he adjusted his position, wishing he'd worn his looser jeans, because his body was at full alert.

"Jimmy is a flirt," Alli said, flipping back the visor and slipping the brush back into her purse. "I just played along. Tessa would have done the same thing if you hadn't been standing there. You were certainly cozy enough in the boat. What were you talking about?"

"Oysters," he said shortly, irritated that she didn't seem to be at all affected by their closeness or the number of oysters they'd both eaten that day. He felt like Jimmy, wanting to demand a kiss to appease his libido.

"Sure, oysters."

He looked over at her and shook his head. "You drive me crazy."

"Well, you'll be free soon enough." She turned

her head toward the window, so he could no longer see her expression.

Free. The word seemed too simple for the complicated emotions running through him. He'd always thought of himself as a straightforward man. He didn't lie. He didn't play games. He didn't cheat. But here he was feeling lust for one woman, at the same time wondering whether or not he still had feelings for her sister.

A long time ago he'd thought of himself as a one-woman man, and Tessa had been that woman. Then Alli had come along and they'd married and shared so many days and nights together that she'd become a part of his existence. She had carved a place in his life, a place that now felt empty, more empty than he would have imagined.

"Do you want to see Tessa again?" Alli asked quietly.

A flash of guilt ran through him. "I'm taking her out on the boat tomorrow," he answered, because there couldn't be any more lies between them.

She turned her head, her brown eyes pained. "On the boat?"

"We need to talk."

"Why can't you just have coffee like everyone else?"

"Tessa can't blink without someone reporting it to the newspaper."

"Well, you'll have all the privacy you want on the boat." Her expression was pure hurt.

"Someday you might have to learn to trust me, Alli."

"It doesn't matter if I trust you or not. I told you I

wanted to set you free, and I meant it. If that means you go to Tessa, then that's what it means."

He tapped his fingers against the steering wheel, feeling more restless with each word. He saw a view point directly ahead and pulled into a parking spot overlooking the Pacific Ocean, because with the way he felt right now he was afraid he would drive them off a cliff if he didn't stop.

"What are you doing?" Alli asked in surprise. "We have a soccer game to get to."

"Oh, we'll get there, all right. But first you and I are going to have a very long-overdue conversation."

Alli turned to face him. "What do you want to talk about?"

"The box of photographs you found in my office."

"Why do you want to talk about that now?"

"Because I do. Because we didn't really discuss it before."

"There's nothing to discuss."

"Of course there is. I didn't collect those clippings, Alli. Your grandmother did. And last year she brought them to me and asked me to keep them for Megan."

Alli looked both surprised and hurt. "Grams wouldn't have done that. She never would have ..." Alli's words faded away as he held her gaze and refused to let go. "Why didn't you tell me this before?"

"Because I didn't want to break the bond between you and Phoebe. I knew you would see it as a betrayal, Phoebe choosing Tessa over you. So I kept the box. I suppose I could have insisted that Phoebe keep them at her house, but I guess there was a small part of me that enjoyed seeing what Tessa was up to."

"So you were interested in the clippings after all?"

He hated the shimmer of pain in her eyes, the trembling quality of her voice. "Was it so wrong to be interested in someone I grew up with, someone I once cared about?"

"Yes. Yes, it was," she said passionately. "Do you know how I felt when I found that box? It was like seeing you in the arms of another woman. And the woman was Tessa."

"Alli—"

"You can't imagine how awful I felt," she continued, the words pouring out in a rush. "It wasn't just the box itself, it was the secret you were keeping. You knew those photographs would hurt me. That's why you hid them away. Isn't it? Otherwise, you would have just set them on the table."

He forced himself to swallow back an automatic denial. Maybe, just maybe, there was a shred of truth in what she was saying. "I never thought I was cheating on you by looking at photographs of Tessa. Half the world looks at photographs of Tessa."

"Half the world isn't married to her sister." She took a deep breath. "You hurt me, Sam. I thought you were better than that."

"Better than what? I'm a man, Alli. I'm human. I make mistakes. So do you. We're supposed to be able to forgive each other when we screw up."

"I know that," she said wearily. "I told you before it wasn't just the box. That was the last straw, not the first. You've looked at our marriage as a jail sentence—a sentence that won't end until Megan grows up. That's what I can't live with anymore, Sam. I can't stay with someone who is never going to love me the way I deserve to be loved. I don't want to mark time for the next ten years. I want to live my life, and I think you want the same thing."

"I've done everything I can to make you happy. If you want to call that marking time—"

"You haven't done everything," she said, her voice rising again with the force of her emotions. "You haven't let go of Tessa, not deep in your heart where it counts."

He shook his head, feeling frustrated and angry. "Maybe *you're* the one who won't let go of Tessa. Have you ever thought of that?"

"I'm trying to let go. That's why I asked for the divorce. Because one person in love in a marriage isn't enough. We can't pretend anymore. We have to be honest with each other."

"I haven't been pretending to care about you the last nine years. Hell, I've always cared about you, even when you made me nuts." He took a deep breath, knowing he had to tell her something he had only recently been able to admit to himself. "Do you really think I would have made love to you all those years ago if I hadn't felt something?"

"You were a teenage boy. You didn't need to feel anything but horny." She sat back in her seat. "I think we have a soccer game to get to."

"Oh, hell, Alli. Why do you have to make everything so damn difficult?" He started the car and pulled back onto the highway, wishing he'd never stopped in the first place. She was hardheaded and stubborn and she wanted too damn much from him. She always had.

The drive to the soccer field passed in stiff, painful silence. Alli wanted to break it, but she didn't know how. Sam kept confusing her with his words, with his actions. On one hand he seemed to be apologizing, but on the other, he still wouldn't ask her to come back to him. So they sat in their separate corners of the car and said nothing until he pulled into the parking lot by the soccer field and shut off the engine.

"I don't want to fight in front of Megan," she said abruptly. "It isn't fair to her."

"I don't want that either."

"Do you think we could call a truce?"

"Sure. Why not?" He started to open the door, but she stopped him once again.

"Wait," she said. She couldn't let things end this way. It was too awkward, too unsettled. Megan would pick up on the tension in a second.

"What now?" he asked.

"I want you to know that I think you're a good father in spite of everything else. Megan couldn't have a better dad. She knows that, and so do I. In case you thought otherwise."

His expression softened slightly. "And you're a good mother, Alli."

Finally, some common ground they could share. She sent him a tentative olive branch of a smile. "Maybe I do ask too much of you, wanting you to give up all your memories, all your feelings for Tessa. But maybe you ask too much of me, too, expecting me to be able to forget her when you can't forget her. You know, I'm glad she's here. Because you have to find out what you are to each other. Until you do that, we're just going to be circling around her the way we always have, unable to move forward, unable to go back. We can't keep running in place. We're not getting anywhere."

"Have you considered the fact that Tessa has moved on? She came back for your grandmother, not for me."

"But, she wants—" Alli stopped. She had no idea what Tessa wanted, not really. She seemed to want Sam, but then again, she had waited an awfully long time to come back.

"You're trying to control it all, Alli. But you can't. I have a mind of my own and so does your sister."

And on that note, they got out of the car and walked over to the field where Megan's team was warming up. Along the way, they stopped to say hello to some of the other parents, and they both smiled and acted like nothing was wrong—the way they always did.

"I hate this," she muttered. "Everyone else seems to have the perfect happy family."

"Don't kid yourself. We're not the only ones with problems."

Megan waved to them from the field. "Hi, Mommy. Hi, Daddy," she yelled.

Alli willed herself to relax as she waved and smiled to Megan, but the truth was her body was so tense it almost ached. Being with Sam but not really being with him was so difficult.

He thought she made things hard, well, he made them even harder.

"Take a deep breath," Sam said in her ear.

She flung him a quick look. "I'm fine."

"No, you're not, you're about ready to pop. We're not going to solve anything in the next five minutes, so try to relax."

"I'm trying. I just feel so restless."

"The oysters sure didn't help," he said dryly.

She sent him a reluctant smile. "Good point."

"Hey, they're kicking off."

Alli looked back at the field and yelled, "Go Honeybees," as Megan's yellow-and-black team kicked off the ball.

And they were off, twenty-two little girls battling for a soccer ball as their parents yelled encouragement from the sidelines, some more critical than encouraging, Alli thought as one parent told her child to get off her butt and run.

It reminded Alli of the beauty pageants she'd participated in before her mother had decided they really only needed one beauty contestant in the family. Before that, there had been a litany of "Stand up straight, Alli; suck in your stomach; throw back your hair; look like you're having a good time." Torture was more like it. Well, she'd never do that to Megan.

Alli turned her attention back to the game, but she became more annoyed as Megan was repeatedly elbowed and pushed by one decidedly bigger child.

"Go forward, Meg," she yelled. "Stay forward."

"She's fine," Sam told her.

"She's supposed to be forward."

"She's helping her defense."

"But she'll get too tired if she runs the whole field. All right, that's the way." She clapped as Megan's team took the ball down the field and Megan took a shot at the goal. In her excitement, Alli grabbed Sam's arm. Unfortunately, the ball just missed. "Oh, darn, she was so close."

"She'll get the next one," he said.

"Hey, come on," Alli yelled as Megan went down on the ground, tangled up with another girl.

"She's okay," Sam told her.

"You think everyone is okay," she snapped. "Megan looks like she's crying. That girl tripped her."

"It's the way the game is played."

Maybe it was, but Alli didn't like it. And the tension of the game only seemed to increase the tension within her body. Concentrate on the game, she told herself again.

"Oh, my God," she cried, as a little girl on the opposing team gave Megan a shove that sent her flying head over heels. "She can't do that, Ref. Come on."

"Alli, let it go," Sam said.

But Alli's eyes were on Megan, who was slowly getting up off the ground, wiping tears from her eyes.

"She shoved her," Alli told the referee, who was standing just a few feet away from her and happened to be a guy she'd gone to school with. "Come on, Larry, that happened right in front of you. Are you blind?"

Larry shook a finger at her. "They were both going for the ball. They just collided."

"No way."

"That's enough, Alli," Larry said. "If you can't keep your mouth shut, leave."

"I'm not going to leave when some kid is deliberately trying to hurt my daughter."

"That's it, you're out of here."

"What?" she asked in amazement.

"Hey, you can't throw her out," Sam interrupted. "She's just concerned about her kid."

"You're out, too, Sam," the ref said.

"Me, what did I do?"

"You're both out. Parking lot now, or your kid's team forfeits the game."

Alli barely heard the murmurs of protest from the parents behind her. "You are such a power freak, Larry. These are eight-year-old girls."

"Last warning. Leave or the game is over."

Sam clapped a hand over her mouth and dragged her away from the field. He didn't release her until they reached the parking lot. She stared at him, her chest heaving, her breathing ragged. "I can't believe he did that."

"I can't believe *you* did that."

She was somewhat surprised by the unexpected gleam in his eyes. "You're not mad at me?"

"Mad? No." He shook his head in amazement. "You, Alli, are a piece of work. You went after Larry like a mother bear protecting her cub. I thought you were going to rip his head off."

"I would have liked to do just that. I swear, he's

been mad at me since I wouldn't let him cheat off my paper in the sixth grade." She paused. "Do you think I overreacted?"

"I think you always overreact."

"So what was your excuse? You yelled at him, too."

"I didn't like the way he was talking to you."

"Really? Then thank you."

"No, thank you." He put his hands on her waist and looked down into her eyes. "For reminding me that caring a lot about someone isn't a crime and doesn't deserve to be punished."

She was confused by his cryptic words, but he was standing so close to her she was too distracted to ask him to explain. In fact, all she could do was look at him, feeling once again hopelessly, helplessly in love.

"This has to stop," she whispered, feeling the undeniable pull of attraction.

"Later. We'll stop later."

"Okay," she tried to say, but her response was cut off by the descent of his mouth on hers.

One kiss wasn't enough, or another. She was addicted to this man, plain and simple. She loved his mouth, loved his body, loved the way he took control, the way he made her feel like the sexiest female on the planet.

"We were always pretty good at this," she breathed when they finally came up for air.

"Better than good."

He lowered his mouth for another taste when Megan's shrill voice interrupted them.

"Mommy, what are you doing?" she demanded.

Alli and Sam broke apart to see Megan and half her teammates in the parking lot for halftime.

"Uh, we were just discussing the game," Sam said.

"You were kissing," Megan said, obviously embarrassed—but also somewhat delighted, judging by the look in her eyes.

"I'm sorry, honey," Alli said immediately, deciding a change of subject was definitely in order. "I shouldn't have yelled at the referee, even though he was wrong."

"That girl pushed me in the back," Megan said with a sense of her own importance.

"I know she did. Are you all right?"

"I'm fine. I can take care of myself, Mommy."

"Yes, you can," Sam said, sweeping Megan into his arms. "You're a big girl now."

"That's right," she said, somewhat appeased. "So what have we learned today?" she asked, repeating her parents' favorite question.

Sam laughed. "Not to let your mother watch your soccer games?"

"Hey, you got thrown out, too," Alli protested.

"Defending you."

"Same thing."

"I think we need something," Megan said pointedly.

Alli looked at her daughter, then at Sam, and saw the twinkle in his eye. "The Triple Decker—" she started.

"Hot Fudge Sunday," Sam continued. "No nuts."

"Extra whipped cream."

"And two cherries," Megan said.

Alli laughed along with Sam, and in that moment she remembered all the good times between them, the simple pleasures of ice cream and shared jokes and late nights by the fire.

Sam set Megan down on her feet. "Do us proud, honey. We'll wait here until you're done."

"Okay." Megan started to go, then stopped. "Are you going to kiss again?"

"No," Alli said. "We're not going to kiss again."

"You shouldn't lie to our daughter," Sam murmured in her ear.

"I didn't."

"Yes, you did."

🕊 *Chapter 14*

𝒯he entire left side of Phoebe's body felt too heavy to move. She closed her eyes, feeling weary. She hadn't slept well the night before. Maybe because she'd been sleeping during the day. Her body seemed to have the days and nights mixed up.

"I'm going to get some coffee," William muttered.

She blinked up at him. "I'm sorry. I can't seem to stay awake."

"Then you should sleep. You've had a busy morning."

He was referring to the CT scan she'd undergone as well as other tests she couldn't begin to remember. Dr. Price had been vague about her discharge date. She hoped it was soon. She didn't like the sounds or the smells of the hospital; they reminded her of the endless trips she'd made to the convalescent home to visit her mother. It was the only year in the past fifty that she'd left Tucker's Landing for more than a few months at a time. Maybe that was why she felt so resistant to leaving again. Vacations were fine, but moves were different. And William didn't just want to take her on a trip, he wanted to move her back to Philadelphia, to the kind of life she'd left a very long time ago.

She'd said no a dozen times, but he hadn't given up. A part of her was immensely flattered by his attention. Another part felt guilty for allowing it to continue. She wished she could return his love the way he wanted, for hurting him had never been part of the plan.

Phoebe felt William's lips brush her forehead and she struggled to stay awake long enough to say good-bye to him. But when she finally got her eyes open he was gone, and the room was empty.

It was also scary, the bright lights overhead making her dizzy. She closed her eyes again, feeling more comfortable in her head, in the dreams she could create, rather than in the reality that faced her. She was getting old; her body was aging. But mentally she still felt like a young woman on the verge of life.

She smiled as she saw images of herself in her wedding gown walking down the aisle behind a trail of pink rose petals. Her father's arm had been strong and secure, but when he'd given her to John, she hadn't felt even a momentary loss, because she'd known so absolutely that John MacGuire was her soul mate. It was supposed to be a marriage of mutual convenience, two families uniting, but it had turned into so much more.

Phoebe could hear John's deep voice repeating the vows, see the twinkle in his eyes as he lifted her wedding veil and kissed her on the lips. It was so real, so vivid, she could almost taste him.

"I love you, John," she whispered, not knowing if she was really speaking or simply dreaming, because he was there again, dressed in his shorts, standing at the edge of the sea, the water pulling at the nearby sand in the age-old relentless movement of the tide.

"I love you, too," he said. "Sometimes I can almost touch you."

"Like now?"

"Yes." He smiled at her, but his expression seemed more sad than happy. "The weather is getting warmer," he continued. "Wouldn't you like to go for a sail with me? We can wade out to the boat; it's very shallow, and the water will feel good against your skin."

He beckoned to her, and she took a step forward, feeling the heat of the sand beneath her bare feet. She looked down at herself, realizing she was wearing a sundress from forty years ago. She felt something on her head and reached up to touch a crown of flowers. She remembered John putting them there during a long-ago picnic by the sea.

"Phoebe?" John questioned.

"We're not dressed for swimming."

"We'll dance on the water, then."

"As if we could."

"Maybe we can," he said lightly. "Would you like to try?"

She did and she didn't. She could feel a pull beneath her as if the ocean was trying to suck her in, and yet the water was still yards away.

"Have the girls found the pearl yet?" he asked her.

"They're still looking."

"When they find it, our family will come back together."

His words seemed suddenly to have a double meaning.

"What do you mean, John? What are you trying to tell me?" His image began to fade. *"Don't go yet."*

"I must."

"Talk to me."

"I will again, dear heart. Soon."

"No, help me," she cried, feeling the sand beneath her feet shift. She was falling, and she couldn't stop herself.

"Phoebe. Phoebe. Wake up!" William's sharp voice pulled her back from the edge of the sea. She blinked her eyes open in confusion. Had she been asleep? Had she been dreaming? Hadn't William left just a few minutes ago?

"You were calling out for help," William said worriedly. "Are you all right?"

"I was dreaming," she muttered.

"About what?"

She shook her head. "I don't remember."

"Well, everything is all right now. You don't have to be afraid. I'm here with you, and I'm not leaving until you can go with me."

"I don't think I can leave the sea," she said abruptly. For how could she leave a place that she continued to dream about.

"You can visit the ocean whenever you want. But I need to live in Philadelphia to tend to my business and my son."

She knew all about his only child from the first of two loveless marriages, for William had shared those stories ages ago. And the stories had only made her feel more guilty, for he had seemed to compare every love to the one he'd thought to have with her. And maybe they would have married if her parents hadn't asked her to at least meet John, consider marrying him. Maybe if she hadn't met John, she and William would have gotten together. But the world didn't revolve on maybes.

She gathered all her energy for a conversation she knew she had to have. "I don't think I can go with you," she said.

"Not now, but soon. When you're better. I love you, Phoebe. You know how much I love you."

She did, and the force of his emotions seemed too strong to rebut, especially since she didn't want to break his heart yet again. She'd thought for a time that she could marry him. He would be a companion, someone to share the days with, to laugh at a joke, to help with a crossword puzzle. But William wanted so much more from her than that.

"I don't love you the same way," she said finally. "I wish I did."

"I'll love enough for both of us."

God, he sounded just like Alli talking about Sam. "I would be cheating you," she tried again. "I'm not the girl who got away. I'm different."

"I know who you are, Phoebe. You're the woman I've loved my entire life. And we would have had our chance if it hadn't been for your parents and your loyalty to them. Maybe if I had been more well-off at the time, I could have taken you away from their plans. But I couldn't, and I am so sorry."

"I loved John. My marriage turned out to be good."

"I'm glad for that," he said gruffly. "I wouldn't have wanted you to be unhappy."

"Then why do you want me to be unhappy now?"

He looked taken aback. "I don't."

"My life is here."

"Your life could be anywhere. We'll spend half the year here if you want. Whatever you want," he said with desperation. "Phoebe, you were going to marry me before this happened. Don't change your mind now."

"I've been dreaming of John," she said helplessly.

"No, don't dream of John, dream of me," he said, pressing his forehead against hers.

"He comes to me," she whispered. "He wants me to go sailing. I don't know what to tell him."

William pulled away, looking very disturbed. "You have to say no, Phoebe. You have to stay here with me, you know that, don't you?"

"Have the girls found the pearl?" she asked, evading his question.

"Not yet."

"They will," she said to reassure herself.

"Maybe they shouldn't," he told her. "You need to hold on to this life, Phoebe, and let go of the one you had with John."

William was right, but Phoebe was torn between them, the past and the future. And what did either matter when her present was so uncertain? She closed her eyes again, and this time she fell into a dreamless sleep.

Tessa sat on the bench seat, clinging to the rail as Sam powered the boat over the waves that made the floor beneath her feet roll with each bounce. The ocean was more turbulent than she had anticipated, especially since Sam had said the water was expected to be smooth and calm. Not that he seemed to be bothered at all by the sudden jerks and pitches.

"Isn't this great?" He turned to her from his position at the wheel. "Don't you love it?"

She drummed up a smile for him. "How far out are we going?"

"Wherever you want."

"This seems far enough."

He sent her a quizzical look, then cut the motors, and she felt their speed decrease until they were simply rocking on the water.

Sam came to sit next to her. "Are you all right?"

"Sure, why wouldn't I be?"

"You look a little . . ." He paused as he peeled her tight fingers off the railing. "White-knuckled."

"Oh, I haven't been sailing in a while. There's so much water, isn't there?"

"It's a big ocean."

"I thought we'd still be able to see Tucker's Landing, but there's nothing around but water. Are there a lot of sharks out here?"

"I don't see your friend Jimmy anywhere."

"That was a joke, ha-ha."

"We're okay, Tessa. You have to relax. I don't remember you being this nervous on a boat. I guess sailing around the world is probably not one of your dreams anymore," he said lightly.

"It would take far too long. Jets are much more efficient."

"There's nothing wrong with a little time on your hands, a little space," he said.

"There's nothing wrong with getting to your destination as quickly as you can."

"What if you have nowhere to go?"

"I always have somewhere to go. I keep myself pretty busy."

"Do you like it?"

"The modeling?"

"All of it."

"Sometimes I do. Sometimes I don't. It's like any job. I have to say that modeling opened up the world to me." She uttered a little laugh, realizing she'd just repeated something her mother had always said to her.

"What's so funny?"

"My mom used to tell me that when I balked at entering another beauty pageant. She'd say that modeling would open up the world for me, that I'd be able to see and do everything, to have more money than I ever imagined and meet incredibly fascinating people and live a life of constant wonder."

Sam didn't say anything.

"Aren't you going to ask me if she was right?"

"I know she was," he said, with a familiar quirk of his eyebrow that set her nerves on edge.

"She didn't tell me that it would be lonely, that people who didn't even know me would hate me for no other reason than that my hair was blond."

"Sounds like you're tired of the business."

"I am tired, tired of being me," she confessed. "At

least the me I've been the last few years. What about you? Do you really like running your business?"

"I do. It has its bad days, but on the whole it's a good life."

Silence fell between them, broken only by the sound of the water lapping against the boat and the occasional seagull squawking about lunch. Tessa didn't know what to say to Sam. She'd been the one to ask for time alone, but now that they had it, she wasn't sure what to do.

"Tell me a story," Sam said. "The way you used to." He leaned back against the rail. "Tell me about your incredible adventures. Take me to where you've been."

After a momentary hesitation, Tessa found herself telling him about her trips to Morocco and Bali and Indonesia, the swimsuit spread taken on the Colorado slopes in the winter, the parties in Manhattan, the time she'd met the president at a fund-raising gala. She must have talked for half an hour, with Sam only interrupting once in a while to express astonishment or ask a question.

It was like all those days and nights in the treehouse when she'd told him stories, only they were true tales, not dreams. She was different, and Sam was different. Despite his attention, she wasn't sure she was really entertaining him.

Finally, she fell silent. "So that's my life."

"You did it all, Tessa. I'm proud of you."

His words made her heart swell with pride, and she blinked back a tear. Aside from Phoebe, there had been no one to share in her success, no one to say, "I'm proud of you, you did good." She hadn't realized how much she'd wanted to hear that until now.

"Hey," he said softly. "Don't cry."

"Sorry. I just—I missed you, Sam."

"Me, too." His smile faded and his expression turned serious. "When you left there was a big hole in my life."

"I wasn't sure you had any regrets."

"I wasn't sure *you* had any. Look at you, Tessa. You're on top of the world. Why would you give a second thought to that small-town guy who treated you wrong all those years ago?"

"Because I loved that small-town guy," she whispered. "I did love you, Sam."

"I loved you, too." He hesitated. "I was going to ask you to marry me that Christmas. I even had a ring. It was a quarter-carat diamond, I think." He gave her a wry smile. "I'm not sure you could actually see the stone, but I thought it would work until I could afford something better."

She was shocked by his words. They'd never discussed marriage, never even mentioned it. "Sam, I don't understand. We were twenty years old. We were in college. We weren't ready to get married."

He looked away from her for a moment, then turned back. "I think I knew even then you were slipping away from me, and I was trying somewhat desperately to hold on to you."

"I wasn't going anywhere."

"Yes, you were. Half the male population at college was in love with you, and those modeling agencies were hot to sign you, and then you got that commercial. I knew you were going places, Tessa, and I thought maybe I could stay up with you if I married you. When you didn't come home with me, I knew it was over."

"Why didn't you ask me before I left?"

"I had this wild idea that you might change your mind and show up in time for Christmas. When you didn't, I got drunk."

He didn't have to say the rest, because she already knew it.

"It was still wrong," she said.

"I know."

She thought about all those years ago, wondering if she hadn't been a bit vain and self-centered back then. The way Sam made it sound, it had always been about her, but she'd thought he was right there with her, enjoying the same things, only he really hadn't been.

"I guess I could apologize, too," she said slowly. "I didn't realize you were feeling left behind. I thought you would always be there when I needed you."

"You didn't need me, Tessa. I could see that. Oh, sure, we talked about me being your business manager, your agent, but I was a twenty-year-old kid. I might have been good at math, but that was pretty much it. Our dreams were crazy dreams, they were illogical, they were foolish."

"But they were ours. I did need you, Sam. You were my anchor. You kept me grounded. You made me feel like there was someone to catch me if I fell." She paused, thinking about their relationship back then. "From the first day I met you I knew I could count on you not to let me down. And you didn't, until, well, you know."

He leaned forward, staring into her eyes. "I would have caught you if you fell, Tessa, but the truth is—you never fell. Not even after . . ." He paused, taking a breath. "You just went on with your life. In fact, you made a success of your life without me. You didn't need me then; I doubt you ever did."

"How can you say that? We did everything together growing up. We learned how to kiss, how to dance. We learned chemistry together." She dropped her voice down to a whisper. "I thought the first time I made love it would be with you. We got so close so many times. But we never made love. Why didn't we?"

"You wanted to wait. You always wanted to wait."

Because she had wanted it to be perfect, to be special, and the time had never seemed right.

"I waited too long, didn't I?" she asked. "You needed the sex. That's why you went to Alli."

Sam's eyes darkened. "No." He got to his feet. "Look, Tessa, the past didn't work out the way either of us wanted it to work out. But it's over. We can't go back."

"We can only go forward," she murmured.

His face tightened, but she couldn't tell what he was thinking.

"I want to know who you are today, Sam," she continued. "Because you're clearly not the boy I remember. I see signs of him here and there, but then there's a man I don't know, who's making me confused, unsure."

"About what?"

"About what he wants. About what I want." She stood up and moved over to him. "Do you want go forward—with me?"

The whirring click caught Alli by surprise. She looked up from her calculator and found herself gazing into the lens of a camera.

"Hey," she protested as Jimmy snapped another photograph. "What are you doing?"

"Photographing the hardworking retail shop owner at work."

Alli put a self-conscious hand to her hair. "I must look awful."

"You look tired, worried, a bit distracted." He glanced around the shop, which was currently occupied by two elderly women browsing through the postcards. "And definitely in need of a bit more business."

"It's just a momentary lull before the weekend tourist storm."

He picked up a framed photograph on the counter and studied it. "Nice. I like the parallel between the old man and the sea."

"It was taken by a thirteen-year-old kid named Isaac," Alli said. "I'm the first to show his work, but I don't think I'll be the last."

"I'm impressed." He set it down and waved his hand around the store. "I was expecting cheap souvenirs, and instead I see quality crafts."

"The local talent. We don't have an art gallery in town, so I try to show off their work."

He picked up a slightly lopsided pink elephant and frowned. "Now, this . . ."

"Was made by Irene Bentley, who is ninety-four years old and still thinking she might be a sculptor when she grows up."

"Maybe for the blind," he said with a wince.

"It's not that bad."

"Sure it is. But you put it out anyway. Why?"

She shrugged, not sure she could explain it to a man as worldly as Jimmy. "Because the people here matter to me. This is a small town. We look out for each other. Most of these artists will never venture even a mile down the highway, but does that make their expression any less important? And who is to judge what's valuable and what's not except the person who's looking at the piece?"

"You feel strongly about it, I can see."

"I just like to give people a chance. Everyone deserves that."

"Except perfect beautiful people like your sister?"

"Well, Tessa doesn't need a chance. She already has it all."

Jimmy didn't reply, he simply gazed into her eyes with an intensity she didn't expect from him.

"You have a nasty habit of staring," she told him.

"Just trying to figure you out."

"Forget it. I can't even figure myself out." Alli set the calculator aside. There was no point in trying to add up profits while Jimmy was within firing range.

Jimmy set his over-the-shoulder bag down on the

counter and pulled something out of the front pocket. "I want you to take a look at this."

She hesitated, then took the photograph from his hand. It was of Tessa, of course, taken in her grandmother's house. Tessa was looking at something with a yearning in her eyes that surprised Alli.

"What do you see?" Jimmy asked.

"I don't know."

"Try harder. Come on, it won't kill you."

"A little girl lost." She stopped abruptly. "That was a stupid thing to say, I don't know why I said it."

He smiled encouragingly. "What else do you see?"

"She appears to be wanting something. But I can't see what she is looking at. When did you take this?"

"Last night."

"Did Tessa know?"

"She was concentrating on something else."

Alli knew he wanted her to ask what that something was, but she was afraid to ask. He was right. She didn't want to look at Tessa.

"What do you think she was looking at?" he asked.

She shrugged. "I have no idea. It could be a million things."

"It was a necklace—actually, it was half of a necklace."

"Oh, God," she breathed, staring once again at the photograph.

"The half she had said BEST."

"And the other half said FRIENDS," Alli finished, lost in the memory.

"This is for you," eleven-year-old Tessa said. "Because we're not just sisters, we're best friends. I'll wear one and you'll wear the other and no matter what else happens to us, we know we'll always have each other."

Alli let out a breath, feeling the pain right down to the tips of her toes. "She gave me the necklace for my birthday. It was my first birthday after our parents died. I can't believe she still has her half."

"Do you still have yours?" Jimmy asked.

She straightened, suddenly realizing she wasn't just talking to herself. "I don't know," she lied. "I haven't seen it in years." She looked past him to the two women, who were ready to make their purchases. "Can I help you?"

While Alli rang up their postcards, Jimmy wandered over to the window, taking a few shots through the glass at some activity on the pier. When the women left, Alli picked up the photograph once more, wondering why Tessa would be looking at a silly little necklace with so much heart in her eyes. Tessa hadn't cared about their friendship in years. Long before the incident with Sam, they'd been more enemies than friends.

"It doesn't make sense," she murmured.

Jimmy returned to the counter. "Do you want to keep that?"

"No," she said hastily.

"I'll take it, then."

Despite her words, Alli felt a momentary loss when he put the photograph back into his bag, as if she were losing Tessa again, which was ridiculous, because she'd lost Tessa a long time ago.

"Do you want to get some lunch?" Jimmy asked

"My assistant won't be back for another fifteen minutes."

"I can wait."

"You must have something better to do with your day."

"Not really."

"Oh, that's right, Tessa is sailing with Sam." And the thought drove any lingering affection for Tessa right out of her heart.

Jimmy smiled. "Bugs the hell out of you, doesn't it?"

"No. Sam and I are getting a divorce."

"So I hear. I can't quite figure that one out, though. You got him. Why don't you just hang on to him?"

"Because hanging on isn't enough anymore, not that it's any of your business." She took a deep breath. "I need to stay here, finish up some work, especially since we need to look for oysters again this afternoon. Although I heard there might be a storm coming in."

"Tessa says we have to hike down to this oyster farm. I tell you, I didn't know your sister was such a country girl."

"She isn't."

"But she *was*."

"I guess. Tessa liked exploring. She was convinced that smugglers had once used Tucker's Landing to sneak in their treasures. She'd lead scavenging expeditions during the summer. They never found anything, though."

"Sounds like a fun sister."

"Not really. I wasn't included in the adventures."

"Then how do you know about them?"

"Because I followed, of course," she said, hating the knowing smirk on his face. "Like you never followed your brother."

"Oh, I did all the time, but he wasn't nearly as interesting, too concerned with toeing the line."

"Well, Tessa didn't break any laws, but everyone followed her anyway. She was the pied piper around here."

"Because she was beautiful?"

"Yes, but . . ." Alli paused, suddenly realizing that wasn't the complete truth. "She could make the other kids believe they were about to discover a pirate's stash of treasure. She had a gift for telling stories."

"I wonder why she doesn't tell them anymore?" he mused.

The phone rang, and Alli picked it up. "Alley Cat," she said. "Hi, Josie. How are you today?"

"Terrible," Josie replied. "Your husband was supposed to be back twenty minutes ago."

Alli's heart jumped into her throat. "You don't think something has happened to Sam?"

"Don't be silly. But he's turned his radio off, and, well, I wouldn't care, except that I've got a tank full of fish waiting to be unloaded and Petrie's restaurant needs it by two or they don't need it at all. Everyone is out, Alli. Gary is on another tour, Mike is sick, and Billy has disappeared again. I don't know what to do. I can't unload the fish myself.

"Okay, calm down. Try Sam on the radio again. I'll be down there as soon as Mary Ann gets back. I'm sure he just lost track of the time."

Alli hung up the phone and frowned at Jimmy. "Sam and Tessa were supposed to be back twenty minutes ago."

"I'm sure they're fine."

"Of course they are. It's just that Sam doesn't usually turn off the radio." *Unless he didn't want to be interrupted. Oh, God. Were he and Tessa making love?*

"Don't think about it," Jimmy advised.

"You don't know what I'm thinking." She wandered over to the window and looked out at the harbor.

"Oh, yes I do," he said dryly. "But Tessa wouldn't sleep with a married man."

"Unless that man was Sam." Alli turned her head. "For him, I think Tessa would do just about anything."

Chapter 15

Sam looked into a pair of beautiful blue eyes set in the prettiest face he had ever seen—a face that was offered up to him with a mouth begging to be kissed. He'd never refused Tessa anything. And he didn't know how to start now.

He lowered his head and allowed his mouth to touch hers, a brief, chaste kiss, much like the very first one they'd shared when they were thirteen years old. Her lips were cool. Or maybe his were.

It felt strange to be this close to her after years of separation. He started to slide his arms around her waist, then hesitated. She was taller than he remembered. Her body felt too thin, too angled. She was perfect, he reminded himself. The whole world thought so. But it didn't feel right. Not at all.

Tessa pulled away from him. "You kissed me like you were afraid I was going to break."

Her eyes were worried. She looked as unsure as he felt.

"Maybe I am afraid you'll break, or that you'll disappear. Maybe this is all a dream."

"I'm here, Sam. I'm not going anywhere."

Her words became a lie as the boat pitched suddenly, sending her into Sam's arms. He caught her as a gust of wind rocked the boat back and forth on the water.

Tessa rested her hands on his shoulders. "Fate," she said with a small smile. She took the initiative away from him and kissed him firmly on the mouth. He wanted to kiss her back, but there was something unbelievably awkward about their embrace.

"I'm a fool," he muttered. He sat down on the bench seat across from her. "You know where I've been the last nine years in terms of women. What about you and other men? Have you . . ." What the hell was he trying to say? Of course she'd made love to other men. She was twenty-nine years old and gorgeous.

"Have I what?" she prodded.

"Forget it."

"I don't want to forget it. We're trying to get to know each other again. How can we do that if you don't talk to me?"

"Not another MacGuire sister telling me I don't talk to her," he said with a groan.

"If you're this quiet with Alli, I can see why she'd have a problem."

"You're on Alli's side now?"

"I'm on your side, you know that. So what were you going to ask me? About other men? Yes, I've been with a few. Some I liked a lot, others— maybe I just thought I should have a relationship. So I had one. But have I been in love? Really, truly in love? Once."

He met her stark gaze and knew what she was saying, but he didn't want her to say it.

"You're not going to ask, are you?" she said.

He shook his head.

"Taking the easy way out, Sam? That isn't like you."

"I'm married, Tessa."

"Not for long. Even Alli says she's letting you go. Unless you don't want to go. Is that it, Sam? Have you fallen in love with Alli? My God, is that possible?"

Her voice was filled with disbelief, sarcastic wonder. And it bothered him, more than he would have thought. "Alli isn't the monster you make her out to be. She's changed. She's a good mother, a great friend, a smart businesswoman. She's grown up, Tessa."

"All right, okay, more defense of Alli. I guess she is your wife and you feel you have to do that. But I'm her sister, and I know her."

"You knew her back when. You don't know her now."

"And I don't know you and you don't me. I want to move forward, Sam, but dammit, you keep pulling me back to the past." She turned away from him and looked out over the ocean. "Can you tell me that you still love me and you want another chance with me?"

She said the words so softly he was afraid he hadn't heard them correctly. But they were there, hanging on the wind, awaiting his response.

"Is that what you want me to say?" he asked. "Is that how you feel?"

She turned her head to face him. "I asked you first."

Before he could reply another wave hit the boat hard. He suddenly realized that he'd been so caught up in their conversation that he hadn't paid attention to the changing weather, a stupid mistake for any sailor. Dark thick clouds were blowing in from the west, stirring the waves into white menacing tops.

"We should head back," he said. He glanced down at his watch and saw the time. "Shit! I was supposed to be back forty minutes ago."

She followed him to the wheel, her eyes widening as she looked at the turbulent ocean. "Are we going to be all right?"

"We're fine. I just want to get back to the harbor before the storm blows in."

She wrapped her arms around her waist as he powered up the engine and turned toward home. "I don't like this," she muttered. "Everything feels so out of control out here."

"Man against nature."

"This doesn't bother you?"

He shook his head. "I like the ocean in all its moods, but I do respect it. And I don't take unnecessary chances."

"It scares me. I don't think you ever knew, but I never liked swimming in the ocean. The waves crashing over our heads, the current pulling against our legs. I was always happy when the weather was too cold to go in."

He sent her a quick look. "Why didn't you ever say that before?"

"I didn't want you to laugh at me. You were such a fish, and Alli was always willing to go in with you if I didn't."

"She liked challenging the ocean," Sam replied, seeing Alli in his mind charging full steam ahead into an oncoming wave. She'd been an avid body surfer, and she still loved to take Megan down to the beach in the summer and go swimming.

"Alli liked challenging everything and everyone," Tessa said. "And I'm not saying that to insult her, before you jump all over me again. Sometimes it was a good thing. I have to admit her forthrightness with the nurses at the hospital is good. She makes them answer her questions. I barely get more than a nod or a mumble. But Alli doesn't let up."

"Nope." Sam reached over, realizing the lights on the radio were off, meaning he'd either neglected to turn it on or he had a problem with the radio.

"Something wrong?"

He fiddled with the buttons on the radio, annoyed when he got only static. "Looks like the radio is on the blink."

"Is that a problem?"

Again, he heard barely concealed panic in her voice. "We're fine, Tessa, relax."

"I'm trying, but the motion is making me nauseous. I wish we'd stayed at Grams's house. I don't know why I agreed to come out here."

He was beginning to wonder why he'd asked her. He'd thought she'd enjoy the sail, but she'd been tense and on edge since she'd come on board.

"We should have brought someone else to help you sail," she said.

"I don't need anyone's help," he replied with irritation. "It's a small boat, not a cruise ship, for God's sake."

"The last boat I was on was a cruise ship. We went to the Caribbean. It was beautiful and warm, and you could hardly feel the motion of the boat. I felt like I was in this big, beautiful hotel."

"But this is better, because you actually get to feel the water beneath you. That's the point of sailing."

She shrugged. "I guess." Her nonchalance vanished as the boat went up the face of a wave and down the other side, much like a roller coaster. She grabbed his arm so hard he had to fight her to regain control of the steering. "I don't like this," she said, her voice shaking.

"Talk to me, Tessa. Tell me about your life. Tell me about Jimmy," he said, trying to distract her.

"Jimmy. What—what do you want to know? He's a photographer I work with sometimes."

"He seems pretty interested in you, and not just for business purposes."

"He's a flirt," she said dismissively. "I've never seen him stick with a woman for longer than a month. I think that's the length of his attention span."

"So you two aren't dating?"

"No."

"Then why is he hanging around?"

"Well . . ." She seemed thrown by the question. "I don't know. I guess he considers himself a friend and he thinks I could use one right about now."

"I think he looks at you with more than friendship in mind."

"Perhaps there's a little attraction, but it's nothing serious."

"You still don't get the fact that you're every man's dream girl, do you?"

"Most of it is an illusion. You know what I really look like, Sam. The magazine covers are of some woman with not a line on her face or a blemish on her skin or an ounce of fat on her body. It takes about four people to get me to look that good. I don't think most men would like the real thing." She let out a breath as they entered the far end of the harbor, protected at last from the rising waves. "This is much better."

He was amazed by her description of herself. "Are you kidding, Tessa? I'm looking at the real thing right now and it's pretty damn incredible."

"Then why couldn't you kiss me? Afraid you wouldn't like it or afraid you wouldn't be able to stop?"

Both, he decided. Because there was a fantasy of Tessa in his mind that he didn't want to lose, and yet here he had the opportunity to make that fantasy a reality and he couldn't seem to move forward.

"It was so good before," he muttered.

"It could be good again. Don't you think we should find out, Sam? Once and for all?"

"When I see Sam, remind me to kill him," Alli told Jimmy, who was standing on the dock taking photographs of her as she stood in the middle of a flat-bottom fishing boat next to a pile of squirming, smelly fish. She lowered her arm, encased in a yellow vinyl glove up to her elbow, and pulled out another fish and tossed it into a waiting crate.

"This is great stuff, Alli," Jimmy said. "You look terrific, your hair whipping around in the wind, your eyes on fire, your hands in a bucket of fish. I could sell this shot."

"To whom—*Fisherman's Quarterly*? You know, you could help."

He lowered the camera. "I don't think so. Can't mess up these lily white hands."

"You're such a hero."

"Like Sam?"

"He's not my hero," she said. "At the moment, he is lower than scum. And I plan to tell him that as soon as he gets here. If he ever gets here," she muttered, sneaking a quick look over her shoulder. She wasn't worried. She *was not* worried. Sam was a capable sailor. He could handle any boat. Still, the winds had kicked up and dark clouds were blowing through. The weather could change in a second on this part of the coast, and the thought of Sam getting caught out in a bad blow did nothing to ease the growing tension in her body.

"So, tell me again why you're doing this for him?" Jimmy asked.

"Because the fishing business is still half mine, and dammit, I'm not going to lose money because Sam and Tessa lost track of the time."

"So your motives are purely business oriented."

"Absolutely."

"You're not just saving Sam's hide because you still love the guy and you don't want to see his business take a hit?"

"Absolutely not."

"Right."

Jimmy didn't believe her. Well, why should he? She didn't believe herself. Why was she here? She hated messing about with live, icky, squirmy fish. But someone had to do it. The fish had to be in Petrie's truck by two o'clock, and she was bound and determined to make that deadline.

Alli leaned over and grabbed another one, only to find the fish ripped in half. She now had fish guts dripping all over her jeans.

"Yuck, yuck, yuck," she squealed.

Jimmy laughed as she tossed the fish into the water next to the boat.

"I hate Sam Tucker," she cried.

"Well, here's your chance to tell him," Jimmy said as Sam's boat pulled into the slip next to them.

Alli saw Tessa step off the boat, looking pristine clean in her white jeans and tank top.

"Hey, babe," Jimmy called out to her.

Tessa walked over to them. "What on earth are you doing, Alli?"

Alli glared at her. "I'm playing with the fish, what does it look like I'm doing?"

"And what are *you* doing here, Jimmy?" Tessa asked.

"Waiting for you. Have a good trip?"

"It was all right."

"Anything exciting happen?" Jimmy asked.

Alli saw Tessa shake her head, then tuck her hair behind her ear the way she always did when she wasn't telling the truth. Damn her. Something had happened on the boat. Something between Tessa and Sam? Had they made love? Was that why they were late?

The sickening truth overwhelmed Alli, and she felt like throwing up. What was she doing—saving Sam's business when he was more concerned with fooling around with Tessa. She was an idiot, a stupid, helplessly in love idiot.

Sam finished tying up the boat, then came over to her, his expression wary. "Where's Billy? He was supposed to help with this."

"He's disappeared again and Josie said you turned off your radio."

"I didn't turn it off. It's broken."

"So you say," she said, tossing another fish into the crate. "Fifteen more minutes and your order with Petrie's was history."

"I appreciate your doing this."

"You're such a good little wife, Alli," Tessa said mockingly. "And I've never seen you look better."

"Oh, just shut up," Alli said. And on impulse she drew back her arm, and instead of tossing the fish into the bucket, she aimed it straight at Tessa.

Tessa screamed and jumped aside as the fish writhed at her feet. "Get it away from me. Get it away from me," she said, closing her eyes, apparently frozen in place.

Jimmy reached over and picked up the fish, tossing it back into the bucket. "It's okay, you're safe now, Tessa." He put his arm around her and flashed a smile Alli's way. "I'll protect you," he said to Tessa.

"I just want to get out of here," Tessa replied, and without even bothering to say good-bye to Sam or to Alli, she let Jimmy lead her up to the main road.

"I'm surprised you didn't jump in front of her, protect her from her nasty little sister," Alli said to Sam.

"I don't think I need to get between you two any more than I already have."

"Is that where you are—between us? Or are you with Tessa now? You never run late, Sam. You never forget about your business. Oh, you can forget to come home for dinner or buy me a birthday present or show up for our anniversary, but you never forget business—until now. I guess Tessa must have kept you occupied."

"It wasn't like that. We were talking."

"Oh, sure, talking. God, I hate you." She felt the anger rage within her, and she just couldn't stop it from bursting out. She picked up a fish and threw at him. "I hate that you took her out on our boat." She threw another fish at his head, as he stepped around the first shot. "I hate that you can lose track of time with her but not with me."

Sam sidestepped another throw. "Alli, calm down."

"And I hate it when you tell me to calm down," she cried, launching another fish in his direction.

This time he caught the fish, tossed it into the crate, and jumped onto the boat next to her. "Don't," he said, grabbing her hands with his. "Don't."

She looked up into his face, her eyes blurring with furious tears. "I hate you."

"No you don't," he whispered. Then he put his mouth over hers and she was lost.

His kiss was hungry, seeking, demanding. She tried to resist. She tried to keep her lips closed, but his tongue teased her mouth and she couldn't help but open, letting him slip inside, letting him taste her the way she wanted to taste him. She threw her arms around his back, forgetting that her gloves were soaking wet, forgetting that they were standing literally in a pile of snapping fish. Forgetting that he'd just come off a boat trip with her sister. No—

She yanked her mouth away from his, her breath coming out in ragged, jerky gasps. "Did you kiss Tessa like that? Did you kiss her like she was the only woman in the world and you couldn't live without her. Oh, God! Why do I let you do this to me? Stay away from me, Sam. Just stay away from me."

She peeled off her gloves and tossed them onto the deck. "I don't want you anymore. I don't want to be second choice, second best, second whatever. I don't want to be the one who trails after you like some stupid lost puppy dog. I don't want to be the one you got stuck with after the one you loved got away. She's here, Sam. Tessa is right here in Tucker's Landing. You want to make love to someone. Make love to her."

⛵ *Chapter 16*

Sam walked into Phoebe's hospital room later that afternoon and said hello to William, who sat in a chair by the bed, watching the news on television. The older man looked tired, but there was still a determination in his expression that refused to weaken.

"Hello, Sam."

"How's Phoebe?"

"Sleeping. They put her through some physical therapy earlier. She's talking better, moving better. I think she's on her way back to us."

"That's good news. Do you want to take a break? I'll stay with her for a while."

"I wouldn't mind stretching my legs, maybe getting a bite to eat. Not that there is much in that cafeteria that's appealing. Still, it's convenient." He got up, then hesitated as he saw Phoebe's eyes flutter open. "Phoebe?"

She smiled sleepily at William, her expression growing sweeter as it came to rest on Sam. He smiled back at her, thinking she looked almost normal. There was color in her cheeks and sparkle in her eyes. "Hi, Phoebe? Are you behaving yourself?"

"As if I could do anything else," she said, more quickly and clearly than she'd spoken the day before.

"I'm taking a walk," William said, giving her a kiss on the cheek. "I'll be back soon. Do you need anything?"

"No, thank you." Phoebe patted the mattress next to her as Sam hovered at the end of the bed. "Come here and sit beside me."

Sam did as he was told, sitting down on the edge of the bed instead of the chair. There was plenty of room. Phoebe was so small, she barely took any space.

"Did Alli and Tessa find the pearl?" she asked.

He wanted to tell her yes, but the truth was that they hadn't.

"I'm sorry," he said, realizing Phoebe was waiting. "We haven't found one yet. But we haven't given up either. So don't worry."

"Tomorrow is what day?"

"Friday."

"We don't have much time left before the Fourth."

"We'll find a pearl. We're going tomorrow at low tide to check the oyster farm by Vista Point. Alli said you used to have good luck there. We'll take Megan, too. She'll get to spend some time with her aunt."

Phoebe smiled. "All of you together. That's nice."

"It might be."

She lifted her hand to him and he took it. "You have to make it all right, Sam."

"I'm the problem, not the solution." He shook his

head in frustration. "Alli keeps throwing me at Tessa, and Tessa seems to think maybe we could have something now that Alli is backing off. They both keep looking at me like I know the answer to some question, only I don't know the answer. In fact, I'm not even sure what the question is."

"What do *you* want? That's the question."

"I don't know anymore. I loved Tessa once. You know I did. But Alli and I married for better or worse. I made those vows in good faith. I always meant to keep them, until Alli decided to change the rules." He sighed. "Still, in my mind, Tessa was always the right one and Alli was always the mistake. Now I look at Tessa and wonder how I could fit into her life. But I look at Alli and wonder the same thing. Alli is moving on without me. Her business is going well. She's more confident than I've ever seen her. She used to need me for that. But she doesn't anymore."

"She still needs you," Phoebe said, patting his hand. "But do you need her?"

"I know I miss her more than I ever thought I would."

Phoebe's eyes softened with the wisdom of her years. "That's a start. The rest will come, as long as you're all talking to each other. Can I tell you a little secret?"

"A secret?" Sam groaned. "Do I really want to know?"

"I gave you that box of photos to shake things up."

"Well, you certainly did that."

"Don't be angry with me, Sam. I couldn't stand

watching you and Alli drift along in unhappiness, never talking about that elephant in the living room, the one named Tessa. And I got tired of waiting for Tessa to wake up and come home. Life is short, Sam. You and Alli were wasting far too much of it." She paused. "I never thought Alli would ask you for a divorce, though."

"It shocked the hell out of me, too."

"Because you didn't know what you had to lose until you lost it. And Alli didn't either. Now the two of you need to stop being stubborn and proud and work things out." She drew a deep breath that seemed to come from deep within her soul. "I'm so tired. I wish I could talk to you longer. I wish I could fix this."

"It's all right. You need to rest."

"If I made things worse, I'm sorry."

"You didn't make anything worse. You just speeded up the inevitable."

She smiled sadly. "I hope that's not true. You and Alli have something worth saving."

"I'm not sure what we have."

"Then it's time to find out."

He nodded. "It would be a lot easier if Tessa weren't around. She confuses things."

"You might think you can choose who you want to love, Sam, but that's not the way it works. Love chooses you."

He leaned over and kissed her on the cheek. "I'll see you tomorrow."

"One more thing." She hesitated, her expression reflecting her worry. "If something happens to me, will you watch out for them both? They don't have anyone else."

"Nothing is going to happen to you," he said confidently, although he felt a ripple of uneasiness run through him. But she was getting better, talking better. He was imagining things.

"Promise me, Sam."

"I promise," he said.

"Thank you."

He watched as Phoebe's eyelashes swept across her cheek and she drifted off to sleep. He hoped he wouldn't have to make good on his promise for a long, long time.

William re-entered the room with a cup of coffee in his hand. "She's asleep," he said with disappointment.

"Yes. She seems so tired."

"I know." He set his coffee down on the side table. "It's awful getting old, Sam."

"I've never thought of Phoebe as old."

"Time passes more quickly than we realize. I look back at all the things I should have said, should have done. Why didn't I?" He gave a regretful shake of his head. "Don't waste time, Sam. Not a second. You'll regret the things you didn't do more than the ones you did, no matter what kind of a hash you made of them. Living is about doing, not watching, not waiting." He sat down in the chair next to Phoebe. "I should know. I've waited forever."

Sam didn't know what to say. He had no words to offer in comfort. He didn't understand the extent of Phoebe and William's relationship, but he sensed there was far more between them than anyone realized.

"Every time Phoebe wakes up, she looks at me as if she wonders why I'm still here," William mused. "Sometimes I wonder it myself. Oh, not because she's sick. I wouldn't leave her like this. But when she's better, maybe...I don't know. I want to marry her. I want her to live with me, travel with me. I think she'd be happy. I think I could make her happy." He stared down at Phoebe's face. "But I can't seem to convince her of that."

"Maybe when she's better," Sam said. "Although Phoebe doesn't really like to travel. She doesn't care for airplanes much, says she always feels better when she has the ground under her feet."

"She doesn't like to fly?" William asked quizzically, looking over his shoulder at Sam.

"Not really. She probably told you that."

"I guess she did."

"But I'm sure if it meant going somewhere near water, she'd manage to get on a plane. She loves the ocean as much as I do."

William's expression grew more depressed by the minute. "You don't think she'd be happy with a lake?"

Sam cleared his throat, having a feeling he was not helping at all. "You better ask her. But she always says the salt air puts roses in her cheeks."

"I have asked. Maybe I better start listening to her answers," William muttered. "Why are women so difficult to figure out?"

Sam smiled to himself. "Don't ask me. But along

those lines, I have some fences to mend. I'll see you later."

"Don't wait too long to mend those fences, Sam. It's amazing how quickly the weeds can grow."

Alli padded around the kitchen in her bare feet as she drained the spaghetti and stirred the sauce. That done, she turned her attention back to the bowl where she was stirring some fudge brownie mix. There was something about cooking that was incredibly therapeutic. She could almost relax, almost forget everything that had happened that day.

The kitchen was warm and cozy, a little nest safe from the rain dripping through the trees in the back-yard and the wind rattling the windowpanes. Alli felt a shiver run through her body despite her warm thoughts, for storms had a way of reawakening the monsters in her head, the ones who had first appeared when her parents had lost their lives in a rainstorm.

Living on the Oregon coast, she had grown used to the unpredictable weather, but no matter how hard she tried to be casual and nonchalant, there was something about Mother Nature in all her fury that made her want to hide under the covers.

"Hi, Mommy," Megan said, coming into the kitchen dressed in a pair of blue jeans and a sweat-shirt. She dragged one of the chairs over to the counter and stood on it so she could see what Alli was doing. "Can I stir?"

Alli handed her the spoon. "Sure, honey."

Megan frowned as she moved the spoon through the heavy, thick mixture. "It's hard."

"Just keep blending the mix until you can't see any of the powder. Do you want me to do it?"

"No," Megan said firmly. "I can do it."

Alli smiled to herself. Megan was as stubborn as she was. Megan saw life as a mountain to be climbed and she took each step with great enthusiasm. "You're doing great," Alli encouraged, because sometimes little mountaineers needed some support.

While Megan was stirring, Alli pulled her daughter's hair back and ran her fingers through the curls, smoothing them with her fingers. "How was summer school today?"

"Ricky said his father said he has a kite that can beat ours this year."

"Ricky's father has been trying to beat your dad since he was twelve years old."

"He has?"

"Yep. But your dad and your grandpa couldn't be beat. They always had the coolest and the fastest kite."

"When are we going to make our kite?" Megan asked. "It's almost the Fourth of July."

"Soon," Alli said vaguely. She knew they had to get on it, but she could hardly call Sam, not now, not after the way they'd parted. She felt guilty, knowing that Megan would be the one to suffer if she and Sam couldn't at least communicate enough to finish the kite they'd promised their daughter they would make together.

"Can I call Daddy?" Megan asked.

"Keep stirring, honey. I want to get this in the oven."

"My hand is tired," she said, handing the spoon back to Alli.

Alli whipped the rest of the batter up in no time and spread it in the pan, then set it in the oven. Megan sat on the edge of the counter, licking the chocolate-covered spoon clean. "No more, honey; you'll spoil your appetite."

"Are we going to look for pearls tomorrow?"

"We sure are. We have to go out at low tide, so we can scoop the oysters off the bottom."

"Do all the oysters have pearls?"

"Only a few very special ones. That's why we have to look at a lot of 'em."

"Okay. Can I watch TV in your room until dinner is ready?"

"Sure."

Alli set the bowl in the sink as Megan got down from her chair and ran upstairs to the bedroom. She had just finished rinsing the bowl and setting it in the dishwasher when the doorbell rang, reminding her that the storm couldn't completely keep the outside world at bay.

She walked slowly to the front door, wearily convinced that there couldn't possibly be someone on her doorstep she wanted to see. Still, when she opened the door and saw Sam she couldn't stop her heart from skipping its usual beat.

Sam wore a bright yellow rain slicker. His hair was slicked back, away from his face, a few drops of water clinging to his cheeks. He carried a plastic bag in one hand and a plastic bottle of something in the other.

"What do you want?" she asked grumpily.

"Peace offering," he replied, handing her the bottle.

She saw that it was almond creme lotion, her favorite kind.

"For your hands, to get rid of the fish smell," he said, still dripping all over her front porch.

"Well, it's a start."

"Big-time groveling is in order, huh?"

"I should have let those fish stink up your boat."

"Our boat," he reminded her.

"For the moment."

"I do appreciate what you did for me." He caught her gaze and held it.

She let out a sigh. "Okay, you can come in."

Sam took off his rain slicker, leaving it to dry on the porch. Then he stepped inside and set the large plastic bag on the floor. "Kite stuff," he explained at her quizzical look.

"Megan will be thrilled."

"Where is she?"

"Upstairs watching television."

"Do you want to call her?"

"In a minute." She walked toward the kitchen, and he followed behind. "Have you eaten? I made spaghetti. It's almost ready."

"Sounds good."

She walked over to the stove and stirred the sauce if for no other reason than to keep her hands busy. Sam leaned against one of the counters, watching her. She couldn't remember when he'd just stood and watched her without heading for the table and the newspaper or flipping on the small television they kept in the kitchen cabinet. There had always been distractions between them. Now it was quiet, too quiet.

"I'm sorry, Alli," he said unexpectedly.

She whirled around, spoon in hand. "For what?"

"Being late today, leaving you to do the fish, throwing Tessa in your face."

"Anything else?"

"I'll start with that," he said with a small smile.

"I don't want an apology for—you know."

"Good, because I wasn't going to offer one."

She felt vaguely ticked off at that piece of information, even though she would have been just as offended if he'd said he was sorry. No wonder Sam couldn't understand her. She couldn't understand herself.

"Why weren't you?" she asked, knowing it was the worst possible question.

He stared at her for a long moment. "What do you want from me, Alli?"

"I don't know," she murmured.

"You used to be pretty clear on the subject."

"I used to have tunnel vision. I'm trying to look around in the shadows now and see what I've missed."

"Have you found anything?"

"Only that it appears to be true that you want what you can't have. You weren't this interested in kissing me three months ago."

He took two steps and he was suddenly right in

front of her, his hands slipping onto her waist, and when she started to back up, she felt the dials of the stove stab into her back. She was trapped by his body, by his eyes. She swallowed hard.

"I've never not wanted to kiss you," he said somberly, as if he were telling both of them some truth that had just appeared between them.

"Why?"

"What do you mean, why?"

"Why do you want to kiss me? Because you're a man and I'm a woman, and it's convenient?"

"You know that's not it."

"But you still can't say the words."

"We don't need words to communicate. In fact, we're a lot better when we don't talk." He kissed her on the mouth, softly, gently, like he was tasting something precious, something he wanted to linger over, enjoy.

Alli closed her eyes and let it happen. She was tired of fighting Sam, tired of fighting herself. His mouth was warm, as cozy as her kitchen, as delicious as the brownies baking in the oven. He was her home, her family, her life, in every breath that she took. She kissed him back, putting her hand behind his neck so he couldn't change his mind, couldn't pull away. But he didn't even try, and each kiss grew more heated, more needy, more hungry, until their hands grew restless, seeking a satisfaction they couldn't possibly find in the middle of the kitchen.

"This isn't going to work," Sam murmured against her mouth when they finally took a moment to breathe. "The steam from the sauce is curling your hair."

"Is that why I feel so hot?" she asked breathlessly. She stepped away from the stove and brushed her hair off her face. He looked at her in a way so intimate, so personal, she wanted to take his hand and race him upstairs. But upstairs, on their bed, was an eight-year-old girl. "We have to stop doing this."

"Maybe we should just do it, and then see how we feel."

"That's not the answer, Sam."

"Then what is?"

"I don't know," she said in exasperation.

"Then how do you know I'm wrong?"

She shrugged. "I don't. But there's a long tried-and-true tradition of divorcing couples not sleeping together."

The beeper on the stove went off, signaling that the brownies were done. Thank God. She desperately needed the interruption. As she opened the oven door and took out the brownies, Sam moved back to his position against the far counter.

"I saw your grandmother today. We had a nice chat," he said.

"I stopped by earlier, but she was sleeping. What did she say?"

"She wanted to know if we found the pearl yet."

Alli sighed. "I sure hope we can."

"We have to. She's not going to give up on it."

"I don't understand why she wants it now."

"She didn't tell me, but she seemed in a philosophical sort of mood. Maybe a brush with death does that to you."

"And with the Fourth approaching, she's got her anniversary on her mind. I don't know if William is too thrilled with the reminder of Grams's first love." She gave Sam an impulsive grin. "Those first loves are damned annoying, you know. They just won't stay in the past where they belong."

He smiled. "Most people don't stay where they belong."

"How was your trip with Tessa? You never said."

"You never asked."

"As much as I may regret it, I'm asking now."

"We caught up on what she's been doing. Talked about what happened among the three of us. That kind of thing."

"Did you kiss her?"

He didn't answer for a long moment. Finally, he said, "No matter what I say it will drive you crazy. If I kissed her, you'll be pissed. If I didn't kiss her, you'll wonder why. You'll imagine all sorts of wild scenarios that could have caused such a lapse on my part or Tessa's part. You'll wonder if there wasn't a kiss, then was there touching involved? And if I say yes, we'll have to discuss where people's hands were, and it will be midnight before we're done."

"You think you know me so well," she said, although inwardly she was giving him high points for insight.

"I do know you pretty well," he said smugly.

"I know you, too. And if you don't change your attitude, I'll have to tell Tessa some of your dirty little secrets."

"I don't have any secrets."

"Oh, yeah, like you don't check your head every day to see if you've lost any hair, because your father's bald spot grows wider by the minute?"

"Every man in the free world does that."

"And you know every bad knock-knock joke and insist on telling them to me."

"To entertain you."

"And you eat those really strong Altoid mints in the car after you drive through Burger World so Megan and I won't know you gave in to your craving for fast-food onion rings."

"Now, that's hitting below the belt," he said, taking a step forward. "I may have to retaliate."

Her heart skipped another beat. "What did you have in mind?"

"I thought you could read my mind."

"I can, and it's not going to happen, Sam." She put up a hand and drew in a breath. "We need to focus here. Do you want to call Megan for dinner while I set the table?"

Before he could do anything, the phone rang. Alli moved over to answer it. "Hello?"

"It's Mark Hayworth, Alli," the man said.

Alli's body suddenly tensed. She didn't like phone calls from local policemen, especially on rainy nights.

Sam looked at her in concern. "What's wrong?" he asked.

She shook her head. "What can I do for you, Mark?"

"It's more what you can do for yourself. The storm is getting worse. The weather service is predicting twenty-five-foot waves by midnight. The harbor is already taking some big swells, lots of water running down the pier. I think you might want to throw some sandbags in front of your shop doors and make sure Sam's boats are tied down."

"Of course. Is it really going to be that bad of a storm?"

"I hope not, but it's better to be prepared. And I'd do it quickly if I were you; the wind is picking up."

"Thanks," she said, hanging up the phone.

"What did he want?"

"Big waves are hitting the coast. He thinks I should sandbag the shop, maybe board up the windows, and you should make sure your boats are secure."

Sam's eyes grew serious. "I'll go. I can do both our places."

"It will take too long by yourself."

He looked at her with compassion and an understanding that came from years of living together. "You don't want to go out in this storm."

She didn't. But she also didn't want to risk damage to her shop or Sam's business. "I can do it. But I don't want to take Megan."

"Can she go next door to Judy's?"

"I'll see."

"Alli, I can call Gary or someone to help me."

"By the time you do all that, we could be done."

"You hate the rain."

"I'm a grown-up now, Sam. I can do this."

"Are you sure?"

"Yes," Alli said decisively. Within minutes, she'd arranged for Megan to spend the evening with

Judy, a middle-aged widow whose youngest child was away at college. "It's all set," she told Sam.

"I'll get Megan."

"Good. I told Judy I'd send the spaghetti and the brownies over with Megan. While you're doing that, I'll get my coat."

Sam caught her by the arm. "It will be all right."

"I just hate leaving Megan alone. It reminds me of me—waiting."

"Do you want to bring her with us?"

Alli hesitated, then shook her head. "No, it's cold and wet, and she'll be all right with Judy. Just promise me we'll come back really fast."

He kissed her on the cheek. "I'll take care of you, Alli." It sounded like a promise. She wished he meant it for more than just the drive down to the pier.

⛵ *Chapter 17*

"*H*ere you go." Jimmy handed Tessa a martini with one green olive floating on the top. "The Jimmy Duggan Special."

She eyed it skeptically. "I'm not much of a hard drinker."

"One drink doesn't make you hard. And eat that olive. You could use a few pounds."

She made a face at him, then took a sip. "Ooh, it's not bad."

"Of course it's not bad," he said, walking over to the fireplace, where Tessa had made little progress with the fire she'd been attempting to start. "Let me guess, you were never a Girl Scout."

"I thought the uniform was very unattractive."

He laughed as he squatted down in front of the fire. He stuffed some newspaper under the logs and lit another match, watching the paper burn away to the wood. A spark caught, then another. "That's better."

"You're good at so many things, Jimmy," Tessa said from her position on the floor, her back against the couch. Actually, she was more impressed by the solidness of his body as he worked the fire. In fact, he had a very nice looking ass. She giggled at the thought and he sent her a sharp look.

"What's so funny?"

"I think I'm feeling tipsy."

"On two sips?"

He came and sat down next to her. "This is nice, the rain outside, the fire inside, a good drink to warm our bones." He picked up his own martini glass from the coffee table and raised it to his lips. "Cheers."

"Cheers," she muttered, taking another sip. The alcohol did send a pleasant warmth through her body. If only she could forget how many calories she was drinking . . .

"I could do this for a while," Jimmy said, staring at the now growing flames of the fire.

"You? Sit in one spot for a period of time? Sorry, I don't see it."

"I can relax."

"Since when? You're like a jackrabbit, always on the move, always popping up where I least expect it."

"Gotta keep you on your toes." He set his glass down on the table and reached for his bag. "By the way, while you were visiting your grandmother this evening, I got some photos developed. Do you want to see them?"

She had a feeling she didn't. "Do I?"

"Relax, they're not of you."

That didn't relax her at all. But she couldn't stop him from placing a stack of photographs in her hand. The one on top was the front of Alli's shop. The next one was of Alli and two elderly customers. So far, nothing too horrible.

"Go on," Jimmy encouraged when she hesitated. "They won't bite."

"Promise?"

The next one was of Alli up to her elbows in fish. The expression on her face was of pure disgust, and it brought a smile to Tessa's lips. "Serves her right."

"Why?"

"Because Alli was always one to make a mess of things."

"This wasn't Alli's mess, it was Sam's. She bailed him out. Don't you wonder why? Since she's divorcing the guy?"

Tessa shrugged. She didn't want to think too long or too hard about Alli's motives. Instead, she flipped to the next picture and caught her breath as she saw a close-up of Sam's face. He was looking at someone or something with desire in his eyes, stark, raging desire. "When did you take this?"

"I can't remember," Jimmy said.

"Who is Sam looking at?"

"I don't know."

She looked over at Jimmy, catching a note in his voice that she didn't like. "You're lying."

"I was studying him through my camera. I wasn't paying attention to what he was looking at."

"Was it me?"

"I told you, Tessa, I don't know."

"Was it me, Jimmy?"

"Do you want it to be you?" he asked, the laughter completely gone from his eyes. "Do you want him to look at you like that?"

Did she? There was a fierceness in Sam's eyes that disturbed her, a wildness that she couldn't place as belonging to him. She set the photograph aside. "You like to stir the pot, don't you?"

"It's amazing what you can see when you're not distracted by what you want to see."

Tessa took another sip of her drink. "Is that some kind of pop photographer psychology?"

"I've learned not to trust my eyes to see what's really there."

"Well, maybe if I had a camera, I could do the same thing."

"Or maybe you could just concentrate a little more."

For a few minutes they sat in silence, staring into the orange-red flames of the fire. It was the first time Tessa could remember Jimmy being so quiet. Maybe it was this place, this small town that brought out the quiet side in men. Where she traveled, the circles she lived in, you had to speak loudly and often in order to be heard, to be seen. Even then it was doubtful anyone was really listening.

Jimmy picked up her hand and played with her fingers, twisting a tiny silver ring on her baby finger. "Why do you always wear this?" he asked.

"My mother gave it to me when I was ten. She wore it when she was a child. It's one of the few things I have of hers."

"Was she like you or more like Alli?"

"Me. At least physically. Although, come to think

of it, we shared similar interests. She's the one who got me started in modeling. She tried with Alli, but Alli never could figure out how to say the right thing at the right time."

"Whereas you nailed it on the first try."

"Pretty much. I felt their expectations grow larger with every contest. Funny . . ."

"What is?"

"My parents have been gone for so long, but I can still hear my mother's voice in my head: 'Straighten up, Tessa. Hold your stomach in, chin up, think of your posture, be proud, there's a good girl.' Silly, huh?"

"No. I can still hear my father's voice in my head: 'When are you going to get a real job? When are you going to put some money in a savings account, grow up, be responsible? You can't live on a plane forever, you know.' "

She smiled at his mimicking tone. "You've never talked about your parents before."

"There's not much to say."

"Is your father dead?"

"Oh, Lord, no."

"So he said those things to you just yesterday?"

"Exactly. No wonder they're so fresh in my mind."

She punched him lightly in the shoulder. "You are such a tease. Is your mother alive, too?"

"Yes, and my brother, the senator, is still kicking as well."

"You're not close with your brother?"

"I'm the black sheep, babe. Nobody gets close to the black sheep."

"You're a lamb in wolf's clothing," she corrected.

"Hey, don't ruin my rep."

"You're not as bad as you make yourself out to be. In fact, you're a pretty good guy, you know that?"

"But not quite good enough?"

She turned sideways so she could look into his eyes. "What does that mean? Suffering from a lack of self-confidence? I find that hard to believe."

"Well, you did ditch me for Sam today."

She sighed and looked toward the fire. "Sam and I have some things to resolve. You know that."

"How was the sailing trip anyway? You haven't said much about it."

Because she didn't know what to say. She hadn't really enjoyed it that much. Being on the ocean had made her uneasy. Being with Sam had felt awkward. They'd almost kissed. They'd almost connected, but not quite. It was so frustrating she could scream. Even now, her insides were in turmoil.

"Yoo, hoo, Tessa," Jimmy said, snapping his fingers in front of her face.

"It was fine. I'm not much of a sailor."

"You must have done some sailing growing up here."

"Not as much as you would think. I was busy with school and friends and did a lot of beachcombing, but I never really liked messing around with the boats. And Sam wasn't all that interested then." She hesitated, thinking back, wondering if she'd somehow missed the fact that Sam liked to sail. "No, I don't remember him that way. Sam hated working for his dad on Saturdays. He was always trying to get out of it so he could play with me."

"Yet he ends up running a charter boat service. Odd how life turns out sometimes."

"I don't think it's what he wanted to do, more like what he had to do after Alli got pregnant. His dad always wanted him to come into the business, and I suppose not finishing college, it was all he could do to support Alli and Megan." She looked back at him. "Sam told me that the business has grown so successful a group of investors wants to buy him out. He could either stay running it or just sell out and move on."

Jimmy's eyes narrowed. "Move on with you?"

"I didn't ask him that."

"Why not? I thought you two could talk about anything."

"We used to be able to. It doesn't seem as easy now," she admitted, reaching for her martini glass. It was almost empty. Oh, well, might as well go for broke, she thought.

"People change." Jimmy paused. "Frankly, not to burst your little bubble, sweetheart, but I don't see Sam selling out. He has deep roots in this community. And he's got a wife and a daughter here. Okay, forget the wife," he said immediately as she opened her mouth to protest. "He still has a kid, and I think he's the kind of guy who probably wants to stick around and watch his kid grow up."

She let out a sigh. "You're probably right. But it's so unfair the way things turned out. Don't you think there is a way Sam could keep his ties with Megan but have a chance at a life of his own?"

"A life with you, don't you mean?" He tilted her chin up with his hand. "What are you going to do, babe? Retire? Settle here in Tucker's Landing? Be a housewife?"

"It could be a home base," she said, shaking his hand away from her face. "I can live anywhere, Jimmy. Most of my assignments take me away from the home I have now. What's to say I couldn't change my address? What's to say we couldn't live in Portland or somewhere nearby, not exactly here, but close enough for Sam to get down to see Megan?"

"You've done some thinking about this, haven't you?"

"I've done little else."

"You're crazy, you know that? You're a supermodel, Tessa—a big-city girl with big dreams and a big bank account. Do you really believe you're going to be happy living here or even in Portland? Open your eyes. This isn't your life, as you told me so definitely the first day I got here. It still isn't."

She knew he was both right and wrong. She'd fled Tucker's Landing because of the pain, the betrayal, but being back home had reminded her that there was a part of her that was still small town. Of course, there was another part of her that liked to go to the theater and out to dinner and shopping. But those things could be had every now and then, enough to keep her satisfied.

Jimmy smiled at her as if she were a young child dreaming of flying to the moon. "Have you even looked at a newspaper since you've been here, Tessa?"

"What does that have to do with anything?" she asked with annoyance.

"Being here is like escaping to a remote island. And it's nice. I'm enjoying it myself. But forever? I don't think so."

"When you're with the right person, it doesn't matter where you live."

"Yeah, and Santa Claus still comes down chimneys. Of course it matters. Part of marriage is being compatible, being able to share a life that makes both people happy. If one compromises too much, in the end they'll both suffer."

"Sam did it. He compromised. Why shouldn't I?"

"I don't get why you suddenly want this guy so much. If you were so hot for him, why didn't you come back sooner and try to reclaim him?"

"Because I didn't know that he wasn't happy," she cried, "that his marriage wasn't all right. I never figured them to be totally in love, but I guess staying together as long as they have made me feel like their bond was too strong to break, and I wasn't interested in being a home wrecker. But with Sam about to be free—don't you see, Jimmy? I suddenly have the chance to have what I lost all those years ago."

"So you think," he said. "But let me give you something else to think about."

"Wha—?"

He didn't let her finish, simply leaned over and kissed her full on the mouth. It was so unexpected, so shockingly hot and tingling. He tasted like vodka. He smelled like fire. He felt like a warm, desirable male and her body responded in kind. Her head told her to stop, to pull away, that he was making a mockery of what she'd just told him. But her body seemed unwilling to move, her lips opening instead of closing, her tongue dancing with his instead of lying dormant. Oh, God, what was she doing?

Jimmy stopped before she did, making her feel even worse.

"Why did you do that?" she demanded, when she could finally put words to feelings.

"I thought you needed something else to think about."

"We're just friends, Jimmy."

"Of course we are."

"I don't want you to kiss me."

"Of course you don't," he said, getting to his feet. "I think I'll head back to the hotel."

It was the right thing to do. He'd crossed the line of their friendship. But still, she didn't like to see him taking the glasses into the kitchen, reaching for his coat, leaving her alone . . .

"You're going—just like that?" she asked, scrambling to her feet.

He met her gaze head-on. "Yes, because you just gave me something to think about, too."

"It's the fire and the martinis and the rain, that's all," she said helplessly. "We can forget it happened."

"What if I don't want to forget?"

"Why are you so serious all of a sudden?"

"It hasn't been all of a sudden."

His hard, sharp words made her wonder if she'd missed more than she realized.

A crack of thunder rattled the house, and Tessa suddenly had something else to think about—the worsening storm.

"I'll see you tomorrow," Jimmy said.

"Wait! Um, are you sure you have to go now?" She glanced toward the windows as a streak of lightning lit up the room.

He sent her a curious look. "You don't like the storm, do you? I remember that shoot we did when the hurricane was threatening. You kept popping Valium. I thought you were a drug addict at the time, but come to think of it, you just didn't like the wind, did you?"

"My parents died on a night like this. It was right before Christmas," she said, squeezing her hands together. "They had a baby-sitter come over so they could do some shopping without us. Their car skidded in the rain and they went off an embankment and were killed instantly. All I remember about that night is the thunder and the lightning and wishing that my parents would come home, only they never did." She drew in a breath as his arms slid around her waist and he pulled her against his chest.

"I won't leave you," he said huskily, stroking her hair.

"I'm sorry. It's stupid. You're going to think I'm an idiot or worse."

"Tessa, sweetheart, you don't want to know what I think, because it will scare you worse than this storm."

Alli felt the dock shift beneath her feet as a swell in the water lifted the boats up half a foot. She pulled the hood of her rain slicker tighter against her head, feeling the wind hit her like a runaway truck. She had hammered boards over her store windows, moved some of her more fragile items away from the door, and was now more than ready to get out of the storm, although she needed Sam's help to put a few heavy sandbags in front of the shop door.

"Sam," she called, putting a hand over her eyes so she could spot him in the driving rain. "Sam?"

She saw him as he hopped off the last of the boats and took another second to check the lines that held it in the slip. Although the harbor was usually well protected, unexpected high swells could rip the boats loose and send them into the wood pilings of the docks. She prayed that wouldn't happen. They couldn't afford damage to any of the boats.

She shifted back and forth as Sam called out "One second" and leaned over to check something on the dock. Thunder rumbled over her, around her, inside her, shocking her back to a night a long time ago when she'd snuck downstairs after hearing the doorbell ring. There had been a policeman on the front steps. He had said her parents were . . . God! She couldn't think about that, not now, not when lightning lit up the sky, reminding her of how she had tried to hide away from the horrible truth, but the lightning kept chasing after her, lighting up every hiding place, until she could do nothing but hear the policeman's words over and over again.

"The storm was bad. Everyone was inside. No one saw the car go into the canyon. We think the woman was alive for a while, but we didn't get to her in time."

Alli felt the familiar bile rise in her throat as his

words came home to her. The thought of her mother, strapped in a mangled car, barely alive, praying for someone to save them, but slowly dying while the storm raged around her, made Alli crazy. She shook her head, trying to dislodge the words that had haunted her for years.

Tessa thought their parents had died instantly. And Alli hadn't ever been able to tell her differently. Because Tessa had been so scared that night, climbing into bed with her as they waited for the front door to open. Tessa hadn't come downstairs with her; she'd stayed in bed, the covers up to her chin.

Alli jumped again as lightning ignited the sky like an angry firecracker. She knew the thunder would follow. She was prepared. She was ready. But even so, she couldn't stop the terror that came with the deafening rattle.

She turned and ran. She thought she heard Sam call after her. But she couldn't stop. She had to get somewhere safe. She ran past Sam's office. It was too close to the water; she had to get higher, somewhere safer. She could go to her car. But, no, then she'd have to drive. And she couldn't drive.

Sam caught up to her as she struggled to put her key in the lock of her store. He took it out of her shaky fingers and unlocked the door for her. She ran inside and tried to turn on the light, but the power was gone.

"Oh, God. Oh, God." She stood in the middle of the dark store, hugging herself.

"It's okay, Alli." Sam switched on a flashlight and lit up the space between them. "You're all right.

We're safe. We're safe," he repeated, reaching out for her.

She didn't walk, she ran into his embrace, pressing her face against his wet slicker, not caring that they were both soaking wet. She just threw her arms around his neck and held on tight. Sam reassured her with a constant stream of words that barely registered, but the soothing tone of his voice slowly eased her tension.

"I'm sorry," she said after a few minutes. She tried to pull away from Sam but he wouldn't let her go. "I'm okay now," she told him.

"I'm not," he muttered.

She looked up at him and saw his eyes gleaming in the shadowy light. He pulled away from her and ripped apart the snaps of his slicker, taking it off and tossing it onto the floor.

"Come back here," he said.

She stared at him uncertainly, suddenly realizing the danger was no longer in the storm but in him, in her.

He cut the distance between them when she didn't move and put his hands on her hips in a way that reminded her of the way he held her when they made love, so she could feel him, all of him.

She could almost feel him now, the anticipation of knowing what could come, how she could feel, overwhelming her senses. And when he took one hand off her hip to unzip her jacket, to toss it on top of his, all she could think of was how close their jackets were and how close they could be.

He was warmer now, she thought, as she moved into his arms with a sweet familiarity. His shirt was soft against her cheek, and she could hear his heart beating, strong and fast. She breathed in and out, hoping for calm, for sanity, but her breath brought in his scent, his appeal, and with each molecule of air she wanted him more.

"We—we can't," she forced herself to say, but she once again tightened her grip on his neck as the thunder rattled the display cases. "You're taking advantage, Sam. I wouldn't be hugging you like this if it weren't for the storm."

"I know. It's the storm that's holding us together. It's not you—or me."

Lightning lit up the store like the flash of a camera. For a minute Alli almost thought Jimmy had once again caught her on film. But the light faded, and when Sam turned off his flashlight they were surrounded by darkness.

She wanted to let him go. She tried to let him go, but her body seemed to have a mind of its own, her fingers playing with the curls of hair at the back of his neck.

"Megan—" She tried again to distract him.

"Is fine. I don't want to drive in this. Do you?"

"No." She paused. "You can really stop holding me now."

"You can stop holding me, too."

She was going to do just that when she felt Sam's lips touch her hair and her heart did a somersault at the phantom, feathery kiss. Her pulse began to race even as she told herself she didn't want this. She couldn't want this. But when Sam tucked a kiss into the curve of her neck, she shivered in anticipation, her body a traitor to her thoughts.

"You still have that couch in your office," Sam murmured.

"We're not going into my office," she said automatically.

"It will be safer away from the windows."

She wasn't afraid of the glass breaking. She wasn't even afraid of the storm anymore. She was afraid of herself, terrified of what she wanted to happen next.

Sam moved her backward as if they were in a dance and he was steering her around a ballroom. Only they weren't waltzing past other couples, they were moving in between the aisles of her shop. Her shop, she tried to remind herself, her business, her new focus. She'd poured so much energy into her marriage, and it had all been a waste of time. Now it was going into the shop.

But as Sam turned her around, as he shuffled them toward the office door, all she could think about was the man who was holding her, whose hands and eyes and lips promised her the world. The next thing she knew they were in the office, and the couch was hitting her in the back of her legs.

Sam stood in front of her, holding her hips against his, and she could feel his body hardening just as hers was beginning to soften. He swayed against her. She moved with him, her thighs pressing against his, her breasts tingling from contact with his chest, her lips seeking his mouth as he sought hers.

How she loved the way he ran his hands through her hair, trapping her head with his fingers so he could kiss her the way he wanted to, the way she wanted him to. It was a hot, carnal kiss between two people who knew each other inside and out.

Their bodies moved in perfect accord, as if to music playing somewhere in their heads, in their dreams, in their memories. They had made love a thousand times, but while tonight felt the same, it also felt different, as if they'd never been together, as if they didn't know each other's bodies by heart. Maybe it was the intense darkness, the shadows that kept reality safely hidden away. Maybe it was the storm, the drumming rain on the ceiling that made their other life seem so very far away. Maybe it was that she wanted one last time with him.

Sam pulled her sweater over her head and tossed it in the direction of the couch. She stared at him for one long questioning moment, then slipped her hands under the hem of his shirt and helped him off with it. They stood silently then, their breath rising like the steam from a sauna. There was a chance to change her mind. She knew she should take it.

But Sam was looking at her breasts, worshiping them with his eyes, as his hands slowly crept up from her waist until his thumbs caressed the skin above her bra. She wanted it off—and quickly, but Sam was toying with her bra, running his fingers along the top and then down through the valley of her breasts, playing with the tiny clip that would set her free.

She took in a breath and let it out. He heard her and smiled. His finger flipped the snap and the material came apart. The air hit her breasts like an air conditioner until Sam's hands covered them with his heat, with his desire, with his need. His hands weren't enough. She wanted his mouth, his lips, his tongue.

And then he was there the way she remembered, better than she remembered, drawing her nipple between his teeth until she felt an ache that went straight to the heart of her. Her legs started trembling, and she thought she might fall, but Sam held her steady as he lifted his head from her breasts and looked at her.

He put his hand on the snap of her jeans and opened it. He pushed down the zipper and her pants quickly followed, leaving her standing in a pair of emerald-green silk panties. His hand swept across the silk, caressing her heat, feeling the dampness that told him how much she wanted him.

"I think you should take these off," he said.

She swallowed hard. "And you should take these off." She repeated his motion, opening his jeans, sliding her hands down to the top of his thighs as he kicked them off.

And they stood there again, a second pause, a moment to stop. But how could she stop? How could he?

"Alli," he said huskily, his face barely visible in the shadows, only the light of desire in his eyes showing her the way home.

"Yes," she said, the simple word being cut off by the descent of Sam's mouth on hers, the sudden slide of her panties down the back of her legs, Sam's hands cupping her buttocks, rubbing them, kneading them, each movement getting more frantic. When he moved away from her, she wanted to cry out to him to come back. But he'd dropped to his knees, pulling her panties down to the floor, as he pressed his lips to her belly button, her abdomen, the tight copper curls that graced the apex of her thighs.

She shuddered, reaching for him, but only managing to latch her fingers on to his hair as he began to kiss her there, forcing her thighs apart with his shoulders as he loved her with his mouth until her knees began to tremble and she gasped his name.

The next thing she knew she was lying on the couch while Sam was wrestling with his jeans.

"What are you doing?"

He pulled out a foil packet and quickly ripped it open, sliding the condom on before she could say a word. The familiar action registered like a harsh note in their love song, for even now in the heat of the storm, he couldn't forget about protection. But she couldn't summon up enough strength to protest, not when her body was already on fire, not when he was pressing her back against the cushions and entering her with an aching slowness and completeness that made her heart ache all the while her body sang in joy.

She closed her eyes, feeling him with every fiber of her being, knowing that she would love this man forever, no matter what she told herself or what she told him. With Sam inside her, on top of her, surrounding her, she soared as high as a kite, as free as the breeze, as powerful as the sea. She felt each and every emotion as she matched his rhythm with her own, for in this moment they were in perfect accord, peaking at exactly the same time, collapsing together breathlessly as they came down the other side of the wave.

Tears blurred her eyes, and she wondered if this would be the last time she would hold him, the last time she would feel his body inside hers. She didn't want to let him go now, her hands clasped tightly behind his back.

"I'm too heavy," he said.

"Sh-sh," she said. "Not yet."

He stayed with her for another minute, then rolled off her, the air between them covering her with an icy chill. She sat up on the couch as Sam handed her her clothes. She didn't put them on right away, just watched him get dressed from the dark shadows of the couch.

"It's cold," he said, turning to her. "You should put something on."

"It wasn't cold a minute ago."

Sam sat down on the couch next to her and put his arm around her shoulders. He pulled her to his chest, which was now covered by his T-shirt, she thought with disappointment. But still she rested her face against his shoulder and took a deep breath of him, evoking the scent to memory. She never wanted to forget the way he smelled, the way he tasted, the way he felt.

Sam kissed the top of her head. "You're beautiful, Alli."

His compliment brought another tear to her eye, another ache to her heart. "You're beautiful, too," she said huskily.

They sat in silence for a few minutes, a silence

that gradually began to turn tense as they struggled to find something to say to each other. This had always been the hard part, the moments after they made love, moments when they should have felt closer than ever, yet somehow didn't.

Finally, she raised her body away from him and put on her clothes, fumbling with the hooks and zippers. When she was done, she stood up. "We better go home. I think the rain has lessened." In fact, she could barely hear the wind that had sounded like a freight train only a few minutes earlier.

"Home," he said heavily as he stood up. "Where is that exactly, Alli?"

"What do you mean?" she countered somewhat warily, hearing a note in his voice she didn't like.

"Our home or your home?"

She hesitated. "Do you think things have changed?"

"Do you?"

"We've made love before. Making love has never been our problem, Sam. It's the one thing we do really, really well together."

"But—"

"But you still used a—a condom," she said. "And you still can't say you love me. And I'm not sure you can even say you really wanted this, that if we hadn't come out in the storm we would have even made love."

"I used a condom because the last thing we need to do right now is make a baby."

She turned away, but he put a hand on her shoulder and swung her back to face him.

"You're my wife, Alli. Of course I love you," he

said somewhat awkwardly. "Didn't I just make love to you?"

"So you care about me because I share your name and your bank account? Is that what you mean by 'You're my wife'? That's not the same as 'I love you. I don't think I can go on breathing without you, because without you I'm only half a man, and if you leave me I would probably die from a broken heart.'"

He sighed.

"Oh, forget it," she said. "I'm not scripting it for you."

"That's exactly what you're doing."

"Actually, what I'm doing is going home." She moved out of the office and into the shop. She picked her slicker off the floor and handed him his. Then she opened the door and saw that the rain was still coming down, although not with as much ferocity as before. "Can you help me push a couple of sandbags up against the door?" she asked as they stepped out onto the porch.

The task took only a few moments and they were ready to leave.

"I wonder what would really be enough for you," Sam said somewhat cryptically as they got into the car.

"What do you mean?" she asked.

"I mean, would you even believe me if I told you exactly what you wanted to hear? Because I don't think you would, Alli. I think you believe deep down that no one can love you that way, especially me, because I'll always love Tessa."

Her heart thudded against her chest at his words.

"Is that the truth, Sam? That you'll always love Tessa?"

"You think it's the truth."

"Can you deny it?"

He shrugged. "If I say yes, will you believe me?"

She hesitated for a split second too long.

"That's what I thought," he said.

⛵ Chapter 18

The morning after the storm dawned bright and sunny, as crisp as a new dollar, as fresh as an ocean breeze, but filled with more regrets than Sam would ever have imagined. Besides the regrets, he had a bear of a headache, the result of downing half a bottle of Scotch in the early hours of the morning when sleep had eluded him.

He sat back in his car and stared at his house, at Alli's house, he reminded himself, where his wife—make that his almost-ex-wife—had retreated the night before. He could still see the glimpse of light, of warmth in the house, teasing him just before she'd shut the door in his face—because he didn't love her and he never would.

Damn, he was sick of those words that she wanted so desperately to hear. He didn't remember his father telling his mother he loved her, although everyone had known that was the case. He didn't remember his mother making a big deal out of things like anniversaries and birthdays. There had been a few cakes over the years, a present here and there, but no one had called for a divorce because of a forgotten holiday or a pile of photographs. No one but Alli.

He knew that she was insecure, that she didn't believe in herself. But he couldn't fix what was wrong with her. She had to do that on her own. And maybe he needed to do some fixing within himself.

He would have liked a little time to regroup, but low tide waited for no man, and they needed to be down at the tidal flats by eleven A.M. so they could retrieve the oysters and find the pearl for Phoebe's necklace. He forced himself out of the truck and across the wet grass to Alli's front door.

There was nothing about the day that overtly spelled disaster. The powerful storm had swerved away from the coast just before midnight, returning them to beautiful summer weather. The flowers glistened with lingering raindrops and the wind chimes on the porch played a melody in the soft breeze, but still Sam felt a wave of uneasiness as he applied his finger to the doorbell.

Fortunately, Megan opened the door after the obligatory "Who is it?" She leaped into his arms and planted a big kiss on his forehead. Thank God for small innocent children who loved unconditionally and without restraint.

"Hi, Daddy," she said in her sweet voice.

He smiled into her baby blues. "Hi, honey."

"You didn't come back last night to make the kite," she said somewhat accusingly. "Mommy and I had to sew the fabric by ourselves."

Of course he hadn't come back; he'd been sent home after daring to make love to his wife. Still, he was surprised that Alli could have concentrated on kite building when he'd spent the better part of the evening in turmoil.

"We painted a picture, and now we just have to attach the material to the sticks," Megan continued.

Sam started, realizing he'd missed some of what she'd said. "What?"

"Aren't you listening, Daddy?"

"Of course I am. I'm glad you and Mommy worked on the kite."

"Can we finish it today after we get back from pearl hunting?"

"We'll see."

"That means no," she said with a sigh.

"That means we'll see." He set her down and followed her into the house.

Alli was in the kitchen, standing at the stove and stirring what could only be her favorite apple cinnamon oatmeal. She wore faded blue jeans that clung to her hips, and a short cropped lime-green T-shirt that allowed a glimpse of skin. Her feet were bare and her hair was still damp from a shower. Sam had to make himself keep breathing. He'd seen her like this a thousand times, but he didn't think she'd ever looked sexier. He just wished she'd turn around so he could see her face, assess her mood, but she seemed intent on stirring, determined to ignore him.

"Morning," he said shortly.

"Morning," she mumbled.

Megan sent him a funny look, then sat down at the table to finish her cereal. "Are you having oatmeal, Daddy?"

"If there's enough," he said, his gaze fixed on Alli's back.

She turned her head slightly at that, still not giving him a look into her eyes. "There's enough."

"Great."

She moved over to the cabinet and pulled out two bowls. After filling one with oatmeal, she held it out to him. He didn't take it. He wanted her to look at him, dammit, to show that she remembered every kiss, every touch, every second of their being together.

Finally, she did look at him, and for a split second there was that same sense of awareness, intimacy, desire—then her brown eyes turned defiant, belligerent. Her armor was back on.

"Take it," she said, pushing the bowl at him.

"Thanks."

So they were back to being angry, distant strangers. He should have figured. He sat down at the table and began to eat, listening to Megan talk about her evening at the neighbor's house, about the brownie she'd saved him, and how many oysters they were going to get and what were the odds that they'd find a pearl. And all the while she talked, he barely listened, instead watching Alli take her oatmeal to the kitchen sink, eating while she cleaned up, anything to avoid sitting down at the table with him.

Finally, Megan finished her cereal and at Alli's request took it to the sink. Then she disappeared upstairs to finish getting dressed. Taking his own empty bowl over to the counter, he set it down while Alli busied herself with loading the dishwasher.

He leaned against the counter and watched her. It was all so normal, the way they ate breakfast, the dishwashing soap Alli poured into the machine, the way she loaded each plate, each glass. He remembered when they'd first married, how they'd argued about how to load the dishwasher.

So many fights . . . they'd had so many arguments about nothing—who was going to pay the bills, who would clean the toilet, who would refill the paper towel dispenser. They'd fought over his drinking milk out of the carton, over Alli's forgetting to get the oil in the car checked, over who got control of the remote control, over whether or not they would buy a new washing machine or keep the old one for one more year—all the little things in their lives. But the big stuff, most of the big stuff, they'd agreed on—how to raise Megan, how to build their businesses, how to support their community. They'd never fought over those things.

"What are you looking at?" she asked in exasperation, tossing the dish towel down on the sink. "You're staring at me like you've never seen me before."

Maybe he hadn't. He'd seen her, sure, but *looked* at her—really looked at her—maybe not.

"I'm going to put my shoes on," she said when he didn't reply. "Did you confirm with Tessa what time we'll meet?"

Tessa. Bring up Tessa, it was the last line of defense between them.

"She'll meet us at the parking lot about a half hour from now. But you already knew that, didn't you?"

"Are you trying to pick a fight?"

"Are you?"

"Can we just forget what happened last night? Chalk it up to one more bad decision we made."

"So, you think you can forget it?"

"I don't want to do this right now, Sam. Megan is upstairs. She doesn't need to hear us fighting or see us throwing pots and pans at each other."

"She'd probably rather see us kissing."

"And that would confuse her even more."

"We're all confused. She can join the club."

"You don't mean that."

He slammed his fist down on the counter. "No, I don't mean that. I don't want to hurt Megan, but don't you see, Alli, *this* is hurting Megan."

"But you've been hurting for nine years, Sam. And I've been hurting, too. And that doesn't make for a happy home for our daughter. Please, let's leave this alone for now. There's too much going on now. I can't think straight."

"Neither can I, especially when you're around."

"You've been living with me for so many years. How can you suddenly be this . . ."

"This what?" he asked, moving closer to her.

"This interested. Is it because you don't have me anymore? That now you suddenly want me? Is it to prove that you can make me love you even after everything?"

"That is not it at all. Is it so hard to believe that I'm attracted to you? Have I ever pretended otherwise?"

"Fine, you're attracted to me. It doesn't mean anything."

"It means more than you think." He grabbed her

by the arm. "It means we have something to work with. We can't go on like this, Alli."

"We're not going on. We're getting a divorce."

He looked deep into her eyes. "Are you sure that's what you want?"

"It's what *you* want."

"Don't make my decisions for me."

"Are you saying you don't want a divorce?"

"Maybe—maybe I am," he admitted.

"Well." She drew in a long breath, then let it out. "When you can get rid of the *maybe*, let me know."

"This is completely uncivilized," Jimmy said as Tessa pulled her grandmother's sedan into the parking lot at the top of the rocky bluff. "Tell me again why hiking is involved in this?"

Tessa turned off the engine and looked at him with a grin. "Because we're going down to the tidal flats, where the river breaks off into several strands before it hits the bay, creating estuaries, otherwise known as pockets where the fresh and salt waters mix. When the tide goes out the oysters close themselves up and just sit there in the mud waiting to be scooped up."

Jimmy made a face at her. "This involves hiking and mud?"

She laughed. "You're such a wimp."

"Oh, sure, insult me now that the thunder and lightning have stopped."

"Okay, okay. You were my hero last night, I admit it. And I do appreciate your sleeping on the couch."

"It was the best offer I got," he said dryly. "And I'll have you know that that is not a six-foot couch."

"Sorry, it looked long enough."

"Obviously your judgment where size is concerned is a bit flawed. I'm much bigger than—"

"Than what?" she interrupted, feeling decidedly wicked, but there was something about Jimmy that brought out the devil in her. "Please, do tell me exactly how big you are."

"Some things you gotta see for yourself, babe. And for you, I'll offer a private showing."

Tessa felt her cheeks grow warm. Just like that he'd turned the tables on her, taken her teasing and made it into a dare, a challenge she wasn't quite up to meeting. Although she had to admit that her sleepless night had less to do with the storm and more to do with the emotions curdling her stomach and tensing her muscles. She'd spent half the night thinking about Sam and the other half wondering about the man downstairs, the man who up until a few weeks ago had been just a photographer and a friend, but who had somehow become so much more.

She still couldn't believe she'd told him about her parents, shared her vulnerability about storms. It had taken her years to create a front for herself and in just a few moments of thunder and lightning, she'd completely caved in.

"I take it your silence means the viewing is on hold," Jimmy said.

"You weren't serious anyway. I doubt you would strip down and show me your you-know-what just like that."

"I wouldn't be so sure. Sometimes I think you

need something to shock you out of this rut you've put yourself in."

"I am not in a rut," she protested. "And how would you know anyway?"

"I have eyes and a camera. And by the way, the reason I agreed to shoot a day in the life of you is because I was curious to see what your day was all about."

"Well, it certainly isn't usually about this," she said, waving her hand toward the beach. "I haven't been near the ocean since that shoot in Tahiti last year."

"And you haven't been near family since long before that."

She frowned at him. "Don't start. I've already told you far too much about me."

"What? You have a limit on the amount of information you're willing to share?"

"My personal life is private."

"Oh, so what?" he said with disgust. "You take such care to hide behind this wall of normalcy, but your cover has been blown, babe. I know you think you're in love with a married man, pretty much hate your baby sister, and are terrified that your grandmother is going to die and leave you without anyone to call family."

Her jaw dropped open at his dead-on assessment of her life. "I never told you all that."

"Your eyes did. Am I wrong?" He paused, but when she didn't say anything he moved on. "You're stuck in a rut, Tessa, a deep hole that you buried yourself in nine years ago and haven't been able to climb out of since. You can't admit that you've changed. You can't admit that Alli and Sam have changed. You see everything in this place the way it was, not the way it is. Don't you ever allow yourself to consider the possibility that moving forward isn't necessarily a bad thing?"

She opened the car door and stepped out, slamming it behind her, wanting him to shut up, wanting him to stop analyzing her, criticizing her, getting too close to her.

"You're my photographer, you're not my shrink," she said as he joined her on the edge of the bluff. "Stop trying to get into my head."

"Stop trying to shut me out. You need a friend, Tessa, and right now I'm pretty much your best shot at one."

"And that's what you want—to be my friend?" Adrenaline raced through her body as she looked into his somewhat startled green eyes. "I don't think so, Jimmy." She poked him in the chest. "I think you want to be more than a friend. I think your psychoanalysis is all meant to steer me in one direction—to you. Well, I'm here. And so are you. What are you going to do about it?"

She flung the challenge down like the white glove in a duel. And he picked it up just as quickly.

"Kiss you," he muttered as his mouth came down on hers with a hardness, a hunger, a passion that surprised her. Jimmy didn't kiss her with the casualness that was his trademark. No, he kissed her with intensity, like a fire consuming everything within its reach. And it was the sense of overwhelming need that made her pull away.

She looked at him, still reeling, still struggling for breath, for words, for logic, for calm.

He stared back at her, his eyes dark and unreadable.

"Well," she said finally.

"Well, well," he said somewhat mockingly.

Instantly, she could sense the change in his mood, as if he, too, was afraid of the seriousness between them, as if he, too, didn't know what to do with it. "The other girls were right. You're a very good kisser. I guess you've had a lot of practice."

"Fishing, Tessa?"

"Your reputation precedes you."

"You don't want me to judge you—don't judge me."

"I apologize."

And they were back to wary again. Thankfully, their conversation was interrupted by the arrival of Sam, Alli, and Megan. Tessa's niece bounced out of the minivan with an exuberance that reminded Tessa of Alli at Megan's age. She shook the thought out of her head as she turned her attention to Sam.

In his trademark jeans and T-shirt, he looked good. He was the same Sam, she told herself, refusing to allow Jimmy's comments about being in a rut get to her. This was the man she'd loved her entire life. She saw him the way he was now. She knew she did. But still her heart questioned as Sam glanced toward Alli, as something in that one simple look seemed different from the day before.

"Hi, Aunt Tessa," Megan said, grabbing her hand. "Can I hike down with you?"

The child's hand felt warm and somewhat sticky in hers. Tessa told herself it was adorable.

"Ready?" Alli asked the group in general. "We should go before we lose the tide." She held a pile of burlap sacks in her hand. "We'll fill these up and hope for the best." Without waiting for a reply, Alli headed down the path that would lead them to the flatlands about a mile down the hill.

"Hey, wait up," Jimmy called.

Alli paused as Jimmy joined her. He said something to her, and she laughed. Tessa felt her body stiffen again. Damn Alli. She always wanted what Tessa had. Not that she wanted Jimmy, Tessa told herself quickly. In fact, this was perfect; she would have Sam and Megan to herself.

"Are you going to help us fly our kite on the Fourth of July?" Megan asked Tessa.

"Oh, I don't think so," Tessa replied, wondering if she'd still be here on the Fourth of July. She supposed she could leave once Grams came home from the hospital, but she didn't know when that would be. And maybe Grams would need help. But how could she stay in Tucker's Landing when her life was far, far away? Yet, how could she leave and let Sam go once again?

"I'm going to Mommy," Megan said suddenly. "You're both walking too slow."

"Should I be insulted?" Tessa asked Sam, feeling the space between them vanish with Megan's abrupt departure.

"Megan moves at the speed of light."

"You like being a dad, don't you?"

"I love it. Megan is the best of me, the best of Alli. But most of all, she's her own person with her own strengths, her own weaknesses. Every time I look at her I'm amazed."

"You had her when you were so young. It can't have been easy suddenly becoming a father at age twenty."

"I doubt it's ever easy, though it's true that sometimes I think Alli and I are growing up right alongside Megan. I just hope she doesn't beat us to adulthood," he said with a grin.

"I don't think there is any danger of that. Alli always liked kids," Tessa said idly. "I have to admit I think Megan is cute as can be, but other people's children just aren't that appealing."

"You have more tolerance for your own child than others."

She drew her sweater more tightly about her as the wind came off the ocean. "It's chilly today, but I'm glad the sun is out," she said, changing the subject.

"Were you all right during the storm?" he asked.

"Yes, fine," she lied.

He nodded. "It never bothered you as much as Alli."

She stared at him in surprise. Had he really not noticed all those years ago how much the storms bothered her?

Before she could ask him, her foot caught on a rock, and she felt herself stumble forward. Sam caught her by the arm and held her until she regained her footing. By the time she straightened, she realized that Alli, Jimmy, and Megan had disappeared beyond the next rise and she and Sam were alone.

"Thanks," she said shakily.

"No problem."

He was too close. She was too close. Somebody was too damn close. She took a deep breath and began to walk again. "Are you and Alli really getting a divorce?"

"Why do you want to know?"

"Because—because I do."

"What difference could it make to you? As soon as Phoebe is better, you'll go back to the life you've been living."

"Maybe not. Maybe I could live here some of the time." She couldn't believe the words had come out of her mouth. Sam looked as shocked as she was.

"What are you saying, Tessa? What exactly are you saying?"

"You and me, Sam, a second chance. That's what I'm saying."

⛵ Chapter 19

"Tessa—"

"Daddy, Daddy," Megan interrupted, running back up the path to them, her face flushed with excitement as she held out her hand. "Look, I caught it with my hand."

Sam cleared his throat, turning his attention to Megan. He slowly peeled her fingers apart to reveal a small gold butterfly fluttering against her palm. "It's beautiful," he said. "You have to let it go now. It needs to fly."

"But I want to take it home and keep it in my room."

"I don't think the butterfly would be very happy in your room."

"I would play with it every day, Daddy."

Tessa smiled as Sam flung her a frustrated look. But she couldn't help him out with this one, for the butterfly trapped in Megan's hand could have been herself.

"It would miss the other butterflies, honey," Sam said gently. He stooped down to look into Megan's eyes. "It would be lonely no matter how much you loved it."

"Okay," Megan said reluctantly, opening her fingers and freeing the butterfly.

Tessa watched it soar into the sky with mixed feelings, because the moment of truth between her and Sam had just flown away with that butterfly. Maybe it was better that way. Was she really ready to commit to staying in Tucker's Landing? What would she do here? A vacation was one thing, but a life? It would be nice to be with Grams. But Alli would be nearby as well. And it was such a long drive just to get to an airport. She had to work. She couldn't just do nothing. And her work took her all over the world.

If she stayed in Tucker's Landing, though, she would have Sam. Or at least she thought she would. He seemed as wary as she was to actually say the words out loud, to admit that the love they shared was still there, still simmering just below the surface. Or did she just want it to be?

Tessa remembered Jimmy's telling her she was in a rut, stuck in the past, unable to get beyond what had happened, comparing each relationship to the one she'd lost. Was that the truth? Or was the relationship she'd had with Sam better than any other?

"Don't you think you would miss the other butterflies?" Sam asked quietly.

"I don't know," she whispered.

"Hurry up," Megan said, once again taking Tessa's hand. "Mommy and Jimmy are ready to go into the water."

Sam met her gaze over Megan's small head. "Later," he mouthed.

She nodded. Later was good. It would give her a chance to decide if she really could make a life for herself in Tucker's Landing.

Alli laughed as Jimmy stuck his booted foot gingerly into about one inch of water, then quickly removed it. "I think I'll be the official photographer," he said.

"Chicken."

"Hey, call me anything you want, just call me dry," he replied. He waved his hand at the view before them. "This is spectacular, I must say, the creeks and streams running into the bay, the ocean in the distance with the haystack rocks rising like monuments, the squawking shorebirds, the elegant pelicans," he mused.

Alli watched with him as a pelican soared down into the distant bay, its long neck dipping into the water in search of food. With another flap of its wings, it sailed off with a grace, a sense of freedom that she could only wish she had. Alli drew in a deep breath of fresh air and felt a rush of pleasure. She loved being at the beach, hearing the waves crashing, watching the water ripple, the birds at play. This was her world, and she didn't think she'd ever get tired of looking at it.

"This is the best place on earth," she said to Jimmy.

He raised an eyebrow. "It's pretty, but if you don't mind my asking, have you been many other places?"

"No," she admitted with a laugh. "But it's still the best place on earth."

"Where did you live before—with your parents?"

"San Francisco. We lived in this small, yellow house in the Sunset district. I remember, because I used to think that we'd painted the sun on our house, since most of the time it was foggy outside."

He sent her an indulgent grin. "What else did you think?"

"That the city was crowded, that we always had to be careful not to talk to strangers, not to run in the street. We didn't know any different then, but once we got to Tucker's Landing, it was like we'd been set free. Only problem was, the freedom came with such a huge price tag."

"It must have been rough losing your parents so young."

"It was awful. I missed them terribly. I wished over and over again that I'd wake up and it would all be a bad dream."

"Do you blame Tessa for the accident?"

She looked at him in surprise. "Why would I?"

"Tessa said your parents went shopping for a special doll she wanted for Christmas. Knowing your high regard for your sister, I figure maybe that's where it all began."

"No. I didn't blame Tessa at all. We were close back then. There weren't a lot of kids in our neighborhood so we played with each other. And Tessa was my big sister. She was the one I cried with, the one who held my hand when we came to Grams's house." Alli paused, not liking the warm memories washing over her. She hadn't thought of that night, those days, in years, and she wished she hadn't started now. It made her remember a time when she'd loved Tessa, and loving Tessa wasn't an emotion she was comfortable with anymore. Looking restlessly up the path, she wondered what was taking them so long. "Where are they?" she asked grumpily.

"They'll be along. But since they're not here yet, maybe you can answer a question for me."

"Like what?"

"Like what do you see in the guy?" Jimmy asked with puzzlement in his light green eyes.

"Who?"

"Sam, the boy next door, the love of apparently everyone's life, that guy. He doesn't seem to be particularly rich. He's good-looking, I suppose. Has a business that I think involves a lot of stinking fish. So what is it about him that makes you and Tessa so nuts?"

Alli grinned. Jimmy was probably better looking than Sam, certainly more sophisticated, well traveled, and he had a bit more charm, but in her estimation he still felt short of Sam. Why?

"No one has ever asked me that before," she said slowly.

"Well, there must be a few things about Sam," he said with a mocking note on Sam's name, "that you really like. What are they?"

"He's—he's gorgeous," she said helplessly. "Strong, rugged, handsome. I love his forearms. I know that sounds stupid, but he's got these great muscular arms, and his hands, they're rough and callused, but they can be incredibly—"

"Okay, okay, I get the picture. He turns you on with his hands. What else? And please, let's skip the other parts of his anatomy. There are some things I'd rather not know."

"Sam has a good heart. He's smart and funny. He tells these awful knock-knock jokes that are so stupid but so endearing. And he's good to people, kind, loyal. He's someone you can count on. He's a friend."

"Now you're making him sound like a Boy Scout."

"No, because he's not perfect, he's very human." She thought for a moment. "He can lose his temper, leave his clothes around the house. He can drive me crazy with his need for solitude and the way he keeps his thoughts private, but I guess what I really like best about him . . ." She paused, wondering if she could put it into words. "He makes me better. Or at least he makes me want to try to be better. He gives me confidence. He makes me feel safe enough to just be myself."

"So tell me again why you're getting rid of him?" Jimmy said dryly. "Because it sounds like you have a lot of reasons for keeping him around."

"Tessa is why we're not together anymore."

"Oh, yeah, I almost forgot about her. You know, you'd make me happy if you'd just hang on to Sam."

"So it's that way," she said with a teasing smile. "I sort of figured."

"It's that way for me. Tessa seems hung up on this guy she hasn't seen in almost a decade, who hasn't sent her a Christmas card or a birthday present or listened to her whine about her job or her aching feet. I don't get it."

"It's simple. Sam and Tessa were in love. I got in the way. Megan got in the way. Maybe their love would have lasted if I hadn't been in the picture. Maybe it wouldn't. But they'll never know unless they have a chance to find out."

"It's a big risk," Jimmy warned her, his expression more serious. "I think Tessa could actually talk herself into sticking around here if it meant getting Sam back."

"Really?" she asked, somewhat shocked, although wasn't that what she'd told herself all along might happen?

"But I don't think she can have her career and have Sam. I'm not sure she's figured that out yet."

"She wouldn't give up her career. It's all she ever wanted."

"Tessa has started believing that Sam is all she ever wanted."

Alli stared at him, still not quite sure Tessa would or could give up her career for Sam. "I thought . . ."

"What did you think?"

"I thought if anything Sam would go with Tessa."

"How could he? His business is here. His family is here. And what the hell would he do with Tessa anyway? Hang up her clothes, comment on her hair, follow her around like a puppy dog? She doesn't need a fisherman."

"That's true. I never thought about that part."

"Take him back, Alli. Save us all from this madness," he said dramatically.

"They have to decide for themselves. I can't fight for Sam anymore. It's his turn to fight for me." She paused, sending him a mischievous look. "But that doesn't mean you can't fight for Tessa. I wouldn't mind if she had another distraction."

"I bet you wouldn't. Unfortunately, it's tough to compete with a memory of some out-of-this-world love affair."

"Tell me about it. I've been trying to do it for the past nine years." Alli stopped as she saw Tessa, Sam, and Megan come into view. They were walking like a family, with Megan skipping between them, her hands in theirs.

The scene tore at Alli's heart. It was one thing to lose her husband, but she couldn't lose Megan as well. And it was that thought that made her throat tighten and her words come out sharper than she intended. "About time," she said. "The tide won't stay out forever."

"I think we'll be all right," Sam replied. "What's the plan?"

"Fill up the bags." Alli tossed him a burlap sack. "Megan, you stay close to me or your daddy. The mud can get so thick it will suck you down like quicksand if you're not careful. And the rocks are slippery, so don't go jumping about," she added.

"But have fun," Jimmy interrupted.

"Yeah, right," Megan grumbled.

"We will have fun," Alli promised Megan, softening her voice and her expression. "We're going to find a pearl today and you're going to help us do it."

"Okay, Mommy," Megan said with a blooming smile.

"I'm taking pictures," Jimmy declared, dropping his bag to the beach and pulling out his camera. "You all go ahead."

"I thought you didn't want to miss out on this experience," Tessa said to him.

"I won't miss out. I'll be watching you, Tessa, you little beachcomber you."

Tessa made a face at him, and he snapped her picture.

"Stop that."

"Blackmail, baby. Tessa MacGuire with her hair blowing in the wind and nowhere near her usual amount of makeup. I can see the tabloids getting into a bidding war."

Alli grinned. She liked Jimmy Duggan more by the minute. Why couldn't Tessa see that Jimmy fit into her life so much better than Sam did?

Picking up her bag, Alli walked toward the rocks and pools uncovered by the vanishing tide. Megan moved along next to her, with Sam and Tessa veering off to the right. As they climbed around the rocks, they began to see signs of life in the pools, starfish and baby crabs, sea anemones and all sorts of tiny creatures.

A kaleidoscope of colors, a banquet of smells, and the constant hum of the ocean in the distance combined with the clicking of Jimmy's camera provided a rhythm for their oyster hunt. This particular tidal flat was open and wild, barely managed by one of the old oyster companies, who had made it known that the locals were welcome to hunt to their hearts' content.

The oysters just lay there, closed up tight in their shells, waiting for the water to come back to cover them, nourish them for another day. But these oysters were going to be shucked and probed for that one elusive pearl that would finish her grand-mother's necklace.

"I think we're going to get lucky today," Megan said as she stuck her small hand into the mud and scooped out an oyster. "Look, I got one."

"You'll get more than one before long," Alli promised.

"I can't wait to show Grams a pearl," Megan continued. "Maybe she'll let me wear the necklace when we get it all fixed up and she comes home from the hospital."

"I'm sure she'll let you try it on."

"When is Grams coming home?"

"Soon, I hope."

"What are we going to do with all the oysters after we open them up?" Megan asked.

"Good question," Sam said, startling Alli by his nearness. "I'm not sure I can take any more raw oysters on the half shell, or that it would be advisable for any of us to do so."

She saw the gleam in his eye and remembered their leaping libidos from the last time they'd gone oyster hunting.

"Stew," she said abruptly. "We'll make oyster stew at Grams's house in her big black pot. And what we don't eat, we'll give away to the neighbors like we used to do."

"Tessa," Sam called. "Alli says we're making oyster stew at Phoebe's house tonight."

Tessa looked up in surprise. "Why? Why can't you make it at your house?"

"Because we always did it at Grams's house," Alli explained, although she was irritated that Sam had felt the need to bring Tessa into it at all. She belonged at her grandmother's house as much as Tessa did, if not more.

"I still don't see—" Tessa began.

"You don't have to see," Alli cut in. "That's where we're doing it. Her kitchen is bigger. The table is longer. And besides, we almost always found the pearl sitting around Grams's kitchen table."

"Fine," Tessa said with a sigh. "Let's just get this over with." She wrinkled up her nose as she bent over and scooped several oysters into her bag. "I can't believe I'm doing this. I never thought coming home would include wading in the tide pools. I can feel the water seeping through my rubber boots."

"You'll live," Alli said crisply.

Tessa shot her a dark look. "Of course I will. Did I say I wouldn't?"

"Are you guys fighting?" Megan asked curiously.

"No," Alli said quickly. "We're just talking like sisters do."

"Sounded like fighting to me," Megan muttered.

"Me, too," Sam said, taking his daughter's hand. "Why don't we go look over there? I think I see a better spot."

Alli bit down on her lip as Sam and Megan wandered away. She hadn't meant to snap, to start anything. Why couldn't she just stop putting her foot in her mouth?

Two hours later, their bags full, they began the hike back to the car. Tessa handed Jimmy her bag to carry. "It's the least you can do," she told him.

"Anything for you, princess," he said, swinging

the sack over one shoulder, the camera bag on the other.

"Thus speaks the man who wouldn't get his feet wet or his hands dirty."

"I got some great shots, though. This is a beautiful piece of coastline, and with you in it, it's quite spectacular." His voice turned husky and something inside of her melted. It was nice to be appreciated. Sam hadn't paid her much attention at all, catering to Megan, helping Alli, talking to Jimmy. In fact, it seemed like he'd gone out of his way to avoid her.

"Come on," she said. "I'm thirsty. I just want to go home, put my feet up, and have a really big glass of iced tea."

He sent her a strange look.

"What?"

"You just called your grandmother's house home."

"It was my home," she said slowly.

"Freudian slip?" He didn't wait for an answer, heading up the path with Alli, leaving Tessa once again to bring up the rear with Sam.

"Tired?" Sam asked her as she let out a sigh.

"A little. I'm not used to all this fresh air."

"I don't think I could breathe in a city," he said. "We went to L.A. for a weekend a few years back. The smog about killed me. I don't how you can stand to live there."

"It has other things to offer besides fresh air."

"Which you can't enjoy, because you're dead."

"Oh, hush," she said, knowing he was teasing her by the curve of his lips. "It's not that bad. Maybe if you spent some time there, or in New York—it's such a wonderful city, so much energy and action and things to do. I think you'd like it."

"Manhattan was always on the top of your list of places to see. I'm glad you got there, Tessa."

"Me, too."

He nodded and they set off up the hill. He didn't have much to say and for the moment she didn't either. They'd talked around their relationship in so many circles she wasn't sure if she was coming or going. Her feelings about Sam were just as mixed up, just as confused.

"Sam—"

"Later," he said, cutting her off.

"It is later."

"Alli and Megan are just up ahead."

And he was still concerned about them. Tessa could understand that, sort of. But it was irritating just the same. She couldn't get a handle on this new Sam, the one who didn't put her first, who didn't turn his back on Alli. Not that she selfishly expected him to be at her beck and call, but he'd always been so attentive before, so interested in what she was interested in. Could they ever find that common ground again?

A piercing scream came from up ahead.

"Megan." The word came out of Sam's mouth in a rush. They both burst into a run, turning the corner to see Megan in a swarm of bees.

"Oh, my God," Tessa said, as Alli and Jimmy tried to swat the bees away from her.

"Daddy, save me," Megan screamed, looking directly at her father.

Sam ran straight into the swarm of bees. He gathered Megan into his arms and took off up the path, daring the bees to follow them.

Alli ran after them, and Tessa and Jimmy followed. They didn't stop until they reached the parking lot, where Sam set Megan down on her feet and knelt in front of her, so he could see into her face, run his hands up and down her arms.

"You're okay, honey, you're okay," Sam said soothingly. "They're all gone."

Megan sniffed back a snob. "I don't like bees," she said, then burst into tears.

Sam pulled her against his chest. "I don't either. But they aren't going to hurt you anymore."

"How badly is she stung?" Alli asked, her face white, but her voice still strong and composed as she gently pulled Megan away from her father so she could check her for bee stings.

Tessa was shaking herself and couldn't quite believe Alli could stand there so calmly and deal with her daughter's pain. It suddenly occurred to her that Alli was a mother and apparently a pretty good one.

"I see at least four," Alli said to Sam. "Oh, my God." She stared at Sam in horror.

"What's wrong?" Tessa asked. But she knew, of course, she knew as well as Alli did.

"You're allergic." Both Alli and Tessa breathed the words at exactly the same time.

"Sam, you have to go to the hospital," Alli said. "You've been stung on your face."

"As soon as I make sure is Megan is okay," Sam replied.

"She's fine. Get in the car."

He got to his feet and Tessa saw that his cheeks were beginning to swell. She had a vivid flashback to the last time, when Sam had stepped on a bee at the beach. Within minutes he hadn't been able to breathe. If they hadn't called the paramedics . . .

"Help me get him in the car," Alli said to Jimmy. "He got stung by a bee once before and almost died."

Between them, they got a staggering Sam into the front seat of Alli's minivan, while Megan climbed into the back, crying even louder now that she sensed something was wrong with her daddy.

"It will be okay, Megan," Tessa told her helplessly. "We'll meet you at the hospital," she added as Jimmy slammed the car door and Alli tore off down the road.

"Well," Jimmy said, letting out a breath. "I think I know why you and Alli are so hung up on the guy."

"What do you mean?"

"He almost died from a bee sting once before, yet he still ran into that swarm of bees without a second thought."

"For his daughter," Tessa said slowly.

"He's a hero," Jimmy muttered. "A goddamned hero."

⛵ Chapter 20

*W*ithin ten minutes, Alli was turning into the parking lot by the emergency room. Sam's face was swollen, one of his eyes was shut, and he was already extremely short of breath. But she managed to get him out of the car and through the double doors of the hospital. The receptionist took one look at Sam and had an orderly grab a nearby wheelchair.

"Be okay," Alli said breathlessly, kissing the top of his head. "I'll take care of everything out here." She hesitated. "I love you," she said after him, but he was already gone.

"Is Daddy going to be all right?" Megan asked, tugging on her hand.

"He will be fine. They just have to give him some medicine, and then he'll be good as new."

"I'm sorry, Mommy." Megan burst into tears once again as she buried her face in Alli's stomach.

"It's not your fault," Alli said, stroking Megan's head. "You didn't see the bees."

"I should have looked where I was going," she choked out in between sobs.

Alli pulled Megan's head up and smiled down at

her watery blue eyes. "It's not your fault," she repeated. "I was talking to you, distracting you, remember? If it's anyone's fault, it's mine. You don't worry about it for one second longer, okay? Now, how's your face, sweet pea?"

"It hurts," Megan whimpered.

Alli pulled Megan's hair away from her face and counted at least four bee stings, but unlike Sam, Megan had only slight tender puffs at the sting sites.

"Excuse me, ma'am, but could you fill out these forms on your husband, please?" the receptionist asked. "And I'll need your insurance card."

"Okay." Alli turned her head as Tessa and Jimmy burst through the emergency room doors. Tessa looked frantic, her eyes holding a fear that Alli remembered seeing once before when their parents had died. "He's going to be okay," she said automatically. "They'll give him a shot. It will be all right."

"Are you sure?"

Alli nodded. "I'm sure."

Tessa sent her a searching look, then let out a breath and glanced toward Megan. "How are you, honey?"

Megan's lip quivered once again. "Hurts," she said, drawing a hand across her teary eyes.

The receptionist came back with a clipboard and an ice bag. "I thought you might need this for your little girl."

"Thank you," Alli said. She juggled both items for a minute, then turned to Tessa. "I need to fill out the paperwork. Could you help Megan with the ice pack?"

Tessa looked taken aback by the request. "I—I guess. Let's sit over there." Tessa took Megan's hand and led her over to a row of chairs against the wall.

"You okay?" Jimmy asked Alli.

"I'm fine."

He slowly smiled. "Yeah, you are, aren't you?"

"What does that mean?"

"It means, I think I figured out not only what you see in Sam, but what he sees in you."

Alli wanted to ask him what he meant, but he simply winked at her and went over to join Tessa. First things first, she decided. She had to take care of the insurance, then deal with Megan. She hoped Sam would truly be all right, as she'd predicted so confidently just a moment before.

Megan had chosen to sit in Tessa's lap rather than on the chair next to her. It felt strange to have a child on her lap, to feel a curly head under her chin, to smell baby shampoo and to hear tiny little sobs. Tessa patted Megan, feeling awkward and incompetent. She would have preferred dealing with the insurance forms and letting Alli handle the mothering part. She feared she'd do the wrong thing, make Megan feel worse instead of better.

Tessa sent Jimmy a desperate look, but he gave her a sublime smile that told her he was enjoying her predicament. Well, screw him, she decided. So much for helping her, for being a friend . . .

"Daddy's going to be mad at me," Megan said.

The line caught at Tessa's heart. "Oh, no, he's not, Megan. He loves you. He would never be mad at you for this. It was an accident."

Megan turned to look up at her. "Are you mad at me?"

"Of course not."

"Do you like me?"

"Yes, I do. Very much," Tessa said, wondering where the questions were coming from.

"How come you never came to see me before?"

Tessa licked her lips. "Well, I've been traveling around the world. I just never got back to Tucker's Landing, but that doesn't mean I don't like you."

"I heard Mrs. Conroy tell Mommy that you stayed away because Mommy had me. And you didn't like me."

Tessa stared at Megan in horror, hating the rejected look in Megan's eyes, hating the fact that somehow, however inadvertently, she'd been the one to put it there.

"That's just not true," Tessa said firmly. "I left home to become a model, because that's my job. That's what I do. My staying away had nothing to do with you."

"But you don't like Mommy," Megan said.

"We're sisters. Sometimes sisters fight, just like friends fight. I bet you argue with your friends sometimes."

"Then we make up." Megan put her hands on Tessa's face, and Tessa had to stop herself from flinching. This mothering stuff was dirty business. "You and Mommy have to make up."

"We will someday," Tessa lied, because she didn't know what else to say.

Megan studied her for a long moment. "All right, then." She turned her attention to the nearby television and squirmed around in Tessa's lap until she could lean back against Tessa and watch in comfort.

Tessa tightened her arms around the little girl, realizing she was starting to enjoy the contact. She wondered what it would be like to have a child of her own. It wasn't something she'd thought much about, especially after Sam's departure from her life.

After that, she'd been consumed with staying thin and looking beautiful and getting magazine covers. But she knew that her career wouldn't last forever, not in the business she'd chosen. And then what would she have? Scrapbooks full of photos, clippings of hundreds of parties, two apartments and not one home, not one man?

Did she want children? Did she want a husband? The white picket fence, the carpools, the peanut-butter-and-jelly sandwiches? Right now, holding Megan, she could see some definite advantages to having a child. She'd have someone to love her, someone to belong to her. Maybe that's what Alli had been looking for, she thought suddenly, her gaze traveling to the counter where Alli was finishing up the admittance procedures.

Jimmy didn't think she looked at Alli, and maybe he was right. Because the woman she saw standing in the emergency room was nothing like the pesky little sister she remembered. Alli had grown up. Well, so had she. That didn't solve their problems, but it did add some distance, maybe some perspective.

Jimmy sat down next to her. "How's it going?"

Tessa took the ice pack off the side of Megan's face. "Looks better, don't you think?"

"Yeah, you've got guts, kid."

Megan smiled like every other female who came under Jimmy's charm. "Mommy said I was very brave."

"You *were* very brave," he agreed. "If I ever have a little girl, I hope she'll be just like you."

"Are you planning to have children?" Tessa asked him.

"I'd like to."

"Really?"

"Why so surprised?"

"Children would tie you down."

"I've been pretty much everywhere I wanted to go, sometimes twice. The world isn't that big."

"I'm still not sure I can see you changing a dirty diaper. You're not exactly prone to manual labor."

"My wife will take care of the diapers."

"You are such a chauvinist."

"What's a chauvinist?" Megan asked.

"It's a man who lets his wife change diapers."

"Daddy says he used to change my diaper."

"Now why doesn't that surprise me?" Jimmy said dryly. "Okay, what about you? Any kids in your future, Tessa?"

"Yesterday I would have said probably not."

"But today your biological clock started ticking?"

"Something like that," she said, smoothing down a piece of Megan's hair.

Jimmy followed her movement with his eyes and they softened when he gazed at her. "You look good doing that. Can you believe I actually left my camera in the car?"

"It's about time. You know, it occurs to me that

you're so busy taking our pictures, you don't really participate, you just watch."

He shrugged. "Someone has to be the recorder."

"I don't think that's a rule."

"You like having your picture taken."

"I also like doing stuff with you. So it's okay with me if once in a while you come to me barehanded."

"I'll remember that."

"Good."

"Everything okay?" Alli asked as she joined them. She smiled down at Megan. "Better?"

Megan nodded, pushing the ice pack away from her face. "I'm hungry."

"I think there's a snack machine over there," Alli said. "Come and pick out something with me."

Megan immediately slipped off Tessa's lap and took her mother's hand.

"Anyone else want anything?" Alli asked.

Jimmy said no, and Tessa shook her head, feeling suddenly cold without Megan on her lap.

"What's wrong?" Jimmy asked.

"Nothing."

"Liar."

"I thought I was satisfied with my life until I came here," she said.

"And saw what you were missing? Come on, Tessa, I know Tucker's Landing is a cute little town, but do you really want to spend your life here?"

"I want a husband. I want children. I want some roots somewhere."

He raised an eyebrow in surprise. "You do?"

"I don't think I realized I did until just now." She got to her feet and stretched her arms over her head.

"Everything is all mixed up in my mind. And I find it odd that we're in this part of the hospital with Sam while my grandmother is just a few floors up."

"You want to go see her?"

"I think so. Do you want to come with me?"

"I'll wait here with Alli and Megan. I've been in emergency rooms before, and I have a feeling it will be a while before we see Sam again."

"I'll just stop in and say hello to Grams and tell her we're going to shuck some more oysters. That should reassure her."

Tessa stepped onto the elevator just as Alli returned to Jimmy with a bag of nacho chips and a can of Gatorade. She popped the lid for Megan and handed it over to her, then squeezed open the bag of chips. It was all so ordinary, and she relished the simple movements, feeling more like they were in a park at a picnic than in the emergency room of a hospital.

"Did Tessa go up to see Grams?"

"Yes."

"That's good." She cast another worried look at the double doors through which Sam had disappeared. She wished she could have gone with him.

"He's going to be fine, you know," Jimmy said.

"I know, but that doesn't stop me from worrying. Since I had Megan I've become immensely concerned with my own mortality—and Sam's, too." She dropped her voice, even though Megan had wandered over to a chair closer to the television set. "I don't want her to grow up without both of her parents."

"The way you did," Jimmy said.

"I wouldn't want her to go through that for anything in the world. Losing my parents left me with this incredible sense of panic that kicks in every time someone I love is a little bit late. I know it drives Sam crazy how often I call to check up on him, but he never had the rug pulled out from under him the way I did."

"I can see how you would worry. But he will be all right. You got him here in time."

"I know. You're right." She leaned back against her chair, taking slow, deep breaths. Five minutes passed, then fifteen. Alli stood up and paced. Jimmy went to get a soda. A half hour and no word. She was just about to demand to be taken to Sam when Tessa reappeared.

"How's Grams?" Alli asked.

Tessa frowned. "Tired, worried, sluggish. She was talking better yesterday than she is today. William said she just got back from physical therapy and that makes her too tired to speak clearly."

Alli studied Tessa's face thoughtfully, wondering if there was something her sister wasn't telling her. "Are you sure that's all it is?"

"I think so. She's still focused on us getting that pearl. I don't want to be the one to tell her we failed."

"We won't fail. Maybe you and Jimmy should go home and get started."

"I want to make sure Sam is all right," Tessa said.

"It could be a while."

"I don't want to leave yet."

Alli slowly nodded. "All right. Then we wait."

Fifteen minutes later, the double doors opened and Sam appeared in a wheelchair.

"I told them I could walk," he said as he was rolled up to them.

Alli smiled down at him with her heart filled to the brim with love. Thank God he was all right! His face was still swollen, but his breathing was clear and sharp. "Are you really okay?" She couldn't help taking his hand, and he gave it a reassuring squeeze.

"I'm fine. How's Megan?"

Alli tipped her head to where Megan was engrossed in a television program, completely oblivious to anything else in the room. "Recovered," she said with a wry smile.

"Good. I was afraid she was worrying about me and blaming herself." Sam got to his feet. "Whoa," he said, steadying himself with a hand on Alli's shoulder. She slipped her arm around his waist.

"Okay?" she asked.

"Just got to get my land legs."

"Lean on me."

He glanced down at her with a grateful smile. "Thanks for getting me here so fast."

"Just don't dare to criticize my driving again, or I'll have to remind you that I saved your life."

"Deal," he said with a warm, tender look that stole her breath right out of her chest.

He turned his head as Tessa cleared her throat.

"I'm glad you're all right, Sam," Tessa said.

"Thanks."

"Uh, folks, if we're done here, I think we've got

some oysters baking out in the car," Jimmy interrupted.

"Where do you want me to take you, Sam—to our house or to your parents' house or . . ." Alli suddenly felt like a fool. Where did Sam belong anyway?

"I'll go to my parents' house," he said quietly. "I think I better pass on the shucking until my eyes are completely open. I might chop off my finger."

"And the last thing we need is another trip to the hospital," Alli said lightly.

"Daddy," Megan said, running over to join them. She threw her arms around Sam's waist. "Are you okay?"

"Better than okay, honey bun."

"Your eyes are all weird."

"They'll get better. You ready to go home?"

Megan nodded and they all headed for the parking lot.

"I have an idea," Jimmy said as Alli opened the car door for Sam to get in.

"Uh-oh," Tessa replied.

"It's a good one," he said.

"I'll bet. What is it?"

"Sam lives right next door to your grandmother's house, right?"

"Right," Tessa said warily.

"He could probably use some company and someone to make sure he doesn't suddenly collapse or anything. So I'm volunteering."

"Jimmy, we have hundreds of oysters to shuck, remember?"

"Correction, you and Alli have hundreds of oys-

ters to shuck. As I recall, you said your grandmother specifically asked that you two do it
together. So why don't I keep an eye on Sam, and
Megan and I can play some games while you two
girls open up some oysters and make us some
stew?"

"No," Tessa said.

"Absolutely not," Alli interjected, hating the idea
as much as Tessa. "We're not doing this alone."

"You won't be alone. You'll be together," Jimmy
said brightly. "What do you think, Megan? Want to
play some games with me?"

"Okay," Megan replied.

"Sam?" Jimmy asked. "What do you think?"

"I think that's the best idea I've heard in weeks."
Sam smiled over at Alli. "Just call us when dinner is
ready."

Just call us when dinner is ready. The idiots, the jerks.
Alli searched her mind for more appropriate adjec-
tives, but she was too tired. The last thing she
wanted was to spend time alone with Tessa. What
on earth would they talk about?

"I can't believe they talked us into this," Tessa
said, dumping a bag of oysters on their grandmother's kitchen table thirty minutes later.

"I can't either," Alli murmured, although it struck
her that for the first time in a long time she and
Tessa were actually in agreement. "Do you want to
start shucking or get the stew going?"

Tessa looked at her like she was crazy. "Do you
actually think I remember how to make oyster
stew? If I ever knew?"

"Of course you knew. We made it with Grams all the time."

"I didn't, that was you."

"You were there, too."

"No, I dropped in for a while and left as soon as you and Grams got distracted. You never even noticed I was gone."

How could that be? Alli always noticed Tessa. Tessa took up lots of physical and emotional space. But come to think of it, she didn't recall Tessa being involved in the kitchen much. Then again, Tessa usually had a date—with Sam. Alli took a deep breath. She had to get through this; she couldn't start thinking about Sam and Tessa. It would only drive her crazy.

They were adults now. They could do this. They could be civilized and polite to each other.

Alli picked up the shucking knife and handed it over to Tessa. "Guess you're in charge of shucking the oysters, then."

"Thanks," Tessa said with a sigh, sitting down at the table. She stared at the heap in front of her with an air of hopelessness. "We're never going to find a pearl."

"Think positively," Alli instructed as she pulled a large pot out of the cupboard and set it on the stove.

"If any of us were thinking at all, we would have told Grams this was a ridiculous idea."

"And have her worrying about the necklace instead of getting well? I don't think so."

Alli opened the cupboard and began pulling out ingredients she would need for the stew. She'd picked up a few things at the store on the way in, but knew she could rely on Grams to have the staples on hand. It felt so familiar to be working in her grandmother's kitchen, but it also felt strange, because Grams was usually in the room with her. In fact, she kept thinking her grandmother would walk in at any second and give her some last-minute instruction. The thought was so strong, Alli couldn't stop herself from looking toward the doorway, but it was empty. The house was empty, waiting for its owner to return.

"She's not here," Tessa said, catching her gaze. "I've been looking for her since I got here."

Alli didn't feel comfortable with the eye contact so she looked away. For a long while the only sounds in the kitchen came from the clatter of the knife against the oyster shells and the sizzle of scallions sautéing in the pot.

"My hands hurt already," Tessa complained a while later.

"I guess you don't work much with your hands, do you?"

"Sometimes I model them."

"Really? People pay money to take pictures of your hands?"

"Of course they do, a lot of money," Tessa said, setting down the knife. She got to her feet and stretched. "I'm taking a break."

"Fine, you go rest, and I'll do it," Alli said in disgust.

"I said I was taking a break. I didn't say I was quitting."

Tessa walked over to the refrigerator and pulled out a bottle of mineral water she had obviously stocked earlier in the week—since Grams had never been partial to bubble water, as she called it. "I've never thought cooking was much fun."

"Do you only do things that are fun?"

"That's me. Fun and games. What about you, Alli? What do you do for fun? Oh, I forgot, you steal other people's boyfriends."

Alli set down the knife she was using to chop scallions just so she wouldn't be tempted to throw it at her sister. "You want to talk about it?"

"I didn't say I wanted to talk about it."

"Well, you brought it up, so let's talk about it."

"I just have one question. How do you look at yourself in the mirror every day?"

"I'm not as attached to my mirror as you are."

Tessa set the bottle of water down on the counter, her blue eyes blazing. "How dare you presume to know anything about me?"

"Likewise, and I sleep just fine, because no matter what I did to Sam, I didn't break his heart. You did that before he ever came to me."

Tessa's jaw dropped open. "What are you talking about?"

"I'm talking about that Christmas. He was going to ask you to marry him. He actually thought you might say yes."

"I would have said yes, and how do you know about that?"

"Sam told me."

"He wouldn't have."

"Well, he did. He told me that night before he got drunk so he wouldn't have to think about what you were doing with your modeling friends in Aspen."

"I certainly wasn't doing what you were doing with my boyfriend. And you were my sister, Alli. I knew you were capable of a lot of things, but I didn't think stabbing me in the back was one of them."

"How could I stab you anywhere but the back? You always had your back to me. I was forever chasing after you, because once we moved here, once you and Sam became bosom buddies, you didn't have time for me. I wasn't anyone to you. So forgive me if my sisterly instincts didn't kick in that night."

Alli felt the anger and bitterness of a lifetime rage within her. Her throat tightened so much she wasn't sure she could breathe. In fact, she had to hang on to the counter to stop herself from falling or, worse yet, flying after Tessa the way she'd done when she was a little girl.

"You never had any sisterly instincts," Tessa said bitterly. "You were a conniving little sneak, listening to my conversations, taking my clothes, wearing my jewelry."

"And you were a bitch," Alli burst out, no longer able to contain the anger within her. She wanted to hit someone or something. Her fingers reached for a weapon and closed around the pile of scallions she was about to toss into the stew. Oh, what the hell, she thought as she threw them at Tessa's face.

Tessa shrieked and grabbed the nearest thing to her. It was the bag of flour. Before Alli could move, Tessa had dumped it over Alli's head. Alli sputtered and choked as the floury air surrounded her. Her eyes lit on the pile of oyster meat waiting in a bowl. She grabbed it and threw the contents at Tessa.

Some of the meat splashed on the floor, and when Tessa tried to run, she slipped on the wet, floury tile. As she went down, she grabbed Alli's arm and pulled her down along with her.

Another second and they were rolling around between the counters and the kitchen island, tossing handfuls of flour and oyster meat at each other, until they were both covered from head to toe in the squishy, smelly mixture. Searching for new ammunition, Alli reached into the bag of oysters on the floor and started throwing those at Tessa.

Tessa ducked as the oyster shells clattered against the cupboards and the floor. Any that fell nearby, she tossed back in Alli's direction.

"I hate you," Tessa yelled.

"I hate you, too," Alli screamed back, dodging as one hard shell came close to her face. "You were the worst sister in the world."

"No, you were the worst," Tessa said as she tried to stand up but slipped on the floor and landed hard on her right hip.

Alli gasped at Tessa's sudden cry of pain. "Oh, my God. Are you all right?" She went down on her knees in front of Tessa. "Did you break something?"

"I should break you," Tessa retorted, then her shoulders started to shake.

"What?" Alli suddenly realized her sister was laughing. Laughing! She tried to drum the anger back up again but as she stared into Tessa's flour-covered face, Alli, too, was struck by the ridiculousness of the situation.

"You look awful," Tessa said, pointing a finger at her as she collapsed in laughter.

"And you've never looked better," Alli replied as a laugh snuck past her own lips. "If your fans could see you now."

"I'd probably be out of a job." Tessa wiped a chunk of flour away from her eyes. "Ick. Do you remember that food fight we had with Dad? Mom was at the PTA meeting, and Dad made that spaghetti—"

"Which was awful," Alli finished.

"And he threw the noodle at the wall, and it stuck," Tessa said with a giggle.

"And then you threw a noodle at him, and it stuck to his forehead."

"We had so much fun that night." Tessa's laughter faded away.

"We did have fun." Alli felt strangely empty, as if her body had suddenly deflated.

"Not just that night," Tessa said.

"Not just that night," Alli agreed. She hesitated, then plunged ahead, knowing that what she had to say was long overdue. "I'm sorry, Tessa, sorry for seducing Sam. I know you won't believe me, but I regretted it almost instantly. I didn't just do it to hurt you, I did it because I loved Sam. And I thought it might be my only chance to have him. When you were around, he didn't look at anyone else. And I was crazy about him. I couldn't think straight."

"I thought it was just a crush, something you'd grow out of given enough time."

Alli looked her in the eye. "If I could take it back, I would, and not just because of how I hurt you, but because of how I hurt Sam. It wasn't fair to him.

And it isn't even fair to Megan, because now she has two parents who don't belong together." Alli took a deep breath and slowly let it out. "I've made a lot of mistakes. Saying sorry doesn't make them go away, but it's all I have to offer."

"I've made a few mistakes, too," Tessa said after a moment. "I shouldn't have stayed away so long. I missed time with Grams. And I don't even know my niece, who seems to be a wonderful little girl, in spite of all of us." Tessa leaned back against the counter. "I missed you, too, Alli. When it rained last night, I remembered how we clung to each other the night Mom and Dad died, and it hurt to know that we'd never be that close again."

Alli bit down on her lip as she struggled not to cry. She couldn't believe that Tessa had missed her at all. But why would she say it if it wasn't true?

"I miss the way we used to talk when the lights were out," Alli said after a moment. "I miss the way you used to play the flashlight on the ceiling, putting your fingers over it in weird ways to scare me."

"I don't remember that," Tessa teased, her eyes somewhat misty.

"Most of all I miss having you there to share a memory," Alli continued. "Because not even Grams was with us in the beginning. I lost my childhood when I lost you, because I couldn't talk about it to anyone who would understand."

"I couldn't either. And I wanted to," Tessa said, her mouth trembling.

Alli felt a tear slide down her cheek. "I did love you, Tessa. And I wish—I wish I hadn't hurt you so bad."

Tessa sniffed. "You're trying to make me cry. But I'm not going to cry."

"I've cried lots of times." Alli wiped another tear off her cheek. "When Megan was born, I remember waking up in the middle of the night in the hospital room, and I was all alone. Sam had gone home and Megan was in the nursery, and I looked out the window and I saw this incredible star winking at me, and I remembered all those times we looked at the sky with Grams, counting the stars, trying to decide which one was sending us a kiss from Mom and Dad. And I turned to look at you—but you weren't there."

Alli shook her head as the tears overwhelmed her. "You weren't there. You were my only sister, and I had a new baby, and I wanted you to see her, see how pretty she was, but you weren't there. And I missed you." Alli's voice caught, and she couldn't go on, especially when she saw that Tessa was crying.

Tessa suddenly scrambled toward her, putting her arms around Alli as they knelt on the kitchen floor. "I wish I had been there. My stupid pride wouldn't let me come back. I'm sorry."

Alli cherished the embrace between them, wishing it could go on forever. But as the minutes ticked by, reality began to intrude along with the uncomfortable feeling of wet flour halfway down her back. She slowly pulled away. "Grams would have our heads if she saw this mess."

"I think she'd be smiling, glad we're finally talking to each other," Tessa replied.

Alli slowly stood up as Tessa did the same. They

took a good long look around the room, realizing the extent of the damage. Well, some things didn't come easily or neatly.

"When Jimmy suggested we do this together all I could think of was that you and I would be alone," Tessa said. "I didn't know we were going to throw food at each other, but I had a feeling something was going to happen."

"Probably why Jimmy suggested it. He's a natural-born troublemaker."

"That he is," Tessa agreed.

"He appears very interested in you."

"He likes women; he likes to flirt."

"Seems like more than that."

"It's not. I know Jimmy."

"I'll have to take your word for it." But Alli wondered if Tessa really did know Jimmy as well as she thought. "We better clean this up before the guys come over. I think Jimmy would have his camera out in about two seconds."

"Make that one second," Tessa replied, reaching for some paper towels.

"I don't really want Megan to see this either. She still thinks I'm a responsible adult." Alli picked up a sponge and wiped down the counter.

"Sam thinks you are, too," Tessa said after a moment.

"What?" Alli couldn't possibly have heard her right.

"Sam thinks you're a responsible adult. He told me."

"He did?"

"Does that surprise you?"

"Sam continually surprises me."

"Well, I have to admit that he's right. And Alli, I'm tired of our old fight. It's so over. Can we stop talking about it? Move on with our lives?"

"Yes."

"Good."

Deep down, Alli didn't know what moving on meant exactly in terms of the three of them, but she knew the next move belonged to Tessa and Sam.

"I'll get a mop," Tessa said.

"All right." Alli leaned over to pick up an oyster, and as she did so she saw one that had been split in two after hitting the edge of the dishwasher. Something glittered within it, something shiny and smooth. "Oh, my God! Tessa, come quick."

⛵ Chapter 21

"Nice car," Jimmy said, rubbing his hand over the smooth finish of Sam's Thunderbird. "How does she drive?"

"Like a dream."

"And you're going to sell this beauty?"

Sam nodded, feeling a momentary pang as he took a good look at the car which had been a part of so many of his memories. "It's time," he said shortly. "I could use another boat more than I can use this car."

"That's thinking practically."

Sam had a feeling that thinking practically wasn't one of Jimmy's priorities. "I guess."

"Can I sit in it?"

"Sure."

Jimmy slid in behind the wheel and smiled with appreciation. "This is very cool. Maybe *I* should buy it."

Sam instinctively tensed, seeing Jimmy and Tessa in the car, driving off with a laughing wave. It was the wrong image, and yet . . . He couldn't really see Tessa and himself in the car anymore. Instead he saw Alli asleep in the front seat after she'd spent the night waxing the car for a surprise birthday present.

He'd felt so incredibly touched by her gesture that he'd awakened her with a kiss. Five minutes later they were making love in the car. It had been passionately awkward and fun; they'd laughed at the foolishness of it all. Because they had a perfectly nice bed just up the stairs. But wasn't that the way it had always been with Alli—passion, recklessness, laughter, love? His body tightened at the word *love*, the word she wanted so desperately to hear from him.

"Uh, Sam?" Jimmy asked, snapping his fingers.

"What?" he said shortly.

"Where did you go just now?"

"Just thinking about the car."

"Lots of memories, huh?"

"A few."

"Are you sure you can let the car go?"

He could let the car go. But how could he let Alli go?

"I'm thirsty," Jimmy said as he stepped out of the car. "What have you got to drink?"

"Let's see," Sam said, heading into the kitchen. He opened the refrigerator. "Do you want a beer?"

"Sure." Jimmy deftly caught the beer can in one hand. As he popped the top, he said, "So, do you think Alli and Tessa have killed each other yet?"

"Maybe," Sam muttered, taking out a bottled water. He put the cool glass against his still hot, swollen cheeks. "I'm not sure leaving them alone was a good idea."

"They're sisters. They need to talk." Jimmy's eyes narrowed. "You should sit down. You still look blotchy."

"I'm fine," Sam said, but he did sit down at the table.

"What are you worried about anyway?" Jimmy asked, taking a seat across from him. "Afraid they're telling secrets about you?"

"No."

"You don't have to pretend they're both not in love with you. I have eyes and a camera. In fact, I brought you some photos. I'll get them."

Sam waited in the kitchen while Jimmy retrieved the photos from his camera bag. Sam wasn't sure he wanted to look at any more pictures of Tessa. Wasn't that what had gotten him into trouble in the first place?

Jimmy dumped a pile of photos on the table in front of him, and Sam was surprised to see shots of Alli. He suddenly realized how few photos he had of her, for Alli was usually the one behind the camera. In fact, she did her best to hide away when photographs were taken. But Jimmy had captured her every mood at work, at play, with Megan. There was joy, passion, tenderness, and love in every smile, every look.

Sam drew in a deep breath, feeling like he'd been punched in the stomach.

"Not bad, huh?"

"These are . . ." Sam couldn't think of a word to describe how he was feeling. Alli was beautiful. God, Alli was beautiful. He'd never realized.

"Stunning," Jimmy finished, catching Sam's eye. "Don't you think?"

"You're very good."

"I had the perfect subject, although Alli has no idea that beauty doesn't always come in shades of blond, does she?"

"No."

"It must have been hard growing up in Tessa's shadow."

"I think it was," Sam murmured, knowing he certainly hadn't made it any easier for Alli.

"I tried to give Alli the photos, but she didn't want them. I thought maybe you'd like to keep them—for Megan, if not for yourself."

Sam grinned at the irony of Jimmy's request. Phoebe had given him the box of Tessa's photos with the exact same words, and look where that had gotten him. "You have no idea what you're asking me," he said cryptically. "But yes, I'll keep them."

"Good." Jimmy paused. "So, can I ask you something?"

"Can I stop you?"

"Are you planning to take Tessa back?"

Sam tensed once again. "What's it to you?"

"I want her," Jimmy said flatly. "But Tessa seems to think that she can have you back. Can she?"

Could she? Sam didn't know what to say. "If you want Tessa, you should tell her."

"Oh, I've told her. But she's waiting for you." He paused. "You had Tessa once. Why did you let her go?"

"I didn't let Tessa go. She left me long before I left her," Sam replied sharply.

Jimmy raised an eyebrow. "That's not the way she tells it."

"Well, it's the way it was." Sam left the room, stopping in the hallway to catch his breath, to gather his thoughts. Hell, that's exactly the way it had been. It was all so clear now. He'd blamed himself for destroying their relationship, but in truth their relationship had been in trouble long before he'd slept with Alli. Why hadn't he seen that before?

The front door flew open before he could come up with an answer, and to his surprise, two figures completely covered in white something came running into the hall. "What the hell happened to you two?" he asked.

Alli and Tessa were laughing and crying and talking all at the same time, and Sam couldn't understand a word they were saying. "What? Slow down. You had a food fight?"

Jimmy came up behind Sam, raising an eyebrow at their appearance. "Nice look, ladies."

"Never mind us," Tessa said impatiently. "Show 'em, Alli."

Alli held out the oyster shell. "We found it, Sam. We found the last pearl."

Looking at the two women, whose eyes were lit up with joy, who were so in tune, so happy together, Sam had a feeling they'd found much more than a pearl.

Phoebe leaned back against the pillows on Saturday morning, exhausted after her morning bath and physical therapy session. She wondered if she would ever walk normally again, ever feel the energy that had once made her shun caffeine for fear of running at a hundred miles per hour instead of her normal sixty.

"I hate this," she said to William, who always seemed to be nearby. "I want to go home."

"You will. The doctor said two more days. He wants you to get your strength back before you're on your own."

"Oh, piffle," she said, weary of the whole discussion. "As if I couldn't do this at home. I lay around and sleep half the day." He patted her hand, but she pulled it away from him. "Don't."

He winced at her harsh tone. "I'm sorry."

She softened. "No, I'm sorry. None of this is your fault. I just hate this place. I sleep all day, then I can't sleep at night, and it's so lonely then." What she didn't tell him was that she couldn't sleep because her dreams of John were growing more haunting. He kept going deeper in the water, and she could feel the water lapping at her own bare feet as he called to her with passion in his eyes, in his voice, in his outreached hands—hands that he wanted her to take, only she kept waking up before she could take them.

She loved him so much, but the dreams were beginning to scare her, and she didn't know why.

"I'll stay with you at night," William offered, distracting her from her thoughts.

"You can't be with me twenty-four hours a day or you will wind up in here along with me."

"It would be worth it."

She looked into his comforting brown eyes and wondered for the thousandth time why he was still here. "You should go back to Philadelphia, William."

"I'm not leaving you like this. Once you're on your feet, we'll talk about our plans."

"Maybe you should make your plans without me."

"I don't think so. I'm going to get some coffee. Would you like me to bring you anything from the cafeteria?"

"No, thanks." She sighed as he left the room, wondering why he didn't go when he would be so much happier without her. But he refused to see the truth.

"Grams?" Tessa asked from the doorway. "Are you up to visitors?"

"Tessa, sweetheart, come in."

Tessa came over and planted a cool kiss on Phoebe's forehead. There had always been more distance between them, more formality, than between her and Alli, but Phoebe didn't mind. She understood Tessa just as she understood Alli. But there was something different about Tessa this morning, a sense of excitement that she seemed desperate to hide.

"How are you?" Tessa asked.

"I'm fine," Phoebe said automatically. "I think the better question is how are you?"

"Pretty good."

"You look it. What's happened?"

"Nothing has happened. I'm just happy to see you awake and talking. Your speech is better, isn't it?"

"It seems to be. I thought you and Alli might have found the pearl."

"When we do, you'll be the first to know."

Phoebe's heart sank. They hadn't found it yet. And the Fourth of July was only two days away.

"But I do have some good news," Tessa said quickly. "Alli and I have declared a truce on the past."

"That *is* good news." Phoebe gave a heartfelt sigh. At least something positive had come of her illness.

"I feel like we can all move on now."

"What does that mean?"

"I'm not sure exactly."

Phoebe saw the nervous light in Tessa's eyes, the restless fidgeting of her fingers against her side, and knew Tessa hadn't begun to move on, as she called it. "Do you still love Sam?"

Tessa cast a quick look at the door, as if she were afraid someone was listening. Once she could see they were alone, she took the chair next to the bed. "I think I do, Grams. I think that's why I haven't been able to get serious about anyone else."

"Oh, Tessa."

"I want what you and Grandpa had, a strong, enduring love and marriage."

"With Sam."

"Yes. And before you say anything, I'm not trying to break up Sam and Alli. They were broken up before I got here. You know I wouldn't do anything to get Sam if they were still together."

"Of course you wouldn't." Phoebe looked up as William came back in the room. He stopped when he saw Tessa.

"Good morning, Tessa," he said.

"Good morning."

"Don't get up. I forgot my newspaper. I'll be back in a few minutes."

"He's devoted to you," Tessa said with a smile. "Do you know how much he loves you?"

"How much or how little?"

"What do you mean?" Tessa asked in surprise.

How could Phoebe explain it? And yet she had to explain it, because it suddenly occurred to her that Tessa and William had something in common. "William believes that my parents forced me to marry your grandfather because of money and business connections. While it was true that they wanted the marriage, it was also true that when I met John MacGuire I fell in love with him. John took me on a wonderful adventure. He freed my spirit, Tessa. He made me see that I could be the woman I was meant to be. We had a wonderful life together. He was my soul mate."

"You were lucky."

"I was lucky. But William always thought that if I hadn't been forced to marry John, I would have married him. He believed that his lack of money and social standing had made him unworthy, so he spent the rest of his life amassing money and power. He married twice, had a son, but never felt happy."

"Because he's in love with you."

"No. He's in love with the girl that he thought I was." Phoebe took a breath. "He has asked me to marry him. To move to Philadelphia."

Tessa was shocked. "You love the sea. You love this town."

"Yes, I do. But William doesn't understand. He only remembers who I was that one summer when we were close. He's been stuck there like a broken record going around and around. And no matter what I say he can't see the truth. I love him as a friend, but not as a husband. I know I encouraged him the last few years because I was lonely. That was wrong of me. Because William deserves a true love. And I already gave my love to John."

"That's so sad, Grams. William is a nice man."

"A very nice man. I wish I could love him the way he wants, but I can't."

"Why are you telling me this?" Tessa asked.

"I don't want you to make the same mistake," Phoebe said gently.

"You don't think I see Sam the way he is today?"

"Do you?"

"I know we've changed."

"Do you think Sam knows the real you?" Phoebe paused, feeling weary from the exertion of so many sentences. "If he does, Tessa, if Sam knows you and loves for who you are, and you can say the same, then perhaps you were meant to be together. That's up to the two of you. I won't interfere."

Tessa stood up and walked over to the window, then turned back. "Do you think I could be happy living here again?"

"Oh, Tessa, how would I know that?" Phoebe looked up as William re-entered the room, this time followed by the rest of the family: Alli, Sam, and little Megan, who skipped over to the bed with all the energy Phoebe wished she still had.

"You'll never guess, Grams," Megan said.

"Then I won't even try."

"Did you tell her?" Alli asked Tessa.

"No, I was waiting for you."

"We found it, Grams. Tessa and me. We found the last pearl." Alli felt the words burst out of her, excitement bubbling up inside of her like champagne. She saw the light come on in Phoebe's eyes, the hope, the joy.

Alli's hands were shaking so much she could barely pull the pearls out of the bag. She'd had them strung that morning. "Here is your necklace, Grams. It's done." Alli walked over to the bed and slipped the pearls over her grandmother's head. "They're beautiful," she said.

Phoebe's blue eyes blurred with tears. "My pearls," she whispered. "I finally have them." She looked up at Alli and Tessa. "Thank you. Thank you both." She held out her arms to them. Alli leaned down on one side, Tessa on the other, and they hugged together, the way they'd done so many years ago.

When Alli and Tessa pulled away they were both crying.

"Now, none of that," Phoebe said with a sniff. "It will make your eyes red."

"I love you, Grams," Alli said.

"I love you, too," added Tessa.

"And I love you both. I knew you would find the pearl together."

"You won't believe how we found it," Alli said with a laugh.

"Mommy and Aunt Tessa had a food fight," Megan interrupted. "You should have seen your kitchen, Grams. I told Mommy she was in big trouble."

Phoebe smiled down at Megan. "I think they've learned their lesson." She paused, glancing over at the man who meant so much to all of them. "Sam, come here, won't you?"

Sam moved over to the bed. "You look beautiful in those pearls, Phoebe."

"There's a mirror in the top drawer. Would you hand it to me?"

Sam handed her the small pocket mirror. "What do you think?"

"I think they're perfect." She touched the pearls with a reverent gesture.

And they were perfect, Alli thought, but as mismatched as any strand could be, all different sizes, all different shades of white and ivory, and yet still perfect because of what they symbolized, a lifetime of love. How she wanted that kind of love. The thought of never knowing it almost broke her in two. But this wasn't about her. This was about Grams. They'd found the missing pearl. They'd finished the strand. Now things would be better. Grams would come home, and . . . well, that was a start.

Phoebe handed the mirror back to Sam. Then she pulled the pearls over her head. After looking at them for a long minute, she kissed one and then

held them up to Sam. "I want you to have the necklace."

"What?" he asked, stunned. "I couldn't."

"Both my granddaughters have loved you. And
I've loved you, too. You're part of our family."

"Still, I couldn't—"

"I won't take no for an answer."

Sam looked over at Alli. She didn't know what to
say to him. She was as surprised as he was. Tessa,
too, appeared startled by the request. But what
could either of them say? The pearls belonged to
their grandmother. They were hers to give as she
pleased.

"Sam," Phoebe said, drawing his attention back
to her. "I want you one day to give these pearls to
the woman you truly love. You'll know when it's
right. And you'll know who." She held his gaze
with hers for a long minute, then said, "I'm tired
now. I think I'd like to rest."

Sam leaned over and kissed her on the cheek. "I'll
see you soon." He turned to Megan. "Say good-bye
to Grams."

" 'Bye, Grams, see you tomorrow."

" 'Bye, honey."

Alli smiled down at her grandmother. "I'm not
going to ask you why you did that."

"Nor am I, Grams," Tessa said.

"Good." Phoebe looked at them both. "Remember always that you're sisters above all else. Whatever you have now, don't lose it. Promise me that."

"We promise," Alli and Tessa said together.

"Rest now," Alli added. "We're going to finish our

kite for the festival today, and on Monday you'll be able to sit on your deck and watch it soar higher than all the rest."

"Not so fast," Tessa interrupted. "I found the kite you and Grandpa used to fly. Would you mind if I entered it in the contest?"

"I would love it," Phoebe said softly. "My darling girls. You mean so much to me and to each other. Just like the pearls, you are so much better together than you are apart. That's what I wanted you to know."

Alli followed Tessa to the doorway, feeling a strange uneasiness. She didn't like all the good-byes. They felt too final. "I'll be back tonight, Grams. You'll be all right, won't you?"

"Of course I'll be all right." Phoebe paused, sending her a tender look. *"I can't die yet, honey. I haven't finished counting the stars, and don't you know that you will never be alone, because there is always love, and love lives forever."*

Alli looked at Tessa and saw the instant recognition in her eyes.

"Everything will be all right," Tessa said softly.

"Yes," Alli agreed. "Everything will be fine."

William sat down next to Phoebe's bed and didn't say anything for several long minutes. He'd been so quiet earlier, she'd hardly noticed he was there. Now she wondered if she'd hurt him yet again.

"The pearls were beautiful on you, Phoebe. I only wish John could have seen them," he said heavily.

"Do you mean that?"

"Yes." He let the silence fall again. "I think I'll go back to Philadelphia next week, after you come home from the hospital."

"I'm sorry," she said softly.

"It's not your fault. You've been telling me all along that I couldn't see what was beneath my nose. I finally saw it today. When you looked in the mirror, when you saw the pearls—did you see John in the reflection?"

She saw the pain in his eyes but could only be truthful. "Yes."

"I always thought that our love was the true one. But it wasn't."

"Our love was young. We weren't fully grown. You were different. I was different. Only you never realized that I changed or even that you changed."

"I thought once John had passed, once time had passed, that you might see your way back to me. But I think I've worn out my welcome."

"Never. You are my dearest friend. And I do love you in a way that has always belonged only to you."

He tipped his head, his voice turning gruff, as he said, "I'll always love you, Phoebe. Do you mind if I sit with you for a while?"

"I would like that. I hate to be alone here."

"And when you fall asleep, I'll go." He looked deep into her eyes. "Because you'll be with him then, won't you?"

"Yes," she said softly. "I'll be with him."

They were beautiful, Sam thought, watching as Alli and Megan ran with the wind, trying unsuccessfully to get their kite into the air. He would have helped, but it was far more fun to watch them, their hair blowing in the breeze, Alli's a shiny copper penny, Megan's a glorious blond. Their faces were flushed, their voices pitched with excitement, their efforts broken up with laughter.

Every so often they looked to him. But Alli wouldn't ask him for help. She'd stopped asking him for anything. He felt a deep hungry ache in his soul for the way it used to be. Alli wanted a divorce because he couldn't let go of the past. But now he had a feeling that he couldn't let go of her.

"Sam, do you think you could help me with this?" Tessa asked, walking across the thick grass toward him. Jimmy had stopped to photograph Alli and Megan, obviously as caught up in the appeal of the scene as Sam had been.

He smiled at Tessa. At least someone needed his help. Then he looked down at the twenty-year-old kite in her hand and laughed. "Where did you dig that up?"

"Grams's attic. Do you think it will still fly?"

He took the kite out of her hand and examined the edges for tears, but everything appeared intact. "A little ragged, but it should still fly."

"Some things don't change, do they, Sam?"

He saw the seriousness in her eyes and knew there was more behind the question than the subject of kites. "Some things," he agreed.

"Do you like what you see in me now? I don't mean my physical appearance, but me—do you like the woman I've become?"

Her eyes were worried, as if she were afraid of

his answer. And how could he answer—there were so many facets to this grown-up Tessa he didn't begin to understand. "I like what I see. But isn't it more important if *you* like what you've become?"

"You'd think so, wouldn't you? But I've wanted to ask you that question for a long time. In fact, way back when we first split up, I used to fantasize about calling you and telling you I'd just gotten back from a photo shoot in Australia or that my face would be on the cover of some magazine. I thought how impressed you would be. How bad you would feel for having let me go." She sent him a rueful smile. "Pretty sad, huh?"

"I am impressed by all you've accomplished. I'm proud, too. Proud I knew you when."

Her eyes watered. "Really? You're proud of me?"

"Very much."

"That means more than you know." She paused. "I think you grew up into a fine man. I always knew you had potential, but watching you this past week, I realized you would have never been happy following me around the world. You're part of this place," she said with a sweep of her hand. "This beautiful place where roots grow deep and the sea nourishes the soul. My grandfather once told me that's why he loved Tucker's Landing. And I think you love it, too."

"I do, Tessa. It's a part of me that I've only just recently come to accept."

"I feel like I want to settle down, too."

He felt his stomach lurch. "Settle down here?"

"What do you think?" She looked into his eyes

with a pleading expression that told him she really needed an answer. But what was the right answer?

"Tucker's Landing is a long way from New York or even L.A.," he prevaricated.

"I could make it my home base, the best of both worlds."

"I'm sure your grandmother would be happy to have you here. And you and Alli seem to be getting along better."

"We've declared a truce. I wonder if you and I could do the same thing. And you could stop being angry at me."

"I'm not angry at you, Tessa."

"But that's the problem, Sam. I don't know how you feel about me."

There was a challenge in her words, a call to speak the truth. He thought about the pearl necklace Phoebe had given him, and her instructions to give it to the woman he truly loved. Was that Tessa—his first love? His gaze drifted over to Alli and Megan. Or was it Alli—his wife, the woman who shared his life?

"It's taking you a long time to answer," Tessa said lightly, but there was a pain in her voice that told him she knew the truth as well as he did. "There's a time and a season, isn't there?"

"I think so," he said slowly.

"And this isn't our time. Well." She took a deep breath. "I suspect I already knew that. I just didn't want to admit it, not even to myself."

"Hey, Tessa, babe, are we ever going to launch that thing?" Jimmy called out.

Sam cleared his throat and handed Tessa back the kite. "Jimmy is waiting for you."

She hesitated, then took the kite out of his hands. "I'm going to beat you in the kite festival, you know."

"Give it your best shot."

"Oh, I will, don't worry."

He smiled as she left, feeling an incredible weight slip off his shoulders.

As Jimmy and Tessa, with Megan's help, attempted to launch their kite, Alli came over to Sam, her cheeks flushed, her eyes lit up like a Christmas tree. "Don't you want to practice flying the kite?" she asked.

"You and Megan are doing a good job."

"Nobody does it as good as Daddy," Alli said, mimicking Megan's little girl voice. "You're her hero, you know, especially after you saved her from the bees yesterday."

"I didn't think; I just acted. That doesn't make me a hero." He shoved his hands in his pockets so he wouldn't be tempted to brush the hair out of her eyes or put an arm around her the way he wanted to.

"Actually, that's exactly what it makes you." She paused. "I feel so happy today. We found a pearl, Sam, among all those wild oysters, against all those odds—a beautiful pearl in a muddy, ragged shell. Who would have thought we could have done something like that? Who would have thought you and I could have brought a beautiful child into the world? Who would have thought

Tessa and I could be sisters again? Sometimes life amazes me."

"It is a good day."

"I want to kiss you," she said.

And he stopped breathing then, for her eyes were on his mouth, and her body was so close to his. It was the first time in a long time that she'd admitted to wanting him.

"What's stopping you?" he asked.

She glanced over her shoulder and saw that Megan, Tessa, and Jimmy had disappeared into a thatch of trees, their kite string caught in some branches. "Just one kiss," she told him.

"For starters," he murmured, standing perfectly still, his heart thudding against his chest as she stood on tiptoe to kiss him.

Her lips were warm, shy at first, then growing bolder as their mouths recognized each other in delicious familiarity. He groaned down deep in his throat as he ached for a deeper, harder, longer kiss. But she was gone almost as quickly as she had come. And her eyes were not as happy as they had been a minute ago.

"Don't keep saying good-bye," he told her. "It's not the last kiss."

"It could be," she whispered. "Maybe it should be."

"Since when have we done what we were supposed to do?" His words coaxed a reluctant smile out of her.

"You've got me there." She hesitated. "Sam, I know about the offer you got to buy your business."

"Tessa told you?"

"No, Tessa didn't tell me. You told Tessa?" she asked sharply.

"It doesn't matter, Alli. I'm not going to sell out."

"Are you sure? This could be your chance to start over, Sam, in every way. Maybe you should take it."

"Maybe I don't need to start over, Alli. Most people only start over when they're losing. I don't think I'm losing."

"What does that mean?" she asked in confusion.

"It means you just kissed me."

"So?"

"Like I said, it's a start."

"A start to what?" She held up a hand. "Don't answer that. Not today. I'm feeling too good today, and I don't want to spoil it just yet."

"Daddy, we need help," Megan called, running toward them.

Alli tipped her head toward Jimmy and Tessa. "Looks like it's time for you to be a hero again."

"We're not done talking."

"For now we are. We found the pearl, Sam. And I think somehow everything else is going to work out the way it's supposed to. And for the moment, I'm going to just do what Grams always tells me to do."

"What's that?"

"I'm going to have faith."

Phoebe put a hand to her neck and felt the warm pearls against her skin. She looked at the man standing a few feet from her. "It's beautiful, isn't it?"

"As are you."

"The girls found it together. They're a family again. I wish you could see them."

"I can," he said simply. "And you, my love, are you ready to sail away with me?"

She wasn't afraid anymore. In fact, the water was deliciously warm, and when she reached out to John, she could feel him. No more elusive longing. He was here. He was hers.

"You won't leave me again?" she asked.

"Not ever again. I love you, Phoebe. I've missed you."

"And I've missed you."

Chapter 22

$\mathcal{A}$lli grinned as Jimmy tried to talk Sam into climbing the tree and rescuing the kite entangled in the branches. Before she could suggest that Jimmy make the journey himself, her cell phone rang.

"Hello," she said, flipping it open, expecting to hear Mary Ann's voice, but it was William. "What?" The words rocked her to the core. The group around her fell silent as she tried to make sense of what he was saying.

"Phoebe has had another stroke," William repeated. "They're trying to resuscitate her. Hurry, Alli. Hurry."

She flipped the phone shut, her gaze running immediately to Sam. "Grams has had another stroke. We have to go now."

"No," Tessa cried, putting a hand to her mouth. "That can't be right."

"She'll be fine. We have to believe that." But the word *resuscitate* ran through Alli's head.

"Is Grams going to die?" Megan asked her.

The question hung in the air for a long moment.

"Why don't Megan and I stay here and practice

our kite flying?" Jimmy suggested. "We'll meet you back at the house later. What do you say, Megan? I could use some more practice."

She looked uncertain. "Mommy?"

"It's a good idea, honey." Alli gave Megan a quick hug. "Jimmy is pretty bad at this, and we don't want him to embarrass the family."

"Okay. But you'll tell Grams I love her?"

"I'll tell her."

Alli just prayed they would have the chance.

In the minutes that it took to get to the hospital, Alli went through a hundred different emotions, but the one she kept coming back to was fear. Phoebe couldn't die. They'd found the pearl. It was supposed to make everything all right.

Somewhere between the parking lot and her grandmother's room, Tessa took her hand, and Alli clung to it like a lifeline.

Dr. Price stopped them outside the door to Phoebe's room. His face was a picture of compassion, of pity, of sympathy. Oh, God!

"I'm sorry," Dr. Price said. "Phoebe had another stroke. A massive one this time. And her heart stopped. She didn't make it."

"She didn't make it? What does that mean?" Alli asked wildly. "How could she not make it? She was getting better. You told me she was getting better. She was going home on Monday. I don't understand. She's not dead. She can't be dead. I have to see her."

"Alli," Sam said softly, putting his arm around Alli's shoulders. "She's gone."

"No. No." Alli looked into his eyes and saw the truth but she didn't want to believe it. "I didn't say good-bye. She can't go until I say good-bye." Alli turned her head and saw Tessa frozen in place, staring at the door to her grandmother's hospital room with an expression of pure terror.

Alli slipped away from Sam and put her hand on Tessa's arm. Tessa looked at her in confusion. "Why is this happening, Alli?"

"I don't know," Alli said shakily.

"You can both go in if you want," Dr. Price said quietly. "Mr. Beckett is with your grandmother now, so whenever you're ready . . ."

Alli glanced back at Sam. He nodded in encouragement. "I'll wait here for you."

She took a deep breath and entered the hospital room. It was dark, not only from the closed blinds but because the bright lights that had disturbed her grandmother so were now dimmed in respect. William rose from the chair when he saw them, his eyes anguished, his hands trembling as he put his arms around both of them.

When he released them, Alli looked over at her grandmother, lying flat in the bed, so still, so pale. Her heart broke and the tears streamed down her cheeks. "Oh, Grams," she whispered. "I wanted to tell you that I love you, but now you're gone, and I can't." She sat down on the edge of the bed and kissed her grandmother on the cheek, shocked by the coolness of her skin.

Tessa came around the other side of the bed, keeping some distance between herself and Phoebe. "She looks like she's sleeping, like she might wake up any second and tell us that she can't die yet, because . . ." Her voice broke.

"She hasn't finished counting the stars," Alli said with a sob.

"She told us it would be all right," Tessa said in confusion. "Why isn't it all right, Alli?"

Alli shook her head. "I don't know. I miss her already. Oh, God! I can't believe she's gone." She took a breath, feeling overwhelming sadness. "I can't believe I'm never going to talk to her again. She's never going to walk into her house or kiss Megan or pick a flower in her garden or tell me to stop acting so childishly. I wanted her to see that I've changed, that I've grown up."

"She knows that, Alli. She knew us better than we knew ourselves."

Alli looked into Tessa's eyes. "How can we go on without her?"

"We just will," Tessa said helplessly.

The clocked ticked off another loud minute. It was the only sound in the room, a painful reminder that they had been too late.

"I thought the pearl would save her somehow," Alli said. "But instead I think it set her free. That's why she gave it to Sam. She must have known, must have felt something."

"That's why she sounded like she was saying good-bye to us earlier. She didn't want to scare us but she wanted us to know that she loved us," Tessa said.

"I feel so alone, so terribly alone."

"You're not alone." Tessa held out her hand across the bed and Alli took it. "I'm here."

Alli squeezed Tessa's hand. "Thank God. We can't forget that we're sisters, Tessa. We share more than just blood and memories. We share love. And we are better together than we ever were apart." Alli looked down at Phoebe, feeling a deep and penetrating sorrow. "If Grams taught us anything, she taught us that."

Two days later, on the Fourth of July, Alli walked down the pier toward the boathouse where Sam, Megan, Tessa, and Jimmy waited for her and the silver urn she carried in her hands. It felt strange to be carrying her grandmother's ashes, but then the past forty-eight hours had been surreal as they had dealt with the business aspect of death all the while being frozen with grief and despair.

There had been little time for reflection. They'd been busy answering the phone, receiving casseroles and desserts and filling out forms. Alli wasn't sure when it would all sink in—maybe today, when they spread her grandmother's ashes across the sea that she could never bear to leave.

William met her at the end of the dock, standing away from the others in a stark black business suit. He'd lost weight, and there was a bleakness to his eyes that she would never forget. When she reached him, she gave him a hug, blinking back the perpetual moistness that claimed her eyes every time someone looked at her with sympathy.

"Are you all right?" she asked.

"Never again," he said gruffly. "But somehow I'll go on. We all will." He paused. "I'm not going out on the boat with you."

"You're not?"

"No." He looked out at the sea, then back at her. "I never thought this was where she wanted to be, just where she had been forced to live. In other words, I thought she grew where she was planted," he said, repeating her grandmother's favorite phrase. "Now I know that this was where her heart was always. The last few months, I'd been begging her to marry me. I told her I could give her a mansion in Philadelphia or a mountain retreat in Colorado, but all she ever wanted was her house by the sea."

"I'm sorry. I know what it's like to love someone who doesn't love you back the way you want, the way you hope." She took a deep breath. "I think Grams did love you in her own way."

"The only way she could," he agreed. "But I can't go out on that ocean with you. This was her place. Hers and John's. It wasn't mine. It wasn't meant to be. I hope you won't think me disrespectful, but I need to go home now."

"I understand. You've been a tower of strength for all of us. I just wish it didn't have to end this way."

"So do I. Good-bye, Alli. Take care of yourself and your family." He started to leave, then stopped. "I don't regret loving Phoebe, even though she thought it was a huge waste of my life. She never understood that loving her made me happy, that in a way it was enough for me." He paused, sending her a very direct look. "I don't expect it will ever be enough for you. If Sam doesn't love you enough, find someone who will. You deserve it. Don't sell yourself short."

"I won't," she promised. Alli watched him walk away, then took a deep breath and headed for the boat. Sam took the urn out of her hands as she stepped on board. Jimmy gave her a smile and a hug. Jimmy had been great the past few days, taking care of Megan, making sure they all ate, even making them laugh. Alli wished Grams could have met Jimmy. She felt sure Phoebe would have liked him.

"I'm thinking maybe I should stay on dry land and wait for you," Jimmy said to her as Sam started the engine and Tessa began to explain to Megan exactly what they were going to do.

"No, you should come."

"I'm not family."

"You're a friend, a good friend. Please come."

"Well, I'd like to be here for Tessa."

"Then stay." Alli walked over to Megan and picked her up in her arms. "How's my baby?"

"I'm okay, Mommy."

"She's just like you," Tessa told Alli. "A million questions, and she keeps asking me each one in a slightly different way until she gets the answer she wants."

"That's my girl."

"Everyone ready to go?" Sam asked.

Tessa looked at Alli. "We're really going to do this, aren't we?"

"It's what she wanted," Alli replied.

"I can't believe we're spreading her ashes on the Fourth of July, on her wedding anniversary. She was supposed to be home today."

"I think she is home," Alli said softly. "I think she's with Grandpa."

Tessa nodded and slipped her arm around Alli's waist as Sam took the boat out to sea. It was a bright, beautiful, sunny day, the kind of day when anything seemed possible. The wrong kind of day to bury someone, Alli thought somberly. Or maybe, as the minister had told her earlier, maybe the angels were celebrating Phoebe's coming-home party.

Finally, Sam cut the engines and they drifted on the waves, Tucker's Landing a beautiful harbor behind them, the rest of the world waiting on the horizon.

"Do you want to say something?" Sam asked Alli.

"Grams didn't believe in funerals. She didn't want any ceremonies, no long speeches, no public farewells. So I guess we'll just say, So long, Grams, we love you." And Alli let the ashes fly with the breeze as they sailed across the water and toward a new future.

They weren't going to participate in the kite festival, but upon returning to the docks they found half the town waiting for them, a picnic lunch set up at the park in lieu of the memorial service Phoebe's life-long friends knew she didn't want. But they were all there to talk about her, to celebrate her life along with the Fourth of July.

When the kite festival began at four o'clock, Alli found herself just behind the starting line, waiting for the others to come back with the kites. Sam walked up to her a moment later, his hands empty. "Megan insisted on carrying the kite."

Alli simply smiled.

He put a hand on her shoulder. "Are you okay?"

"Not really. Do you think Grams would mind us doing this?" she asked. "It seems disrespectful."

"I think she'd expect you to go on, Alli. It's what she always did, after she lost her son and later her husband. Even when Tessa left, she told us to get on with our lives, that we weren't meant to stand still in one place, but to embrace whatever life held in store for us."

His words gave her a comfort unlike any other, and she couldn't stop herself from giving him a tender kiss on the lips. It was meant to be a brief caress, but once there, she found herself lingering, tasting, memorizing everything about him. They hadn't talked about anything personal in the last forty-eight hours, and soon they would have to face the reality of their lives. But not now. Now she just wanted to stop thinking and love Sam for just a few more minutes.

When she finally pulled away, she was almost shaking from the intensity of her emotions. She didn't know if she could bear to lose Sam now. Her resolve to let him go, to give him his freedom, had weakened considerably since her grandmother's death. How could she go on alone? But she knew she had to do just that. She had to let Sam have a chance at the life he wanted, whatever that was.

Sam looked down at her, his eyes dark and serious. "We need to talk, Alli."

Her stomach turned over. She couldn't do this now. Couldn't say good-bye to anyone else, not today.

"We can't. They're about to start the kite race."

He hesitated, seeing she was right as Megan, Jimmy, and Tessa drew near.

"Daddy, are you ready?" Megan called, lining up next to Jimmy and Tessa.

"Do us proud, okay?" Alli said lightly.

Sam leaned over and kissed her firmly on the mouth. "I'm going to impress the hell out of you. Just watch."

"I won't be able to take my eyes off of you," she said. *I never could.*

The race took off with the sound of a whistle, and within minutes the blue sky was covered with a kaleidoscope of colors taking a ride on the wind. Alli kept her eyes peeled on the kite upon which Megan had so lovingly drawn a picture of their family. Would this be the last time they were together? Would this be the end of everything?

She tried not to think about it, tried to let the worries fly away as easily as some of the kites, but deep down inside, she knew they were heading toward the moment of truth, for now that Grams was gone, Tessa was free to go or to stay, and Alli wasn't sure she could bear it either way.

In the end Sam and Megan came in second, because somehow Jimmy and Tessa, flying Grams's old kite, caught a breeze that wouldn't quit, and Alli could do nothing but smile, for it was Grams's day after all.

The next night Alli looked out her bedroom window and saw a sky filled with stars. One of them

seemed to give her a wink as if to say, I'm okay,
don't worry about me anymore. Alli blew the star a
kiss and walked over to the bed.

She sat down, staring at Sam's side, so empty, so
cold. They'd barely spoken since the fireworks the
night before. She'd spent the day with Megan down
at the beach, relaxing, trying to breathe some normalcy back into her daughter's life while Jimmy
and Tessa had kept themselves busy somewhere
else.

Alli knew Tessa was planning to leave soon.
She'd mentioned that she had to get down to L.A. to
finish the assignment she and Jimmy had been
scheduled to complete last week. But Tessa had
been deliberately vague about her long-term plans.

Alli started, hearing footsteps on the stairs, heavy
footsteps, a man's footsteps. She jumped to her feet
as Sam filled the doorway. He was wearing a brown
leather jacket over his shirt and jeans. "You scared
me," she said breathlessly, pulling the tie of her
bathrobe, suddenly aware of what she wasn't wearing underneath.

"Sorry, I didn't want to ring the doorbell and
wake Megan up." He took a step into the room and
set a suitcase down on the floor.

Her heart sank to her toes. Was he leaving with
Tessa? Had he come to say good-bye?

"How are you, Alli?"

"I'm hanging in there. I feel like I've been on a
roller coaster this past week." She studied the
intense look in his eyes. "My ride isn't over yet, is
it?"

"Tessa is going back to L.A. in the morning," Sam said.

She held her breath, not daring to ask if he was going with her.

"She said she'd come back to help you deal with Phoebe's house and her things," he added.

"I can't do any of that right now."

"I don't think Tessa is ready either."

He stopped talking, and Alli had no idea what else to say. Sam walked farther into the room and shut the door behind him.

"What—what are you doing?" she asked.

"I have something to give you, Alli."

She swallowed hard. "What is it?"

It took slow, agonizing minutes for him to pull the strand of pearls out of his pocket. He held them out to her, and they sparkled in the night light.

Alli couldn't move. She couldn't lift her hand. Couldn't take them. "You're supposed to—supposed to give them to the woman you truly love," she said breathlessly.

His gaze didn't waver from hers. "I love you."

Oh, God! It had taken a lifetime for him to say the words. Or had he said them? Was she imagining the moment? She blinked, but he was still there when she opened her eyes, and he was waiting. "I think you're going to have to say that again," she told him.

A smile crossed his lips, but his eyes were still incredibly somber. "Fair enough. I love you, Alli. Did you hear me? Do you get it? Because if you need me to say it again, I will, and again, if I have to. I should have said it years ago."

"You love me?" she asked in wonder. "Are you sure? When did you know? When did it happen?"

"I don't know when it happened," he said slowly. "Maybe it happened when we slept together all those years ago. Maybe when you delivered our baby into the world. Maybe when you stayed up all night with me when I was sick. Maybe when you bought that red thong for our anniversary." He smiled gently, tenderly, lovingly. "Maybe it was when you made up with Tessa, when you told me I was free. Or maybe it was when we said good-bye to Phoebe. I don't know when it happened, Alli. Because our love is our life."

A knot formed in her throat, so big she wasn't sure she could breathe or swallow or talk. "Sam," was all she could get out.

He moved closer and put the pearl necklace over her head. "You are the woman I love."

"I want to believe you, Sam, but Tessa . . ." Her insecurities haunted her still.

"Tessa and I would not have lasted. We were young love, but when our love was tested by the very smallest thing, it fell apart. I wasn't meant to follow Tessa around the world, and she wasn't meant to be a fisherman's wife."

"Are you sure?"

He cupped her face with his hands. "You didn't steal my life. You gave me one. Watching you these past few months made me realize how much I'd taken your being in my life for granted. I know now I was holding something back from you, but I hope you realize that I was holding it back from myself, too. When you got pregnant, it was like one life ended and another started. I guess I felt I could only hang on to that past life if I held something back from you."

"But you loved Tessa. You might love her again," Alli cried, knowing she should just take what he was saying at face value, but she had to be sure. "If you come back to me now, I'm never going to let you go. So you better know what you're saying to me."

He smiled. "I do know what I'm saying. You're the one who isn't listening. I don't love Tessa anymore. All these years I remembered her only as I knew her, but she's different. I'm different. So are you. We all grew up. We all grew into ourselves. Tessa and I don't belong together. Her life is not what I want. My life is not what she wants. We flirted with the possibility of what if, because of the way it all ended so abruptly. We never felt like we had a choice. But the truth is, we always had choices, and we made the right ones."

He took a deep breath, but put his finger against her mouth when she tried to interrupt. "I care about Tessa," he continued. "She'll always be my childhood friend. She'll always be your sister. But you— you are the one. I love you, Alli, and I'm not going to let you divorce me. And I'll fight you and Tessa and the whole damn town if I have to."

"You would fight for me?" she asked.

"Isn't it about time?"

"Past time."

"Forgive me for being a little slow?"

"A lot slow. But I do forgive you. I love you, too, Sam. I always have, from the first minute I saw you."

He kissed her tenderly, a first kiss, a promise of a new beginning.

"What's with the suitcase?" she finally asked.

"I'm moving back in. And I've made some other decisions."

"Like what?"

"I'm not going to sell my business. I'm going to make it better. And I'm not giving up on my marriage; I'm going to make that better, too." He smiled at her. "I'm also thinking of selling the Thunderbird to Jimmy. We can use the money to invest in us, in whatever you want, Alli."

"I just want you."

"And—" he began.

"There's more?" she asked with a laugh.

"I'm sleeping in my bed tonight," he said huskily.

"I'm sleeping with you," she replied.

"In that case, neither one of us will be sleeping." He pulled the tie on her robe until the edges fell open and he could slip his hands inside. "Mmm, naked already. I like this."

"I took a shower. It wasn't like I was waiting for you." But hadn't she been doing just that, standing at the window, staring out at the stars?

"I'll be the one waiting for you from now on," Sam said. "I want to have fifty years with you, one for each pearl on that necklace."

"Why don't we go for sixty?"

"You're on," he said with a groan, as she pressed her breasts against him.

"And you're wearing too many clothes," she whispered, making fast work of his jacket and his shirt and his pants, until they were both completely bare. Then she pulled him down on the bed with her.

He pressed her back against the pillows as he kissed her, as he ran his hands down her sides, across her breasts, her legs, her thighs. Everywhere he touched turned to liquid fire, until she could think of nothing else but having him inside her. It wasn't until he'd nudged her thighs apart that she realized there was something missing, something very, very familiar. She pushed him back in shock.

"What's wrong?" he asked with alarm. "Did I hurt you?"

"For God's sake, Sam. What are you thinking?"

"What do you mean?" he asked warily.

"You're not wearing a condom."

"Oh, that."

"Yes, that."

"We don't need one. I want to have another baby. I want to make love to you without anything between us. No more barriers, Alli. It's you and me forever."

"You want another baby?" she echoed in wonder. Would he never stop surprising her?

"Yes." He paused, running his finger down the side of her cheek. "A funny thing happened when my first love came back to town—I discovered I was in love with my wife. And I intend to make her very happy—for better or worse, in sickness or in health."

"Until death do us part," Alli murmured. And she sealed their promise with a kiss.

⛵ Epilogue

"*I* can't believe you're eight months pregnant," Tessa said to Alli.

Alli stared down at her round stomach and felt a huge sense of pride as well as love. "I've never looked better, have I?"

"Unfortunately, no, since I'm the bride, and I'm supposed to be the most beautiful one in the room. But I fear you'll eclipse me today."

"As if that would ever be possible. But thanks for saying it." Alli took her sister's hand. "I am so happy for you. Jimmy is a great guy."

"You're just saying that so you can stop feeling guilty about winning Sam," Tessa said lightly.

It was partially true. Alli had felt guilty about her incredible happiness with Sam, but during the nine months since their grandmother's death, she and Tessa had shared many a conversation on the subject of Sam, and it was clear to Alli that both Sam and Tessa had come to the same conclusion, that the love they shared belonged to the past and only to the past.

"Jimmy is a great guy," Alli repeated. "He's gorgeous, in case you hadn't noticed, but more importantly he's kind and generous and he gets you."

Tessa smiled. "He does understand me. I think sometimes he knows me better than I know myself. It's scary."

A knock came at the dressing room door, and Sam stuck his head into the room. "Can I wish the bride good luck?"

"As long as Jimmy isn't with you. He cannot see me in my wedding dress before the ceremony," Tessa said. "It would be bad luck."

Sam entered the room, his smile growing more appreciative as he took in Tessa in all her beauty. Alli thought her sister had never looked more glorious than she did right now. For a brief second, that age-old jealousy came back, but then Sam looked at her and she didn't just see appreciation, she saw love.

"Will you kill me if I tell Tessa she looks beautiful?" he asked.

"I'll kill you if you don't, because it's the truth."

"I wish you the best," Sam said instead. "You deserve it."

"Thank you," Tessa replied with a slight catch in her voice. "Don't you dare make me cry, either of you."

"Maybe I shouldn't give you this, then," Alli said, pulling out a beautifully wrapped box. "But I'm going to anyway."

Tessa sent her a sharp look. "Should I open it now?"

"You better."

Tessa undid the wrapping paper and lifted the

lid. Her gasp lit up the room. "Oh, Alli, the pearls? You can't give me the pearls." Tessa looked at Alli in disbelief.

"Grams told Sam to give them to the one he loved, and I thank God every day he gave them to me. But we both love you, Tessa, and it's your turn. We want you to have the pearls. You can pass them down to Megan or one of your own daughters as a reminder that MacGuire women pick only the best men and their marriages last forever."

"I love you," Tessa said, hugging Alli. "And I love you, too, Sam," she muttered, giving him a hug as well. "And now I'm going to cry."

Another knock came at the door. "Come in," Tessa said helplessly, patting her eyes dry with a handkerchief.

Jimmy opened the door a crack. "I promise not to look, Tessa, but is everything okay in here? No second thoughts about the old boyfriend?"

"Everything is perfect," Tessa said. She walked over to the door and threw it open.

"Hey, you said it was bad luck," Jimmy protested, just before Tessa threw herself into his arms and kissed him on the lips. "But this doesn't feel so bad."

Tessa laughed and fingered the pearls she now wore around her neck. "We're never going to have bad luck, Jimmy. Not for at least another fifty years."

Alli placed a hand over her stomach, feeling the baby kick, reminding her that she now had everything—a husband who loved her, a wonderful daughter, an incredible sister, and a charming brother-in-law. To think it had all come with that last pearl.

Welcome to the world
of the Avon Romance Superleader
Where anything is possible . . .
and dreams really do come true

We all know there are unspoken rules that govern the acts of courtship. There are the rules of today (if he doesn't call by Wednesday he won't, even if he says he will!) and the rules of days gone by (a lady should never dance more than three times with a gentleman).

But often, what is expected is at odds with what is longed for . . . and how you're allowed to act is different from the way you feel. Heaven help you if you take a wrong step . . . but sometimes it's better to toss the rules away, take matters into your own hands—just as the heroines of these upcoming Avon Romance Superleaders are about to do.

❧

HERE COMES THE BRIDE
Pamela Morsi

JULY AVON ROMANCE SUPERLEADER

Gussie Mudd, the proprietor of a small ice business in
Cottonwood, Texas, has determined that at some point in a
woman's life she must get herself a man, or give up on the
idea entirely. To get her man she decides to play by the
rules . . . the rules of business. And she makes a business
proposition to her employee, Mr. Rome Akers.

"PEOPLE, MR. AKERS, ARE JUST LIKE BUSINESSES. THEY
act and think and evolve in the same way as commercial enterprise. People want and need things. But
when they are vastly available, they prize them differently."

"Well, yes, I guess so," Rome agreed.

"So when we consider Mr. Dewey's hesitancy to
marry me," she continued, "we must avoid emotional-
ism and try to consider the situation logically."

"Logically?"

Rome was not sure that logic was a big considera-
tion when it came to love.

"Mr. Dewey has been on his own for some time now," she said. "He has a nice home, a hired woman to cook and clean, a satisfying business venture, good friends and myself, a pleasant companion to escort to community events. Basically all his needs as a man are met. He has a virtual monopoly on the things that he requires."

Rome was not certain that *all* of a man's *needs* had been stated, but after his embarrassing foray in that direction, he chose not to comment.

"He is quite comfortable with his life as it is," Miss Gussie continued. "Whyever should he change?"

"Why indeed?" Rome agreed.

She smiled then. That smile that he'd seen often before. That smile that meant a new idea, a clever innovation, an expansion of the company. He had long admired Miss Gussie's good business sense and the very best of her money-making notions came with this smile.

"I can do nothing about Mr. Dewey's nice home, the woman hired to cook and clean, his business, or his friends," Miss Gussie said. "But I can see that he no longer has a monopoly upon my pleasant companionship."

"I'm not sure I understand you," Rome said.

"In our business if Purdy Ice began delivering smaller blocks twice a week, we would be forced to do the same."

Rome nodded. "Yes, I suppose you are right about that."

"We would be forced to change, compelled to provide more service for the same money," she said.

"Yes, I suppose that's right."

"That's exactly what we're going to do to Amos Dewey," she declared.

Rome was listening, but still skeptical.

"You are going to pretend to be in love with me," she said as if that were going to be the simplest thing in the world. "You will escort me about town. Sit evenings on this porch with me. Accompany me to civic events."

That seemed not too difficult, Rome thought. He did not normally attend a lot of public functions, but, of course, he could.

"I don't see how that will change Dewey's mind," he told her honestly.

"You will also let it be known that you are madly in love with me," she said, "and that you are determined to get me to the altar as soon as possible."

Rome got a queasy feeling in his stomach.

"Amos Dewey will no longer have a monopoly. *You* will be the competition that will force him to provide the service he is not so willing to provide—marrying me."

Gussie raised her hands in a gesture that said that the outcome was virtually assured.

Rome had his doubts.

"I'm not sure this will work, Miss Gussie," he told her. "Men . . . men don't always behave like businesses. They are not all that susceptible to the law of supply and demand."

"Don't be silly," she said. "Of course they are."

"I'm not sure I'm the right man to be doing this. Perhaps you should think of someone who would seem more . . . well more suited to the task."

Her response was crisp and cool.

"I was hoping for a late-spring wedding," she told

him. "When the flowers are at their peak. But I suppose, in this instance midsummer would be fine. Let's say the Fourth of July; that sounds like an auspicious day for a wedding. It is going to be absolutely perfect. The most perfect wedding this town has ever seen. I do hope you will be there, Mr. Akers."

HEAVEN ON EARTH
Constance O'Day-Flannery

AUGUST AVON ROMANCE SUPERLEADER

For Casey O'Reilly the world was supposed to be an orderly place where you met, married, and had children with the man you love. But nothing had gone according to plan. Mr. Right never made an appearance, and now, at "thirtysomething," Casey figured she had a better chance at being struck by lightning than struck by love ... but then the unthinkable happened ...

SHE WAS MAKING THIS UP. WHATEVER WAS HAPPENING was all in her mind. *It had to be!*

Desperately, Casey rubbed at her eyes and then cupped her hands around them to shelter her face as more lightning, familiar narrow streaks, flashed around her and thunder rumbled.

There was no time for questions as a man slowly, deliberately, walked closer, as though he had no fear of the lightning or the sandstorm. Casey's voice was stuck in her throat. She wanted to ask him who he was, but only garbled noises emerged from her mouth as she watched him unbutton his dark coat above her. His face was hidden by a wide turned-up collar and the cowboy hat pulled low over his brow, but somehow the closer he came, the less she feared him.

He knelt before her and, without a word, wrapped the edges of the raincoat around her, pulling her to his chest and sheltering her from the sandstorm. She could feel the strength of his arms around her back, and immediately sensed peace as she was gathered into the sanctuary of his body. She felt the strong beat of his heart reverberating against her face. She smelled something citrusy, very earthy, about him, and lifted her hand to cling to his soft shirt.

"You are all right, Casey O'Reilly."

She almost jumped at the close proximity of his voice resonating from his chest and into her ear. The low soothing tone sent shivers throughout her body and she found herself clinging even more tightly to his shirt.

"Who . . . Who are you?" she managed to mutter.

"I've come to help," he answered, holding her tighter as another crash of thunder made the ground shake violently beneath them.

"Thank heavens," she sobbed.

Somehow she felt incredibly safe, more so than she had ever felt in her life. Her body was tingling with some strange and powerful energy that was unfamiliar and yet . . . so perfectly wonderful. She felt a renewed strength welling up in her muscles, spreading through her body down to her burning foot. Her chest stopped aching and her headache eased as she held this man who had just walked out of a bolt of lightning and into her life . . .

❧

HIS WICKED PROMISE
Samantha James

SEPTEMBER AVON ROMANCE SUPERLEADER

Glenda knew what was expected of a Highland lass—she must wed a man bold and strong enough to protect her. Love could come later . . . if it came at all. But although she was now without a husband, she had once known the joy of the marriage bed . . . and the pleasure that Laird Egan was willing to reacquaint her with . . .

"WELL, YOU ARE EVER AT THE READY, ARE YOU NOT?"

He cocked a brow. "What do you mean?"

"I think you know quite well what I mean!"

He was completely unfazed by the fire of her glare. A slow smile rimmed his lips. "Glenda, do you speak of my manly appetites?"

"Your words, sir, not mine," she snapped. Her resentment blazed higher with his amusement. "Though I must say, your appetite seems quite hearty!"

"And what of yours, Glenda?"

"Whatever do you mean?"

"You are a woman without a husband. A woman

without a man. I am not a fool. Women . . . well,
women have appetites, too. Especially those who
know the pleasure that can be found in another's
body."

And well she knew. She had lost her maidenhead on
the marriage bed, but she had never found lovemaking
a chore or a duty, as she'd heard some women were
wont to do. Instead, she had found it a vastly pleasura-
ble experience . . . All at once she was appalled. She
couldn't believe what they were discussing! To speak
of her lying with a man . . . of his lying with a
woman . . . and to each other yet!

He persisted. "Come, Glenda, what of you? I asked
you once and you would not answer. Do you not find
yourself lonely? Do you not miss the closeness of a
man's body, the heat of lips warm upon yours?"

Suddenly she was the one who was on the defensive. "Nay," she gasped.

"Nay?" He feigned astonishment. "What, Glenda!
Did you not love Niall then?"

Glenda's breath grew short; it seemed there was not
enough air to breathe, for he was so close. *Too* close.
So close that she could see the tiny droplets of water
which glistened in the dense forest of hair on his
chest. Niall's chest had been smooth and nearly void
of hair, and it was all she could do not to stare in min-
gled shock and fascination.

She was certain her face flamed scarlet. "Of course I
did! You know I did! But I"—she made a valiant stab
at reasoning—"I have put aside such longings."

He did not take his eyes from her mouth. "Have
you?" he said softly. "Have you indeed?"

A strong hand settled on her waist. In but a half
breath, it was joined by the other. His touch seemed to

burn through the layers of clothing to the flesh beneath.

"Egan," she floundered. "Egan, please!"

"What, Glenda? What is it?"

She shook her head. Her eyes were wide and dark. Her head had lifted. Her lips hovered but a breath beneath his. The temptation to give in, to kiss her, to trap her lips beneath his and taste the fruit of her mouth was all-consuming. Almost more than he could stand.

She wanted it, too. He sensed it with every fiber of his being, but she was fighting it, damn her! Yet still he wanted to hear her say it. He *needed* it.

"Tell me, Glenda. What is it you want?"

She shook her head. Her hands came up between them. Her fingers opened and closed on his chest . . . his *naked* chest. Dark, bristly hairs tickled her palm; to her the sensation was shockingly intimate. Yet she did not snatch back her hands—she did not push him away—as she should have.

As she could have.

"Egan? Are you here, lad?"

It was Bernard. They jerked apart. Egan moved first, stepping back from her. Did he curse beneath his breath? Glenda did not wait to find out.

She fled. Her heart was pounding and her lungs labored as if the devil himself nipped at her heels. Her feet did not stop until she was safe in her own chamber and the door was shut.

'Twas then that her strength deserted her. She pressed her back against it and slumped, landing in a heap on the floor.

Thrice now, Egan had almost kissed her. *Thrice.*

What madness possessed him? Sweet heaven, what madness possessed *her*?

For Glenda could not deny the yearning that still burned deep in her heart. Just once she longed to feel the touch of his mouth on hers. Just once . . .

∾

RULES OF ENGAGEMENT
Christina Dodd

OCTOBER AVON ROMANCE SUPERLEADER

Miss Pamela Lockhart knew that proper behavior could guide a governess through any trying situation. The rules were straightforward: never become too familiar with your employer, always take your meals upstairs on a tray, and remember your station at all times. But what happens when your employer is devastatingly handsome . . . and his behavior is anything but proper?

"YOU CONSIDER MARRIAGE THE SURE ROUTE TO MISERY."

"Not really." He stroked his chin, a gesture he had adopted from his grandfather. "The trick to marriage is not letting expectations get in the way. A man needs to understand why women get married, that's all."

Her mouth drew down in typical Miss Lockhart censure. "Why, pray tell, do women get married?"

"For money, usually." He could tell she was offended again, but with Miss Lockhart he didn't have to worry overly much about offense. After all, she didn't. Besides, he thought his assessment quite fair. "I don't blame them. The world is not fair to a spinster. She has no recourse but to work or starve. So if she's asked, she marries."

Obviously, *Miss Lockhart* did not consider his assessment fair. She slapped her mug on the table so hard the crockery rattled. "Do you have any idea how insulting you are? To think a woman is single because she has never been asked, or if she is married she has done so for monetary security?"

He found himself entertained and very, very interested. "Ah, I've touched a nerve. Are you telling me there is a man alive who dared to propose to you?"

"I am not telling you anything." But swept along by her passion, she did. "A man can convey financial security, but whither thou goest, I shall go, and all that rot. A woman has to live where her husband wishes, let him waste her money, watch as he humiliates her with other women, and never say a word."

"Men are not the only ones who break their vows."

"So fidelity is a vow *you* intend to keep?"

Of course he had no intention of keeping that vow when he was forced to make it, and falling into that trap which had so neatly snared his father. "I've supported more women than Madame Beauchard's best corset maker. If I let marriage stop me, think of the poor actresses who would be without a patron."

She wasn't amused. "So nothing about your wife would be sacrosanct, not even her body. Your wife will cherish dreams that you never know about, and even if you did they would be less than a puff of wind to you."

Women had dreams? About *what*? A new pair of shoes? Seeing a rival fail? Dancing with a foreign prince? But Miss Lockhart wasn't speaking of the trivial, and he found himself asking, "What are your dreams?"

"You don't care. Until I spoke, it never occurred to you that a woman could have her dreams."

"That's true, but you are a teacher, and already you have taught me otherwise." Leaning back in his chair, he gazed at her with absolute sincerity, and then said the most powerful words in the universe. "Tell me what you want. I want to know about you."

She had no defense to withstand him. She leaned back, too, and closed her eyes as if she could see her fantasy before her. "I want a house in the country. Just a cottage, with a fence and cat to sit in my lap and a dog to sleep at my feet. A spot of earth for a garden with flowers as well as vegetables, food on the table, and a little leisure time in which to read the books I've not had time to read or just sit . . . in the sunshine."

The candles softened the stark contrast between her white complexion and that hideous rouge. Light and shadow delineated her pale lips, showing them in their fullness. Her thick lashes formed a ruffled half-circle on her skin. When she was talking like this, imagining her perfect life, she looked almost . . . pretty. "That's all?"

"Oh, yes."

"That's simple enough."

"Yes, very simple. And mine."

Careful not to break into her reverie, he quietly placed his mug next to hers. "Why do you want that?"

"That's what I had before—"

She stopped speaking so suddenly he knew what she had been about to say. Moving to the side of her chair, he knelt on the carpet. "Before your father left?"

At the sound of his voice, her eyes flew open and she stared at him in dismay. She *had* been dreaming, he realized, seeing that cottage, those pets, that garden, and imagining a time when she could sit in the sunshine. Her countenance was open and vulnerable, and his instincts were strong. As gently as a whisper he placed his fingertips on her cheek. "There's one dream you didn't mention, and I can make it come true." Slowly, giving her time to turn if she wished, he leaned forward . . . and kissed her.

JUST THE WAY YOU ARE
Barbara Freethy

NOVEMBER AVON ROMANCE SUPERLEADER

Allison Tucker knew that today's women were supposed to face their ex-husbands in a modern way—cordially, friendly, and with the attitude that you didn't have a care in the world. But every time she looked into Sam's eyes, she still felt a longing for what might have been if they stayed together—and what could still be . . .

"DID YOU EVER LOVE MOMMY?"

Allison Tucker caught her breath at the simple, heartfelt question that had come from her eight-year-old daughter's lips. She took a step back from the doorway and leaned against the wall, her heart racing in anticipation of the answer. She'd thought she'd explained the separation to her daughter, the reasons why Mommy and Daddy couldn't live together any-more, but apparently Megan still had some questions, and this time it was up to Sam to answer.

Sam cleared his throat, obviously stalling for time. For the life of her, Alli couldn't move away. She hadn't meant to eavesdrop, but when she'd arrived to pick up Megan after her weekend with her father, she had been caught by the cozy scene in the family room.

Sam sat in the brown leather reclining chair looking endearingly handsome in his faded blue jeans and navy-blue rugby shirt. Megan was on his lap, her blond hair a mess in mismatched braids, her clothes almost exactly the same as Sam's, faded blue jeans and a navy-blue T-shirt. Megan adored dressing like her father.

"Did I show you the picture of Mommy when she dressed up like a giant pumpkin for the Halloween dance?" Sam asked, obviously trying to change the subject.

They were looking at a yearbook, Alli realized with dismay. There weren't just pictures of Sam and Alli in the yearbook, there were other people in there, too.

"Did you, Daddy? Did you ever love Mommy?" Megan persisted.

Answer the question, Sam. Tell her you never really loved me, that you only married me because I was pregnant, that your heart still belongs to—my sister.

Alli held her breath, waiting for Sam's answer, knowing the bitter truth, but wondering, hopelessly, impossibly wondering . . .

"I love your mother very much—for giving me you," Sam replied.

Alli closed her eyes against a rush of emotion. It wasn't an answer, but an evasion. She didn't know why she felt even the tiniest bit of surprise. Sam would never admit to loving her. She couldn't remember ever hearing those three simple words cross his lips, not even after Megan's birth. Or after, in the days and weeks and years that followed, not even when they made love, when they shared a passion that was perhaps the only honest part of their relationship. Sam always held a part of himself back, a portion of his heart and his soul that he would never give to her.

Alli clenched her fists, wanting to feel anger, not pain. She'd spent more than half of her twenty-seven years of life in love with Sam Tucker, but he didn't love her and he never would.

✌

THE VISCOUNT
WHO LOVED ME
Julia Quinn

DECEMBER AVON ROMANCE SUPERLEADER

If there's one place a proper young lady should not be, it's in
an unmarried gentleman's private study . . . crouched under
his desk, desperate to escape discovery. Yet that's exactly
where (and in what position) Kate Sheffield finds herself. Even
worse, Anthony Bridgerton has brought a potential paramour
back with him, and Kate is forced to wait out the entire
encounter . . .

ANTHONY KNEW HE HAD TO BE A FOOL. HERE HE WAS,
pouring a glass of whiskey for Maria Rosso, one of the
few women of his acquaintance who knew how to
appreciate both a fine whiskey and the devilish intoxi-
cation that followed, and all he could smell was the
damned lilies-and-soap scent of Kate Sheffield. He
knew she was in the house—he was half ready to kill
his mother for inviting her to the musicale—but this
was ridiculous.

And then he saw Kate.

Under his desk.

It was impossible.

Surely this was a nightmare. Surely if he closed his eyes and opened them again, she'd be gone.

He blinked. She was still there.

Kate Sheffield, the most maddening, irritating, diabolical woman in all England, was crouching like a frog under his desk.

"Maria," he said smoothly, moving forward toward the desk until he was stepping on Kate's hand. He didn't step hard, but he heard her wince.

This gave him immense satisfaction.

"Maria," he repeated, "I have suddenly remembered an urgent matter of business that must be dealt with immediately."

"This very night?" she asked, sounding dubious.

"I'm afraid so. *Euf!*"

Maria blinked. "Did you just grunt?"

"No," Anthony lied, trying not to choke on the word. Kate had removed her glove and wrapped her hand around his knee, digging her nails straight through his breeches and into his skin. Hard.

At least he hoped it was her nails. It could have been her teeth.

Maria's eyes were curious. "Anthony, is there an animal under your desk?"

Anthony let out a bark of laughter. "You could say that."

Kate let go of his leg, and her fist came down on his foot.

Anthony took advantage of his release to step quickly out from behind the desk. "Would I be unforgivably rude," he asked, striding to Maria's side and taking her arm, "if I merely walked you to the door and not back to the music room?"

She laughed, a low, sultry sound that should have seduced him. "I am a grown woman, my lord. I believe I can manage the short distance."

She floated out, and Anthony shut the door with a decisive click. "You," he boomed, eliminating the distance to the desk in four long strides. "Show yourself."

When Kate didn't scramble out quickly enough, he reached down, clamped his hand around her upper arm, and hauled her to her feet.

"It was an accident," she said, grabbing on to the edge of the desk for support.

"Funny how those words seem to emerge from your mouth with startling frequency."

"It's true!" She gulped. He had stepped forward and was now very, very close. "I was sitting in the hall," she said, her voice sounding crackly and hoarse, "and I heard you coming. I was just trying to avoid you."

"And so you invaded my private office?"

"I didn't know it was your office. I—" Kate sucked in her breath. He'd moved even closer, his crisp, wide lapels now only inches from the bodice of her dress. She knew his proximity was deliberate, that he sought to intimidate rather than seduce, but that didn't do anything to quell the frantic beating of her heart.

"I think perhaps you did know that this was my office," he murmured, letting his forefinger trail down the side of her cheek. "Perhaps you did not seek to avoid me at all."

Kate's lips parted, but she couldn't have uttered a word if her life had depended on it. She breathed when he paused, stopped when he moved. She had no doubt that her heart was beating in time to his pulse.

"Maybe," he whispered, so close now that his breath kissed her lips, "you desired something else altogether."

Rita Award-winning Author
BARBARA FREETHY

"A fresh and exciting new voice."
Susan Elizabeth Phillips

JUST THE WAY YOU ARE
0-380-81552-4/$6.50 US/$8.99 Can
Take a romantic journey with Barbara Freethy to
Tucker's Landing, Oregon, where Sam and Alli
Tucker have made a life together . . . a life about to
be tested by the return of the only woman who can
break them up . . . Alli's sister, Tessa.

Also by Barbara Freethy

ALMOST HOME
0-380-79482-9/$6.50 US/$8.99 Can

THE SWEETEST THING
0-380-79481-0/$6.50 US/$8.50 Can

ONE TRUE LOVE
0-380-79480-2/$5.99 US/$7.99 Can

DANIEL'S GIFT
0-380-78181-9/$5.99 US/$7.99 Can